R.I.P.

...'Til We Meet Again

R.I.P.
...'Til We Meet Again

Sonya Senell Wash

ARA Publishing
Morrow, Georgia

ARA Publishing
P.O. Box 511
Morrow, Georgia 30260-0511

Copyright © 1999 by Sonya Senell Wash
ISBN: 0-9703122-0-2
Library of Congress Card Number: 00-191554
All Rights Reserved

Cover Illustration: Gregory Wynn

Email: snywash@aol.com

Printed in the United States of America
First Printing

*This novel is dedicated to my parents,
the late Elder Willie L. Wash, Sr.
and Mrs. Elizabeth King Wash*

NURTURE NOW

ARISE AND REJOICE MY SISTERS
JOIN ME AS WE SHED MEMORIES OF PAIN
REACH FOR THE PROMISES THAT FORGIVENESS OFFERS.

RELEASE THE CAPTIVE...YOUR HEART
RECEIVE THE LOVE THAT AWAITS YOU
RECEIVE THE LOVE YOU WERE DESTINED TO POSSESS.

GROW, PRUNE, GROW
GROW IN HAPPINESS
GROW IN HEALTH
GROW IN LOVE.

RECEIVE THE BLESSINGS OF FORGIVENESS
AND
BREAK THE CYCLE.

LET US NURTURE AS WE HAVE NEVER BEEN
BREAK THE CYCLE

CLAIM THE POWER OF FORGIVENESS MY SISTERS
NOW.

BY: PHYLLIS DUMAS-COMBS

Acknowledgments

First, I would like to give honor to God, who has blessed me with a mind to fulfill my aspiration of writing.

To my late father, Elder Willie Lester Wash, Sr. whose spiritual teaching and guidance led me to make "good" choices in life. My mother, Elizabeth King Wash, who continues to be a blessing to me.

To my sister, Selena Wash-Cage. Thank you for the countless days and nights you spent "cleaning up" my drafts, (although you resigned a few times, you came back in full force ☺).

To my editor, Teresa Fowler-Walker. Thank you for providing your professional critique and at the same time, keeping my story, my story.

To my illustrator, Gregory Wynn. Thank you for your patience. Your talent is phenomenal. Keep that pencil in hand. You never know where it might take you.

A quick hello to the rest of my siblings: Harold, Larry, Freddie, Willie Jr., Sherease, Nazamova, and my two brother-in-laws, Dexter and Kenneth.

To my three precious God-children, Ashley, Rekyia, and Andres (ARA). I can not express enough how important it is to read. It can take you places you have never been before.

Special thanks to friends that provided me with either feedback on some of my chapters or information to help bring my novel to a completion: Phyllis Dumas-Combs, Myra Holliday, Erik and Gena Jordan, Sonia Marrero, Tonya Poiter, Yvette Sanples, Rochelle Smith, Carlis Tarrant, and Mari Wynn.

Another special thanks to my book club members, Friends and Readers of Atlanta: Selena, Rhonda, Bolynthia, Ravii, and Dina. I still have fond memories of Mary; Verdi and Roe; Emma Lou and Alva; Adele and Lucien; Malcolm, Simon, Ariel, and Teddy; and several other characters that kept us debating.

An extra special thanks to some published authors whom willingly opened their doors to me as I traveled along the 'aspiring author' path: Timmothy McCann, author of 'Until' and 'Always'; Trevy McDonald, author of 'Time Will Tell' and co-author of 'Nature of a Sistuh'; and C.Kelly Robinson, author of 'Not All Dogs'.

Sherea, Darlene, keep moving forward. Don't give up. Realistic goals are attainable.

What's Going On

Chapter 1

Indigo

Notable black businessman found to be the number one suspect. My mind still recalls that first line of print as it did two years ago. *How do I rid myself of the guilt I've fixated in my heart? Silence...My silence cost two important people to walk right out of my life. I've got to stop thinking about the past. Besides, my mind should be focused on what's normally considered a pleasurable occasion. Unfortunately for me, I'm receiving no satisfaction.* I sighed and shifted my mind to another undesirable circumstance.

Tomorrow is another workday and just the thought of Sean, the student from hell, makes me wish for an early spring break. I hope Mrs. Smith calls him to the office first thing tomorrow morning. He has no self-control. He doesn't even...

A drop of sweat grazed my left eye and suddenly interrupted my thoughts. *Any day now*, I thought, as Aaron vigorously worked himself into a heated frenzy.

The ringing of the telephone diverted my attention from the rather unpleasant situation I was experiencing. I stretched my arm from beneath his soggy body in hopes of reaching it. It was no use. Each stroke pinned me deeper and deeper into the mattress.

Evidently he was clueless about my non-compliant disposition. There were no movements, moans, or groans from my end since we began. *Does he even care?*

"What's my nameee?" he bellowed in ecstasy.

Why is he asking me such a witless question? Tony, yes, Tony, I thought. *That's what I would like for your name to be. Tony,* I thought again with a partial smirk on my face. *How is he doing? Who is he dating? Does he love her? Has he taken her...?*

My remembrance of the past was abruptly interrupted. This time by a boisterous "OOHHH BAABBYY!"

At that point, I thanked God the fiasco was finally over. Never again will I submit myself to 'love-making' for the pleasure. If there is no 'love', there will be no 'making'.

"Was it good baby?" He rolled over on his back and pulled me toward his chest for the feeling of closeness.

"Yes," I responded. *Why am I lying to him? How could he possibly think I enjoyed myself when my body was as stiff as a corpse?*

Laying my head on his chest gave me a feeling of awkwardness. I was in no mood to cuddle. I faked a coughing spell. *Quick thinking,* I thought. That was the perfect alibi to place distance between us.

"Are you okay?"

"Yes, you know I've been dealing with this cold for the past couple of days. Let me get up and check my medicine cabinet for something."

As I opened the cabinet, I noticed a reflection of Aaron's tall, muscular, dark-chocolate body through the mirror. He walked up behind me and planted a kiss on the back of my neck. His arms gently enclosed around my waist. A slight chill slowly crept upon my skin. The annoyance I felt made me want to elbow him where it hurts.

"We need to talk," I said, turning around to face him. He's not bad looking at all. As a matter of fact, he portrays most of the physical characteristics I desire in a man. He's the right complexion, height, and weight. But there's something very important missing from the romance.

"Okay, I'll be in the bed waiting for you," he responded gleefully, smacking my butt with his hand before walking off. *Ugh!*

I felt my way to the kitchen in the darkness while sliding my fingers along the hall wall. *Yes, something very important is missing,* I thought. *He just doesn't have enough sexual stamina to really turn me on.*

As soon as the cold medicine stopped fizzing in the cup of water prepared for it, I gulped it down. After emptying my full bladder, I slipped back under the comforter where Aaron waited.

He was laughing at one of the comedian's jokes on television. At that moment he seemed to be the happiest man alive.

"Aaron." I said, feeling the blues of dismissing yet another *good* man.

"What's up baby?" he responded. His eyes were still glued to the television set.

"You really are a nice person and I do enjoy hanging out with you, but I don't think this relationship is going to work."

"What are you trying to say?"

"Well, do you remember me telling you about Tony, the guy I dated before you?"

He didn't respond. He just sat there anticipating what was next.

"I have to be honest. I'm still in love with him."

"Have you spoken with him recently?"

"No. I just need some time to work out my feelings. I don't think it's fair to be involved with you when my heart isn't really in it

My decision to discharge him from my life wasn't *all* about Tony, but I had to tell him something. Don't get me wrong, I really do like Aaron. I want so badly to care for him and have a relationship with him, but it's just not happening. Priscilla would tell me to work with him. Rashondra would consider me insane for going back after the first affair.

"I guess I have no choice but to accept your decision. I was really starting to care for you deeply," he said wearing a look of somber.

He removed the comforter away from his body and exited the bed. Evidently he didn't like the news I delivered because he slammed the bathroom door behind him.

Taking a sigh, I began to wonder if I was doing the right thing. What justifiable reason do I have to continue a sexual relationship with him when there is no real gratification in it for me? I know I made the right decision.

Aaron was fully dressed when he returned from the bathroom, which led me to speak before thinking. "Are you leaving?" I asked. I still wanted him to spend the night, just for the companionship.

"Yes, I mean, why should I stay here if you don't want to be involved with me?"

He does have a point. Who cares? Put on your clothes, walk out my door and never call me again, I thought as I watched him gather his belongings.

Aaron placed his overnight bag on his shoulder and headed down the dark hall, leaving me under the comforter. I launched out of the bed, switched on the hall light, and strolled behind him. When he opened the front door, I uttered a soft, "I hope we can keep in touch."

"Cool," he responded as he walked down the steps, disappearing into the darkness of the night.

After switching the hall light off, I felt my way back to the bedroom and checked my Caller ID. *Oh, it was only Walter. I wonder what he wanted. He was probably doing his monthly check to see if I've spoken with Priscilla and Rashondra. Maybe he was calling about Tony. Who knows? Who cares right about now? I'll give him a ring tomorrow. I'm too disgusted to converse with anyone tonight... I'm really missing you Tony. I want you back in my life, desperately. Are you thinking of me like I'm thinking of you?*

* * * * *

Sometimes in life we make decisions based on our own personal morals. It's really not a matter of right or wrong, but what we believe in as individuals. My conception of what was *ideal* for me six months ago ended my relationship with the man that was *right* for me...Tony.

On the other hand, the empathy we carry can temporarily brainwash our minds into making decisions based on sorrow, not facts. My sudden emotional state for one friend's pain over another caused the walls to tumble on a friendship we thought was unbreakable... Priscilla and Rashondra.

* * * * *

With the realization of my misjudgments in mind, I set the alarm clock earlier than usual and crawled back into bed. Hopefully the 'sandman' will visit very soon to replace the thoughts of tonight's disaster and past events with sweet serene dreams.

Chapter 2

Rashondra

Due to the census at the hospital being extremely high, I've been working sixteen-hour shifts lately. Tonight was slightly different. We're down to twelve patients with six respiratory therapists on the clock. I was delighted at the news of me being the 'chosen-one' to leave at eleven tonight. *I hope my baby has made it home.*

Derrick's flight should've arrived from Japan around nine. His job as a city councilman placed him in a position to attend an International Peace Convention. I was unable to pick him up at Hartsfield because my shift was supposed to end at seven tomorrow morning.

He's been away for two weeks and I miss him dearly. He's the best thing to have ever walked into my life. Without him by my side, I can't imagine how I would've made it through the trials and tribulations I've encountered over the past two years. He's been my sole support in dealing with the loss of my two best friends. Now if I could just get Mama out of the picture, Derrick and I can work toward the fairy tale life I've always dreamed of.

Derrick is going to be so happy to see me tonight. My mind was so entangled with thoughts of my man that I almost missed the turn into our apartment complex.

My eyes meandered to the top floor of the building as I parked the car. The lights were still out in our bedroom. He hadn't arrived yet. A delayed flight wouldn't be the ideal situation right now.

Accepting the disappointment, I clutched my bag and mounted the two flights of stairs. Just before reaching the door, Billy, our neighbor from across the hall, yanked his door open and jumped out in front of me. He landed on both feet; slightly bending his knees and elbows. Curving his fingers in a clawing position, he released an obnoxious, "RAAAHHH!" He almost scared the hell out of me.

Inhaling deeply as I calmed myself down, I playfully pushed him on the shoulder. "Billy you play too much. You need to stop that mess before somebody hurts you."

Without uttering a word, he grabbed his shoulder length, blonde hair with both hands and pulled it straight up on his head. His erect tongue protruded from his mouth as he rapidly shook his head from side to side. Within five seconds he'd vanished back into his apartment, slamming the door behind him.

"Crazy fool!" I mumbled while unlocking my door.

The entire apartment was unusually dark. Even Mama's room bared the sight of darkness. She always left a lamp on until she was ready to retire for the night.

Listen to me, referring to it as Mama's room. You would think she lives with us. The supposedly two weeks visit for Christmas had turned into three months. I guess you can say she lives with us.

"Mama, when are you going back home?' I had asked her back in January.

"Shut yo mouth gul!" she shouted back. "You think you is all high and mighty cause you gots you a good paying job and a good man. I needs to git myself together. Told ya gul, I'm tired of the lifestyle I had in Fote Ladadale. You don't rush yo Mama for nothin gul. You hear me? I brought yo high yellow, big butt, wavy-headed self in this here world, and I sho nuff can take you out," she added.

Rambling on and on, she would talk about how I was her pride and joy when I was a baby. "Prettiest little thang in the hood," she would continue.

Whenever she got on her road of babbling, I would just walk off. I had heard it many times before. That didn't take away the fact that she'd overstayed her welcome.

I turned the light switch on and a purple emanation filled the living room.

Damn! This purple light doesn't help. I forgot Mama changed the light bulb the day after Derrick left for his business trip.

She claimed Leroy, some man she'd met at the bus stop, was coming over to visit. She wanted the living room to have a romantic scene.

"No!" I protested during the confrontation we had. "You can't just go to changing things around in here for some man you don't even know."

"Leroy's a good man. He got hisself some good curly hair too. Kinda minds me of yo daddy. Met him today getting off the bus. He a hard workin man. Just standin thar showin all that curly hair on his chest, sweatin, tryin to sell his last bags of apples and oranges. Says he grows em in his own backyard."

"Mama, please don't bring that man into this apartment while we're not here. Derrick would have a fit if he knows what you are up to."

"Derrick ain't here. He ain't got to know nothin. He don't call no shots from Japan. Besides, this yo stuff. He moved in wit you, member? Who paid the first three years' rent here? Huh? Huh?"

Shaking my head in disgust, I walked off to discontinue the spat we'd created.

"Well all right then," she yelled down the hall loud enough for me to hear. "Til he pays mo rent than you already did, he don't make no rules."

That was my Mama. Always on the defense about something.

I made my way to the kitchen to place my unfinished sub sandwich into the refrigerator. The kitchen had a very clean, fresh aroma, as if a bottle of pine cleaner was sitting around topless.

Soft music sifted my ears as I started my way down the hall. A few more steps placed me in the area from which the music came.

Why is our stereo on? I don't recall having it on before leaving for work today. Maybe Mama left it on, although she has no business in our room.

Derrick and I bought her a nice sized boom box for Christmas because listening to music was one of her favorite past-times. She lost it last month. Well, that's what she claimed.

"Mama, how could you loose a big boom-box?" I asked when she reported the loss to us.

"Gul, I'on know. I thank I left it at the park or somethin. Can't remember," she replied.

Sensing bad vibes before entering the bedroom, my body trembled as I slowly turned the knob to view what was lurking on the other side. To my dismay, every working organ in my body seemed to instantly shut down. I observed the silhouette of a nude woman's body highlighted by the moon beaming through the mini-blinds. She was bouncing in an upright position, in the middle of my waterbed. In total awe, my voice must have been on shut down also because the scream that tugged at the back of my throat was prohibited by paralyzed vocal cords.

Chapter 3

Priscilla

It is two-thirty in the morning and Marlon has not returned from work yet. Constantly staring at the clock created a faint haze of vision for me. My thoughts are slightly obscured as well.

Where could he be? He did call to tell me he would be working a little late, but my God, this is ridiculous. It was strange enough that I found out he was going in on a Sunday while I was in the shower this morning.

The split second it took him to slide the glass door of the shower open and yell through the splattering water and steam, "Honey, I'm headed to the office. I have a lot of paper work to catch up on," was all he needed as he immediately closed it and we went on about his business.

"I didn't know you were going in today," I yelled in hopes of him hearing me. "You promised to attend church with us this morning." There was no response.

Instantly I jumped out of the shower with water still dripping from my nude body. My attempt to catch him was to no avail. The soft *bang* heard from him slamming the front door shut confirmed that he'd already left.

There is no problem with Marlon working extra hours, but when a work Sunday runs into a Monday morning, it's only a matter of time until the panic alarm is pulled.

Calling all the major hospitals from the affluent Northside down to the county owned Grady Memorial yielded nothing. I've paged him several times; he has not responded. Enough time and thoughts have been placed on tragedies. This situation brings one other thing to mind, Sarita. *Oh God, please don't let it be what I think. He promised to never cheat again. As much as we've been through over the past few years, how could he? He promised that this time was for the making.*

My head throbbed as tears swelled in my eyes. *Lord, if you could only tell me that it is not so...* I received no answer.

In an attempt to pull myself together, I decided to check on the kids. I staggered down the hall to find Marlon III fast asleep. He drifted off around nine. A smile slowly stretched across my face as I watched his little chest rise up and down to the rhythm of his wheezy snores. He looked just like his father lying there. My heart refilled with anxiety. Quietly sobbing, I removed myself from his room to allow my little angel to continue his sweet dreams, uninterrupted.

The weakening of my knees shortened my visit to the bedroom next door where the twins, Marlissa and Marlonda slept. Their soft sighs were enough to reassure me that they were okay.

How did I fall so deeply in love with a man who has brought so much grief into my life? The same man who's failed to adhere to his wedding vows. I have prayed to God over and over again, asking him to take the hurt and pain away. If it was not meant for Marlon and I to be together, I've begged to have the deep-rooted love I possess for him taken out of my heart. The number of times I have prayed and the quality of my prayers have done nothing to remove this painful love.

As I unsteadily walked back toward my bedroom, a beam of light flashed through the window. Picking up speed, I dropped to my knees and peeped from the corner of the curtains to view what was taking place below. *It's Marlon. Thank you God.*

As he exited his car, a dark-colored Land Cruiser pulled up in front of our house, stopping by the mailbox. Marlon swiftly jogged down the driveway to meet the female who stood near the passenger side. With only the glaring lights beaming from the other side of the street, I couldn't make out who that tall, slim female was. She was wearing a baseball cap and a dark sweat suit.

She handed him an item that he placed in his back pocket. She leaned toward his face before strolling back to the driver's side of her vehicle. My chest twined with knots as Marlon jogged back up the driveway.

Thank God for the serenity of this neighborhood. No one seems to have witnessed the evidence of my rendezvous, Marlon thought, allowing a beguiling smile to stretch across his face as he walked up the steps that led to the front door.

The sound of his keys clanging against the doorknob as he unlocked it snapped me out of the short daze I'd thrown myself into. *I wonder why he didn't park in the garage.* Quickly, I entered the bed before he made his way up the spiraling steps to our bedroom.

Gradually inhaling and exhaling, I allowed my palpitating heart to slow down. There I was, whimpering softly, in hopes that he didn't realize I was awake, feeling undesirable pain.

Was that Sarita or was it someone else? I really couldn't tell. What did she give him? Did she kiss him? Where has he been? God, please take this pain away.

Peeping from underneath the comforter, I found myself staring at him as he undressed. His dark, silky, hair was a perfect match to that displayed on his chest. His physique had not changed since he was a star football player in college. Five foot-eleven. Small muscular body frame. Just perfect. His smooth, milk chocolate complexion complimented the horseshoe brand that bulged from his shoulder.

I just love him so much.

The spraying of the water from the shower alerted me that it was safe to get out of bed.

'PI Check', I thought.

Indigo and Rashondra would be very surprised to know that I'm now a faithful partaker of PI Checks. Indigo was a master at it. She once told me that there are times in a relationship that you have to investigate for your own personal satisfaction.

"You have to be calm because it requires a lot of concentration," she had said. "You have to be sure you place everything back in the order you found them."

When we were in college, every attempt I made to do a PI Check failed due to me always leaving something out of place. It was difficult for me to lie after being confronted, therefore, I decided not to be so inquisitive. I concluded that if Marlon were lying, his guilty conscious would advert him to tell the truth. If the truth was never told, then there was nothing ever going on, or God didn't want me to know about it.

Oh I would love to talk to Indigo and Rashondra. I miss them both dearly. I somehow wish I could delete the past two years from existence.

Without having Indigo and Rashondra for backup over the last two years, I've taken on the responsibility of checking behind Marlon for myself.

Inhaling deeply, I rubbed my forehead with my fingertips and headed toward the Versace shirt he had thrown on the chaise. With trembling hands, I checked the right pocket. Nothing's there. I placed the shirt under my nose and inhaled for any foreign scents. There was a wee feeling of relief as the familiarity of Hugo teased my nostrils. Carefully placing the shirt slanted across the chaise as he had left it, I reached for the pants.

Front pockets all clear, nothing but a few coins. Back pockets checked out okay as well. Nothing there but his eel-skinned wallet. *Well what did he place in his back pocket? Was it his wallet? Why would she have his wallet?*

At the weakening of my knees, I sat on the edge of the chaise before fingering through his wallet. The palpitation of my heart increased as I began pulling items from it. To my surprise, the wallet checked out okay. Nothing different since I checked it three weeks ago.

Only after finding chewing gum paper in his jacket, I double-checked to be sure every item was back in its proper position and, tediously approached the edge of the bed where his briefcase was placed.

Carefully dialing the combination I'd memorized, I flipped it open and frantically began the last phase of my PI Check.

I was bewildered as the bathroom door swung open with the sound of water still splattering from the shower nozzle. Shock waves moved through my body leaving a feeling of rigidity as my mouth gaped open. There stood Marlon, nude and wet, holding only a washcloth in his hand. He looked at me as if I was some evil spirit attempting to possess him.

How will I get out of this one?

Chapter 4

Rashondra

Not clearly concentrating on my surroundings, I walked back down the hall and out the front door, almost tripping over Billy, who had taken a seat on the top step. I didn't know where I was going, as a matter of fact, I didn't care. Leaving the scene I had just witnessed behind was of most importance to me.

Before taking the last flight of steps, my fast paced walk increased into a jog. As soon as my right foot touched the walkway, I collided with a gentleman attempting to come up. He fell backwards, losing the belongings he held in his hands as I tumbled on top of him.

"Derrick!" I yelled with tears streaming down my face.

"What happened baby? Did someone hurt you?" He grabbed my face with both hands setting his eyes deeply into mine.

Tiny specks of blood trickled from the back of his left hand. He must have scraped it on the cement in an attempt to brace himself from the fall he'd just taken.

How do I tell him I just saw Mama in 'our' bed with some strange man? He hates the fact that she's even here. We've had several bouts in reference to Mama over-staying her welcome. I've always agreed with him, but she's my Mama. It's hard for me to just kick her out on the streets. She has no place to go. It's bad enough that she was evicted from her apartment in Ft. Lauderdale. He just doesn't seem to understand that.

While smothering my face into his chest, I held him tightly, not wanting to answer. I missed him so much.

"Baby, I asked you a question. What happened? Why are you crying?"

My lips stiffened. I still didn't answer. I continued to hold on.

He pushed me away as he scrambled to get up from the ground. He stood there for a moment, brushing dirt off his pants and jacket. Traces of blood from the scratches he wore on his hand stained his clothes.

"Damn, I've messed up a new suit," he said, reaching to assist me from the ground. Before my feet were leveled completely, he grabbed both of my shoulders and shook me. "Rashondra, what the hell is going on? Tell me now dammit!" he demanded.

Reluctantly I said, "Okay." I began to tell him about walking into the dark apartment, the music, and what I saw when I opened the bedroom door.

"Mama!" I had screamed after finally regaining my composure. "What do you think you are doing?"

She quickly grabbed the sheet and wrapped it around her nude body.

"Shondra? Is that you gul?" she asked. "Whatcha doin home so early? I was speckin you da morrow mornin. Sorry bout this gul."

"How could you? I can't believe this!"

"Gul I said I'm sorry. Damn, you cain't hear! That twin bed in thar is too lil for me and Leroy. We was in thar doin our thang and rolled rite on the flo."

At that point, I closed the door and walked away.

"We getting up gul!" she yelled before I exited the front door.

"Your Mama has lost her damn mind! That's it! She's got to go!" Derrick raced up the steps, leaving his briefcase and travel bag behind.

I grabbed his coattail and trailed him. "Derrick wait! Please calm down. We don't know that man in there. There's no telling what he might do to us," I uttered in a semi-hysterical voice.

"This is my home. Right now I don't give a damn what he *tries* to do because I know what he's *going* to do. He's getting out whether he likes it or not."

As Derrick opened the front door, we viewed Mama and Leroy standing in the hallway kissing as if nothing had ever happened. They were fully dressed and didn't seem to have any interest in leaving.

It has to be drugs, I was thinking. *Mama must be consuming drugs again. I can't imagine any other reason why she would do something so humiliating.*

*   *   *   *   *

Mama has been an addict for as long as I could remember. Grandma once told me that every man she dealt with was a dealer, except Papa.

If only Papa had stayed around, things would've been different. Mama loved him so much. She still talks about him today.

Grandma told me that Papa was sent back to Cuba when I was five years old. He and a group of Hispanic men were working for a farmer. They were paid tax-free money. The field was raided one day. Papa was not a citizen; therefore he was exported back to Cuba.

Mama and Papa were never married, but we lived like one big happy family, Mama, Papa, Zach, and me. Zach is only ten months younger than I am. Strangers used to think we were twins.

When Papa left, Mama would not tell me he was gone back to Cuba. I can remember asking, "Mama, when is Papa coming home from work? He's been gone a long time."

"Sugar I'on know. He musta be lost out thar in them big ole tall fields. If his boss cain't find him, he mite not come back home."

After two weeks of waiting for Papa to return, Zach and I decided to go looking for him.

One Saturday morning, we woke up very early and crawled out of our bedroom window while Mama was still sleeping. We ran down the street to the building where Papa and the other men used to wait for the truck to pick them up.

"Where them people at?" Zach had asked, almost out of breath from running.

The only person we saw was a good-for-nothing beggar woman sitting on the ground with her back against the building. She was smoking a cigarette.

"Excuse me lady," I said. "We looking for our Papa. He comes here every morning to go to work. His name is Armando Hernadez. Have you seen him?"

"Yall chillums git outta here," she said, picking a bottle up off the ground and throwing it at us. "Gon mess round and git yall selves kilt comin out hem like this hem."

Scared nearly to death, I grabbed Zach's hand and we sprinted back home. After crawling back through the bedroom window, we both jumped in our beds still dressed. To this day, we never said a word about that lady trying to kill us, well that's what we thought.

Grandma told me when Papa left, Mama started using drugs heavily. She used to hang out at the fancy nightclubs flirting with the men who were spending the most money.

I witnessed at least thirteen men playing temporary papas for us. As soon as one moved out, it wasn't long before another one moved in.

Mama had taken an overdose because Harold, the last step-papa I knew, was shot and killed, right before her very own eyes.

Harold and Mama had smoked almost three thousand dollars worth of crack that Harold was supposed to sell. When his supplier came for the money, he didn't have it.

I was twelve years old the day it happened. We were all sitting in the kitchen eating dinner. There was an unusual knock at the door.

"Get the children out of here," Harold told Mama after spying through the peephole.

Mama took us out the back door and told me to knock on Miss Louise's, our next door neighbor, door. Before she answered my knocks, Mama had disappeared back into our apartment.

About twenty minutes later, a police officer knocked on Miss Louise's door and told her to detain us at her apartment for a while. Through the front window I was able to see Mama. Blood was splattered all over her clothes. She was crying hysterically.

Miss Louise scurried us away from the window to divert our attention from the activities taking place outside. Zach and I sat on her bed while she held Nayla, my baby sister, in her lap. She rocked her back and forth as she began to tell us about Harold's untimely death. He was Nayla's papa.

The next day Miss Louise took us over to Grandma's house. We were told that we would only stay for a few days. Those few days turned into six years for me.

* * * * *

"Get out of my damn house!" Derrick yelled. He grabbed Mama by the arm, interrupting the intimate kiss she was sharing with Leroy.

"We ain't in y'all bed no mo. We was goin in the livin room until Leroy put a grip on my booty with his hand that made me turn round and kiss him," she said, laughing.

"The only place you're going around here is out that door. You have some nerves bringing this stranger into our home. On top of that, you took him into our bedroom. You have lost your damn mind."

"Hold up now boy. Don't talk to the pretty lady like that," Leroy snapped, giving Derrick a quick thrust to the chest. "Watcha mouth boy, you hear me, watcha mouth."

As a natural impulse, Derrick took the buckling of his five right fingers and sent them smashing into the side of Leroy's head.

Leroy stumbled backwards a few steps before he reached inside his vest to pull out a small handgun. "Boy, don't never swing my way unless it's deadly. I don't play boy. I'll blow yo brains out." His firm hand clutched the gun as he pointed in our direction.

"You ain't gonna kill my gul is you Leroy? That's gonna mess up our thang. I can't be wit you if you kill my gul."

"Let that drunk fool..." Quickly I muzzled the completion of Derrick's retort by placing my hand over his mouth.

"Are you crazy?" I whispered in his ear. "That's a real gun he has." For a minute I thought Derrick was trying to get both of us killed. Apparently his knowledge of guns had withdrawn from his memory bank. Guns kill. On several occasions at work I've had to place gunshot victims on the ventilator. Very few made it off.

"Naw. I won't shoot em. A lil punk like that ain't worth going no jail over. He better recognize though," Leroy said, placing the gun back inside his vest. "You coming wit me or what?"

"I better wait til da morrow. Need to let thangs cool off round here first," Mama said. "Just call me da morrow."

After World War III, Leroy went into the kitchen and opened the refrigerator. He pulled out a half full bottle of Cisco that I didn't noticed earlier. "My liquor can't stay if I can't stay," he said.

Before walking out the door, he grabbed the back of Mama's head and pulled it toward his face. He placed his lingering tongue into her mouth. She sucked it for enjoyment a few seconds before he suddenly released his hold and walked out the door. *My goodness, how disgusting.*

Derrick and I stood in astonishment as we watched Leroy's last few moves before he left. I'm glad Derrick didn't say anything else to Leroy. Maybe it finally sunk in that Leroy could've been deadly.

"You done made a good man walk out on me," Mama screamed at Derrick.

"Betty, you've got about fifteen minutes to pack as much as you can and get out of here."

"That ain't nothin but a thang. I always wanted to leave anyhow. I'm tired of you tryin to boss me and Shondra round. You don't do nothing for me no how. When I need clothes, Shondra buy them. When I need to go somewhar, Shondra take me. She need to divoce yo tar-baby lookin ass and go wit that fine, high-yellow, repatory therpist she be talkin bout behind yo back."

"You can say what you want, you just need to leave. You have some nerves bringing that crazy fool in here as if you are some low-life prostitute. You..."

Derrick was stopped in mid-sentence by a loud 'WHACK!' in the mouth with the back of Mama's right hand.

"Now you done said too much. That's one thang I ain't is a prossitute. I been good lookin and fine enuff all my life to git whatever man I want. I'on half to sell my body to nobody."

Derrick jacked Mama by the shirt and backed her into the wall. White flesh lined his arms as a result of scratches from Mama's long, acrylic nails.

"Let her go before you hurt her," I said.

Instantly relieving the grip he had on her shirt, he headed for the front door.

"Where are you going?"

"Y'all can have it in here. I just can't deal with you and your family problems anymore. Didn't you get enough when Zach was here? I'll be damned if I continue to go through this bull with you and Betty. I'm tired of it. It's either going to be your family or me. You need a few days to make some decisions."

Ohh. He makes me sick doing that. Every time he gets mad at Mama, he brings up Zach. He just won't let the past stay in the past. How dare him trying to give me an ultimatum!

He continued down the steps as I followed. Billy was still sitting on the top step, this time smoking what smelled like marijuana.

"What y'all arguing about? I hear it all out here. You show nuff beat him up pretty bad."

Without responding to Billy, I hurried down the steps trying to keep up with Derrick.

He picked up his travel bag and briefcase en route to his car.

After closing the car door behind him, I tapped on the window for him to roll it down. "Where are you going? Don't do this to us."

He cranked the car and said, "I'll call you tomorrow from the hotel."

"Hotel? No baby, I want you here with me. We need to talk about this." I couldn't believe he was leaving me. He'd just arrived home. What was he thinking? I wanted him home with me. I felt an urge to fall to my knees and beg him to stay. But my pride prevailed.

"I'll call you tomorrow," he said and drove off.

There I was, standing in the middle of the parking lot, crying like a baby as my husband's car disappeared, leaving a trail of smoke behind.

My mind became cloudy as I thought about his reactions. He's been by my side in worst situations; therefore, I was appalled by his departure.

Taking a deep breath, I attempted to calm down to pull myself together. Mama... Derrick... Mama... Derrick... My mind was made up. Mama had to leave. I love Derrick too much.

As I reentered the apartment, I noticed Billy standing in the hallway near Mama's room talking to her. He is one character who needed to mind his own business. I had no idea he even knew her that well.

"Leavin ya gul," Mama stated as I walked past her doorway.

"Where are you going?"

"Don't worry bout that. You don't care bout yo Mama anyhow. All you care bout is that damn black ass Derrick."

How could those words even come out of her mouth as much as I've done for her? Did she care about her children when she left them at her mother's house and never came back to get them? It's two in the morning and I'm too exhausted to endure anymore arguing.

"Mama, I'm going to purchase you a one-way ticket back to Fort Lauderdale tomorrow. I'll call Grandma to see if you can stay with her."

"Ain goin back down thar. Who you thank you is? You thank you can just ship me off to Flada? Well ain goin. You hear me. Ain goin."

You're getting out of here, I thought as I walked into my bedroom, closing the door behind me.

My bed was unmade, the comforter was on the floor, and the top sheet was balled at the edge of the bed. *She could've at least had the decency to make my bed. Is there anything decent about Mama?*

Not able to withstand the condition my room was left in, I u-turned and made a beeline to the kitchen.

Billy was sitting on Mama's bed. She was still babbling about me not caring about her. I didn't even entertain the thought. I continued my way up the hall.

A slight feeling of relief hit me when I noticed the bottle of Asti Spumante still in the refrigerator. It was just what I needed. In a matter of seconds I popped the cork and turned the bottle up.

That champagne should have been used to celebrate Derrick's return and our love for each other. But instead, there I was, forcing it down, in an attempt to soothe the pain.

Damn you Derrick. How could you leave me? Why couldn't we have talked like we always did?

* * * * *

The flickering of sunlight through the vertical blinds awakened me from a deep sleep. It was eleven-fifteen. I must have drunk too much. I gently massaged the side of my neck to relieve the discomfort that resulted from poor positioning on the sofa.

A sharp emotional pain went through my body as I thought about Derrick. Racing to my bedroom to check Caller ID ended in disappointment. The only name on my box was Walter Lucas. I really had no desire to chat. I decided to phone him later. I wanted my husband to call. That was the only voice I wanted to hear.

Mama's room was empty. Where could she have gone this morning? I must have really been knocked out to have not heard her leave. There was a piece of paper in the middle of one of the twin beds that drew me in to investigate. *'I'm gone Shondra'* it read. Gone where, I wondered. Checking her closet, I noticed a few pieces of her clothes missing. Where did she go?

Back on the living room sofa again, I began to think about everything that transpired last night. After about two hours of lying around, pouting, and waiting for Derrick to call, I decided to make some calls myself before cleaning up.

Derrick was in a meeting. His administrative assistant informed me that he would be held up for a while. Billy didn't answer his door when I went to inquire about Mama. Grandma wasn't surprised when I told her what happened last night. Then I sat, holding the phone, wanting so desperately to make other phone calls. *Indigo and Priscilla, I know I wouldn't feel half as bad if you two were around. I just can't do it,* I thought and placed the phone back on the receiver.

Within another hour or so, the apartment was clean from top to bottom. Every time I thought about Derrick, that same emotional twang went through my stomach. *What kind of meeting are you in Derrick? You said you were going to call me. When?*

Out of options, I thought about Indigo and Priscilla again. *Nobody will really understand how I feel about Derrick's behavior but the two of them. My two best friends. I still love and miss them dearly, despite what happened two years ago. I really wish I could talk to them.*

Thinking about my friends gave me a change of heart about returning Walter's call. As soon I as dialed his area code, I decided not to again.

He's only going to inquire about Indigo and Priscilla. I just don't want to deal with it right now.

Down on my knees, I began to pray. Hadn't done that in almost two years. *My dearest God. Please give me the strength you've instilled in me before. Please help...*

The ringing of the phone interrupted my prayer. I quickly answered without viewing the Caller ID. "Derrick, is that you?" I said anxiously.

Chapter 5

Walter

Two years have passed and it's still hard to accept the fact that my little sisters have made no attempts to make amends. It continues to tear me apart. I've pondered over the events numerous times to determine if there was anything I could've done to prevent the breakup. I came up with nothing.

The three of them disclosed good intentions on their own behalves, but evidently, those good intentions weren't enough to satisfy the others.

Rashondra, Indigo, and Priscilla, R.I.P. is what I called them. They had a lock on their friendship no key could unlatch, even if it was specially made.

I was there from the very beginning. As a matter of fact, I'm the one to thank for bringing those three together.

* * * * *

Too much partying with my frat brothers caused me to overlook a history class I should've taken during my freshmen year. So there I was, a winter-quartered junior, sitting in a class with a bunch of freshmen, feeling somewhat embarrassed, but doing what I had to do.

Dr. Turner, the professor, was a frat of mine, therefore he allowed me to pre-select three students for a group project. Of course I chose the prettiest and finest females in the class, which happened to be RIP. *Shhh, Now that was Dr. Turner's and my little secret.*

They didn't know each other, therefore, the first thing on my agenda was *not* trying to figure out who would research what part of The Boston Massacre; but which one of them I would *bone* first. That was just the dog in me. It wasn't long before they figured out my game and put me 'in-check' with the quickness. So you see, that history class was the beginning of an astounding relationship between RIP and me.

Just thinking back on that Saturday afternoon we met in the library to start our research. A curly headed, gigolo-looking senior was rapping pretty hard attempting to get a date from one of them. After accepting their denials with little shame, he walked away saying, "Damn, y'all just *ripped* my heart apart."

RIP, I thought as I approached the table. *Rashondra, Indigo, and Priscilla, RIP,* I continued to think, chuckling as I pulled out a chair.

"What's happening RIP?" I said as we all laughed when they realized the connection I'd made with the gigolo. From that point on, they wore that acronym as if it were a monogram on a sweater.

* * * * *

Rashondra, the prettiest and finest of them all, had a body to die for. She was every bit of 36-24-36, awwh what a winning hand. Her complexion reminded me of butter. She stood about 5'9", slimmed and trimmed. Her silky, jet-black, wavy hair descended toward the middle of her back.

Rashondra was also the wildest. She did things she dared not to share with the other two and trusted that her secrets were safe with me. She practically lived in the frat house during Christmas break of her freshman year. She was a slick ole something. She had a strong voice that she didn't mind speaking if you moved her the wrong way. She exerted a 'rough-neck' attitude. If you stepped on her toes, she most definitely stepped back on yours, with lead in her shoes. She brought a sense of independence to RIP. She felt free, under no one's control. She didn't have a mother or father to run to for support. She knew about survival first hand.

Indigo was what I called cute. She was the most attractive of the three. Her make-up was always neatly placed on her face. Not too much, not too little, just enough to blend in with her smooth, milk chocolate, complexion. She was about 5'7", slimmed and trimmed as well. Now the sister kept her hair laid. It never grew below shoulder's length.

Indigo was a little blunt herself. Although she didn't 'beat-you-down' like Rashondra did, she had a little abruptness about herself that kept you off her back. She had more of a sarcastic overtone, which left you wondering how to take her sometimes. She brought intellect to RIP. Don't get me wrong now, they were all smart, but Indigo seem to be the one who diverged in mental thinking. She always came up with the perfect plan, or always knew how to handle a situation. For some unknown reason, my bond with her was just a teeny-weenie bit tighter.

Priscilla was just plain ole gorgeous. Her jet-black hair cascaded just below her shoulders. She and Indigo shared the same height and complexion. Gucci, Coach, Tommy, you name it, she had it. The sister came to college with 'big bank'.

Priscilla was the most meek and humbled person I'd ever met. She was very soft spoken and had a very pleasant personality. I'd often wondered how she was able to keep up with Indigo and Rashondra , but some how, they broke her in. She brought integrity to RIP. She always preached that 'honesty was the best policy'. If ever backed into a corner, she hardly ever lied her way out. She felt it was prosperous to tell the truth. She even angered me at times with her virtuosity. She exemplified the perfect little princess who did no wrong.

* * * * *

Over the last two years, I've maintained contact with RIP, at least on a monthly basis, if not more. They've all expressed how much they miss one another, but are too stubborn to initiate a call.

There is one thing I don't understand about a woman. She will beg a man back in a heartbeat; I know this from experience, but exerts too much pride to forgive her own kind. This is very true, just think about it. A woman can catch her man cheating. She's ready to knock the life out of the other woman, and will hate her for the rest of her life. But the cheating man, on the other hand, is back in her arms the next week. Sometimes the next day.

* * * * *

Viewing the clock as I reminisced about RIP, I didn't realize it was so late. Forty-five minutes was all I had to get to the airport and board my plane before it took off without me. I attempted to contact RIP earlier, but was unsuccessful.

What trick will I pull from my sleeve to bring them together? Nothing comes to mind at the moment, but believe me, before my plane lands, I will have the perfect solution. Oh yes, it's time RIP. It's time to reunite.

Chapter 6

Priscilla

"What would you like for breakfast honey?" I asked Marlon while sitting next to him still undressed. My lips protruded as I bent over for a passionate kiss.

While Marlon was sleeping soundly earlier this morning, I weaseled out of bed and telephoned our part-time nanny. She quickly agreed to pick up the kids earlier when I offered to double her pay for today.

"Karla you are a blessing,"I said after explaining why she shouldn't ring the doorbell. "Meet me at the back door, nine o'clock sharp."

With Marlon working those long hours yesterday, along with the episode we created last night, he needed to rest, undisturbed.

* * * * *

...Overflowed with tears after being caught red-handed going through his briefcase, I explained to Marlon, once again, the doubt and distrust I had in him. I felt he wasn't going to tell me who the female was, what she gave him, why he didn't return my pages, and where he had been.

He went on to argue about how he was so tired of living on 'pins and needles'. "Sometimes I just want to leave and never come back. No matter what I say, you will never trust me. It doesn't seem like you will ever be happy with me. There's always a complaint about something. I'm so tired of having to answer to you every time I blink my eyes. Enough is E-DAMN-NOUGH!"

The petulance displayed by both of us continued for hours. He soon slipped his pants on over his pajamas and threatened to leave.

"I'm sick of your interrogation!" he protested.

At that point, I was so overcome with weakness that I collapsed onto the bed. There I lay, in fetal position sobbing, hoping that each tear I shed drained the love I deeply possessed for him.

Why couldn't he just admit he was wrong? He always reversed the matter at hand, and pinpointed my nagging as the source of all of our problems.

The sensitive side of Marlon must have gotten the best of him because he laid next to me and kissed my salty face. The recitation of his love for me was comforting.

"I was thinking foolishly when I threatened to leave you and the kids. I'm sorry baby. I'll never do that. I love my family too much."

He eventually explained to me that he and some partners were closing on a business deal that led them out for drinks. My pages went unanswered due to mistakenly leaving his pager in the car. The female was a waitress who followed him home because he left his wallet at the bar.

His apologetic disposition transformed to an exotic, sexual demeanor. He slowly undressed me layer by layer. Then we spun a web of love making that I never wanted to break out of.

*   *   *   *   *

The deadbolt lock connected with ease after I kissed the kids goodbye. I stood for a moment, smiling. A rush of joy fluttered my emotional state as I headed back upstairs where Marlon rested like an angel.

My robe gently flowed to the floor before I stepped back into the bedroom. *I love you so much,* I thought as I stared at his beautiful face. Completely filled with excitement, I made my way back into the bed interrupting his snores.

The gasping of his breathing cycle was evident of how tired he was. That didn't stop me. I wanted more of what I had last night. I removed the comforter from his nude body and twirled my tongue delicately in his ear as I crawled on top. My body welded ideally with his. I watched our complexions blend together. He reached from under me, gently sliding his hands down the middle of my back. He planted gentle compressions on each side of my buttock. It wasn't long before Marlon sat me in an upright position, and then laid me back on the bed.

"I'm sorry for hurting you," he whispered in my ear before continuing to advance his way to my breast. His lips worked dynamically at my firm nipples. I excitedly anticipated his next move. Leaving my breast, his slithering tongue descended through the middle of my stomach until it reached the warmth of my womanhood. He placed his hands underneath my buttocks and elevated my body, allowing my legs to dangle on his back. Adjusting his mouth to fifth speed, he drove me deeply to places I love to frequent. Powerful vibrations dispersed throughout my body repeatedly until I became limp. That was always Marlon's cue to enter me with unsteady movements until he became limp as well. Within seconds, he was snoring again.

After lying in his arms, recreating thoughts about the events that had taken place within the last eight hours, I still found it hard to believe the story he had concocted. I decided to let it go and move on because we'd made up. Even if he were with Ms. Slim last night, he couldn't have possibly made love to her after the double dose he'd given me.

Upon returning from a tinkle in the restroom, I noticed Marlon looking over at the clock. It was ten twenty. *If everyday could start off like this, I would be the happiest woman in the world,* I thought right before asking him what he wanted for breakfast.

* * * * *

"Baby you know I've overslept. I should've been at the office two hours ago. I'll have to grab a bite to eat en route to work."

"Do you have to go in today? Karla came to get the kids early. We have the house to ourselves. Don't go in, please. Let's enjoy each other and the time we have in isolation."

"I'm sorry baby. I've got to go. What's today? Damn, it's Monday. Aww baby, I forgot to tell you that I have a flight to catch this afternoon."

"What? A Flight?" *I can't believe this is happening.* "Where are you going Marlon and why didn't you tell me earlier?" I was nearly hysterical now with tears pouring down my face.

"Come here baby." He reached out and grabbed me. My body felt so weak that I caved into his. "I don't know how I could forget such an important business meeting like this one. I'm going to Key West to meet with a potential client about an extension on the company."

"When are you coming back?" I asked with tears still swelled in my eyes.

"Well, I'll be gone until Monday."

"Monday? Next Monday? That's a whole week. So what I'm hearing is you have a planned business meeting out of town that will keep you away for an entire week and you forgot to tell me about it."

"Baby, you are starting to trip like you did last night. See what I mean. I knew you would react like this. That's why I waited until the last minute to tell you."

"This is not right Marlon."

"Baby this questioning session is not right. It has to stop. You've got to trust that I'm doing the right thing or this relationship will not work."

There he goes making that subliminal threat to leave me again. What should I say next to ease the tone?

"Can we go with you, the kids and me?"

"I'm not going to have time to wait for you to get the kids from Karla, clean them up, and pack their bags. After I leave the office, I'm heading straight for the airport."

"Well, can we get on the first flight out tomorrow and just meet you there? This will be very rekindling for the family, especially Marlon III. He hardly ever sees you."

"Naw, not this time. This is a business trip. I'll take you all to Disney World this summer, okay."

Oh I feel so much pain. Why doesn't he want us to go with him? We've gone before. Not recently, but we have gone with him.

"Who is she Marlon? Is it Sarita? Is it the female from last night? Who are you taking with you?"

"See, this is what I mean about walking on 'pins and needles'. I can't keep going through this mess with you every time I go somewhere."

"My intent is not to pressure you about your every move, but you have a history of committing adultery. The last time I found out about your infidelity, I vowed to never let you back into my life again. You deceived me, leading me to believe you'd changed. You are still the same. I can't help it Marlon. My instincts tell me there's more to this trip than just business."

"I've got to get out of here," he said, flinging the comforter onto the floor as he jumped out of the bed. "This could go on all damn day long if I let it," he added and headed for the shower.

With my back against the headboard, I turned slightly, rubbing my fingers against the beautiful, intertwined carving. I have yet to figure out the meaning of the exquisite ornamentation that was trimmed so perfectly. This bed was the first piece of new furniture Marlon had purchased for our home.

"Babe, you're not going to believe this," he'd excitedly said, after returning from a business trip in Canada with my father. "We're going to have a solid mahogany, Louis XV bed shipped straight from Sashatchewan, Canada," he continued. Surely Father played a major role in Marlon's sudden taste in antiques.

During the midst of his excitement, I smiled and pretended to be just as thrilled, not reminding him of the English Tudor bed I'd left in my bedroom in Bloomfield.

Well things are totally different now. Very seldom do I get excited about anything Marlon does these days.

I wrapped my arms around my bent knees. Rocking back and forth, I pondered over how I was going to handle the predicament I was in.

* * * * *

Three years ago Rashondra called because she spotted Marlon's then brand new Mercedes parked four houses down from Derrick's mother's house. After inquiring about the resident, Derrick informed her that the parents of Sarita, a high school friend of his, lived there. He admitted to seeing the Mercedes there a few other times.

Now Rashondra, who was slicker than a fox, made up some excuse about having an unexpected visit from 'Mother Nature'. She headed for 'Quick Trip' down the street and placed a call to inform me of her newfound information. After sharing her bit of news, I called Indigo on three-way. Master minded Indigo knew exactly what to do.

Tactfully planned, Indigo picked me up in Tony's car. After safely buckling Marlon III into his car seat, we drove all the way up I-75 north, which seemed to have taken eternity, until we saw a sign that read 'Cartersville City Limits'.

Slowly cruising down the street, I was nearly blinded by the sunrays beaming off the silver Mercedes parked in the driveway. I took a deep swallow to help oppress the pain, but the ball of saliva seemed to halt midway before it slowly trickled down my throat.

Rashondra had already given Derrick a good reason as to why I was in Cartersville and why she had to baby sit for a short time frame.

Indigo parked behind two tall trees in front of Sarita's mother's house.

"Calm down girl. Just leave all the talking to me."

"Okay, I'm doing the best I can," I whimpered.

My body quivered as we strolled up the walkway to knock on the door.

A petite lady with graying hair answered. "May I help you sugar?" she said, directing her attention to Indigo while opening the screen door.

"Yes Ma'am. I'm sorry to disturb you, but my car stop running as we were riding down the street." Indigo pointed in the direction of the car. "If you have a cordless phone, I don't mind standing here on your porch so that I can call Triple A."

"Oh y'all babies just come on in here. Ain got no cordless phone I can hand to you, but you more than welcome to use the phone in the kitchen." She led us through the living room.

The moth ball smell that met us at the front door soon faded as we closely approached the aroma coming from the kitchen.

Indigo reached back and touched me. To this day, I'm still not certain why she did it. I just assumed she wanted to be sure I was still behind her.

In your name Jesus, let me stand this storm. I had to pray because every little step I took felt as if I was leading myself to destruction.

The telephone was on the opposite side of the kitchen, which lead to the doorway of the dining room.

Laughter poured from within as the little old lady pointed us to the telephone.

"These two young ladies car done broke down on them. They came in here to call Triple A." She pointed to the people sitting at the table. "This here is my daughter, Sarita. That's her handsome boyfriend, Marlon, sitting next to her. And that old man sitting on the end over there is my husband. We been married for thirty-eight years," she added, handing Indigo the phone and laughing at the same time.

Devastation hit me like a bolt of lightning. Keen pains went piercing through my body as I stood, watching my husband eat dinner with another woman. He didn't quite recognize us at first due to Indigo's suggestion to wear shades and baseball caps. "It's not that I think he won't figure it out. It's just that instant recognition. Also, you don't really want her to know what you look like," Indigo said.

A minute had not passed before Marlon started coughing and choking on the wine he was sipping. Sarita stood up to assist him by wiping his mouth with her napkin.

"Are you okay darling?" She lifted his chin with her right hand.

Marlon didn't respond, he only nodded. His eyes appeared to be bulging out of their sockets as he continued to wipe his shirt, even after there was nothing on it.

"Y'all young ladies have some dinner," said Sarita's mother after Indigo placed the phone back onto the receiver ending her fake phone call.

"No thank you. Triple A was able to dispatch a trucker that's already in this area. He should be here within the next minute or so," replied Indigo.

"Y'all want to sit in the living room and wait. Sarita and Marlon can keep y'all company. Y'all young folks can have it in there. Us old folks will clean up in here."

"No Ma'am." My silence was finally broken. I could barely hear my own voice due to being so distressed by the whole ordeal.

When we reached the car, I cried from my soul, overpowered by grief. "Why? Why Lord? Why me? Why, why, why?" Tears poured from my eyes while Indigo rubbed my back.

"You'll get over him in time". Her quick response was as if she knew it was finally over. That's the way is should have been.

A good fifteen minutes had not passed before Marlon hurried out the front door. We ducked as he drove by, with Sarita on the passenger side.

By the time we returned to Indigo's apartment, Marlon had already called and left three messages. When Rashondra came over, she said Marlon had called her apartment looking for me also.

My dear friends and I sat up for hours talking about the healing process. My heart was weak. I had endured enough.

The next day while Marlon worked, Rashondra and Indigo came over with boxes to help me pack his things. The six boxes were neatly stacked on top of one another in the car garage with a note attached that read," I've shed my last tear."

Arriving home that evening, Marlon's attempt to come inside was curtailed by the change of locks on the door. He tried the windows but was still unsuccessful. He soon gave up and left.

The following day I received a certified letter from Marlon, asking that I give him a chance to explain the situation. Part of me wanted to listen, but I couldn't. The daily phone calls continued for weeks, but went unanswered. Soon the calls deceased.

Marlon's mother phoned me two months later asking to spend some time with her grandson. I suspected Marlon to be the culprit of this request. He had temporarily moved in with her. That one visit turned into every other weekend.

If was difficult not to think about Marlon because I saw him twice a month. He came over for the first time since his barring for Marlon III's second birthday party. *I miss you so much,* I thought as I watched him maneuver through the kids trying to take pictures.

Eight months after our initial separation I heard a knock on the door. There stood Marlon, about ten pounds lighter, crocodile tears and all, beseeching a return home. After two hours of talking and making up, I forgave him.

Well that was three years ago. If this so called business trip is fictitious, Marlon will be on his way out the door, for good this time.

* * * * *

Marlon departed from the bathroom as I continued to sit on the bed, carried away by events of the past. He dressed and packed his suitcase without uttering a word to me.

Slowly exhaling, trying to maintain a calm demeanor, I wondered why he was mute. You'd think he would want to leave on good terms, considering he'll be away for a week. But there I sat, in total silence, watching him pack.

After placing the locks on his Hartman suitcase, garment bag, and carry-on satchel, he walked over to the bed where I'd been sitting all along and kissed me on the cheek.

"I'll call when I'm settled in okay." He lifted my chin to catch a glimpse of my eyes.

How could he not see the pain I'm feeling? My eyes are swollen with tears, my head is throbbing with pain, and my jaws are sagging with sadness.

He received no response from me except the expression I portrayed. He picked up his belongings and walked out the door.

Sorrow spanned through my entire mental, physical, and emotional states. I continued sitting on the bed and allowed the tears to flow freely. My thoughts reflected the good as well as the bad aspects of our relationship. Which outweighed the other?

Drifting even further into the past, I thought of Indigo and Rashondra. Oh how I missed them so much.

In an attempt to relieve the uneasiness I was feeling, I decided to shower, get dress, and leave the house.

Phillip's Plaza welcomed me with open arms. I went back and forth to my car, each trip with over- loaded shopping bags. Soon afterwards, I zoomed across the street, toured and purchased from Lenox Mall until I felt satisfied.

Five hours of shopping and three thousand dollars worth of receipts were good reasons for me to head back home, just in time to beat the Peachtree traffic.

My bouts of joy quickly ceded as soon as I stepped into the house. I hoped Karla would keep the kids overnight. I felt remote. I needed isolation. My brain seemed to be experiencing a mini explosion.

Am I losing my mind or what? Marlon did this to me. I'm feeling a lessened need for existence, I thought as I gradually strolled toward the nightstand.

The hard, cold object I retrieved seemed to smelt with the warmth of my hand. I rubbed my index finger across the barrel, wondering if this was the only path to solace... *Who will raise my children if I pull the trigger?*

Chapter 7

Indigo

Leaving for work at five-fifty sure did have its advantages. I took a left onto Powers Ferry Road out of my complex. Made another left onto Windy Hill Road and jetted onto I-75 south without any delays.

"I've got to get away. I've got to get a way-ay" I sang along with Bobby as I turned the volume of the radio up. It had been a while since I heard that song.

Spring break was only three weeks away. Just the thought of it cracked a smile upon my face. Two months later, I'll be punching out for the summer. Where will I go, I wondered as I thought about the reality of not traveling to Hawaii with Tony.

* * * * *

Tony had assured me that Hawaii would be the spot for our next summer's vacation after we spent a very romantic evening on the shores of Nassau, Bahamas the year prior.

"This is so wonderful baby," he said to me as we nestled on our quilt, listening to the clamorous waves thrust into the boulders.

I still remember the way his head tilted in an effort to grasp my lips for a passionate kiss. The delicate movement of his body into mine created sensuous warmth as we simultaneously expressed our love for one another.

As we lay in each other arms, mesmerized by our complacent love making, I felt water creep upon my toes.

"Tony baby, look. A few more feet and we'll be carried away by the currents of the ocean."

We had slid away from the cozy little resting spot that protected our bodies from the sandy soil.

"We can drift off to Senegal for all I care, as long as I drift with the one I love." He rolled over and kissed me once more before pulling me up.

Before gathering our quilt off the ground to return to our room, he stopped directly in front of me. He allowed his sandy hands to slide down both sides of my face as he cupped my jaws and said, "I love you Ms. Indigo Duncan. I've had a wonderful time with you. I wish we could stay like this forever."

* * * * *

'Honnkkk! Honk! Honk!' screeched from my horn. I spotted a blue Oldsmobile attempting to cross over in front of me. That interrupted my daydream.

Oh look at that fool, just driving, not even paying attention to where he's going. He probably doesn't even know I'm behind him. Oh, he most definitely will get 'the eyes'.

My attitude instantly changed as I drove past the little old man. He looked at least eighty years old. Reminding me of Granddaddy, he was slumped over the stirring wheel straining to see the road.

Bless his heart, I thought as I waved at him with a smile.

I sighed and realized I needed to stop thinking about a worthless cause, which was Tony. He was a done deal.

The volume of my radio was turned up even louder. I continued to sing almost every song on the radio until I reached the school's parking lot.

* * * * *

A quick chill met me at the door as I walked into my classroom. Being so frustrated with Sean on Friday, I totally forgot to leave the heater on over the weekend. My bookbag was placed on my desk right before I reached over to turn the switch to 'on'. I headed upstairs for a fresh cup of coffee to stimulate my brain before the students arrived.

By eight-fifteen, Sean was called to the office and my mood was in high swing. It wasn't long before that changed due to a call to my room from the principal. She wanted to meet with me during my planning period.

This has to be a serious offense because Mrs. Smith barely spoke to me unless she felt a need to flash her authoritative voice around.

"Duncan!" she had once addressed me, purposely deleting 'Indigo' or 'Miss' in front of my last name. "You need to teach your students proper table manners!" she had yelled across the cafeteria. Boy did she strike a nerve.

After evaluating my actions over the pass couple of weeks, I was not able to come up with any sufficient reason that warranted such a short-noticed meeting with the principal.

One of the first things she addressed to the faculty last year when she arrived as our new principal was, "Don't say the words 'shut-up' to the students because those harsh words can lead them to become very rebellious".

I reminisced about the times Momma used to tell us to 'shut-up'. Sometimes she reinforced it with a backhand slap. It never caused any of us to become rebellious. As a matter of fact, those same two words that the educational system calls harsh knocked us back into submission.

But anyway, I abided by Mrs. Smith's command and always told the students to 'close their mouths', or 'be quiet'.

What if she finally wanted to compliment me on the acknowledgement I received in the county newspaper about the strategies I use to keep my class reading scores up? Not hardly. She would have done that two months ago when it was printed.

* * * * *

My steady heart began to palpitate as I walked into her office, noticing the counselor and assistant principal already seated. The only sources of light seen in her office were those seeping through the closed mini blinds as well as the light pouring from the eight-inch lamp settled on the left corner of her desk. She claimed that bright, direct light affected her ability to learn accurately. She even had us cover half of our ceiling lights with colored crepe paper. This was to allow those students with similar characteristics to better adapt to their learning environments.

"Duncan," she said, opening a manila folder on her desk. "In speaking with Mrs. Rogers, Sean's mother, she gave me a story totally opposite of the one you gave about Sean pushing a kindergarten to the floor on Friday. She claimed you falsely accused her son of wrongdoing. I'm not disputing your words, but you need to know that she had several other complaints about you as well," she added, tilting her head down in an attempt to glance at me over the glasses that sat on the tip of her skinny, wrinkled nose.

"Mrs. Rogers stated that Sean exemplifies undesirable behavior in your classroom because he's bored."

"Miss Duncan, we're here to assist you in ways to motivate and challenge Sean," interrupted Miss Axel, the counselor.

"The parents want Sean taken out of your classroom and placed..." Mr. Cobb was stopped in mid-sentence by my abrupt interruption.

"Excuse me," I said, sitting at the edge of my chair, very angry. "My intentions are not to be rude, but I feel a need to break in. It appears to me that you all have already thrown a guilty verdict on me and is now giving me my probation terms."

"I think you are misunderstanding us," said Mr. Cobb.

"Well, I would like to comment on this inappropriate behavior I've observed over the last seven months. Bored is the *last* label I would place on Sean. He keeps himself very busy in my classroom. Yes, he does rush through his assignments in an attempt to be the first one finished, which results in careless mistakes." *Believe it or not, I've left the edge of my chair, now standing, with all kinds of hand movements going on.*

Continuing to utter about the student from hell, I added, "He's very disruptive. While I'm teaching, he's either talking, out of his seat, or throwing things across the classroom. This is guaranteed behavior on a daily basis. If you ask me, he's a true candidate of ADHD."

"Have you met with the Student Support Team in reference to your suspicions of Attention Deficit Hyperactivity Disorder?"

"Yes I have. I've also had several personal and phone conferences with Mrs. Rogers. I've recommended a daily checklist, but she refused, stating that if Sean is in a classroom that adverts her attention to monitor his behavior daily, then something is wrong with the classroom management, not Sean. And yes, I have that in writing. Pull your files for office referrals this year," I added, now diverting my attention to Mr. Cobb. "You should have six referrals on him." I rested my case and sat down.

After spending my entire planning period in that so-called emergency meeting, I took my students outside for recess, not even concerning myself with the time. Of course I would be breaking one of Mrs. Smith's school rules if I stayed out too long.

"Ten minutes is the maximum amount of time allotted for recess on the days your students don't have PE. Staying out any longer takes away valuable instructional time which is needed to raise the test scores," she said.

At this point in time, I could care less about rules and test scores. This break is all about me regrouping and getting my head straight before going back inside for instruction. Yes, teachers experience stress also.

Mrs. Rogers have some nerves, I thought while watching my students rip and run around the playground as if they had just escaped from a locked cage. She was trying to make it appear as if I was incompetent. The truth of the matter is, she has a corrupted son and doesn't want to admit it. If I receive one more irrelevant note from her, I'll probably shove it down Sean's throat... *'Why didn't Sean bring his math book home? What happened to Sean's lunch money? You have no right sending Sean to another classroom to work without my permission. Since when is asking, "Why do I have to sit down?" is disrespectful? Why did you take free time away from Sean? He was reading, not talking. He deserves extra free time today. Call me about this at two o'clock.'...* Oh this mess has been going on ever since the day she stepped her raggedy looking, trying to act high-classed, bleached-blonde head into my classroom during open house back in September. Sometimes I can't decipher who's worse, Sean or Mrs. Rogers herself.

* * * * *

When Sean returned to my class after lunch, it was rather difficult to disregard the conference I had earlier. Every time I had to discipline him, an unpleasant attitude went alone with it.

As I taught math, he threw a spitball across the class and attempted to argue with me when I moved him to the back. Then he started banging on the tape recorder in the reading center, which gave me no choice but to send him into the hall. Continuing his rude behavior, he jumped up and down, making faces through the window of the door, which created an abundance of laughter within the classroom.

Getting really fed up with his nonsense, I told him to go to the class across the hall to complete his assignment.

"It's not fair!" he yelled. "My momma told me I don't have to go!"

"Just go!" I insisted, stretching my arm as I pointed in the direction he should walk. I closed the door behind me.

This little fool has really lost his mind, I thought while swinging the door back open after he slammed his math book into it.

"What's your problem Sean? Pick up the book right now!" I said firmly, clinching my teeth together, which muzzled the loudness of my harsh tone.

He was a rather chubby kid for a second grader. He stood about five feet and weighed about one hundred thirty pounds.

Surprisingly, he bent over and picked up the book. Instead of continuing to hold on to it, he elevated both hands above his head and hurled it, full force, in the direction of my head. Quick thinking allowed me to duck just in time as it entered the room and rested on the classroom floor.

Ramming his head into my stomach, he yelled, "Stupid teacher! Stupid teacher!"

I felt like the life was knocked out of me as I maneuvered him into a bear hug.

One student had sense enough to push the red button on the wall that alerted the office staff there was trouble. I continued with the struggle.

Resisting every hold I placed on him, the twisting and turning caused us to bump into the closet door where his shoulder scraped the pencil sharpener.

Oh God, this big grizzly bear is so strong. I can barely keep up. Do I allow myself to get 'beat-up' by a seven-year-old student, or do I continue to retain him? It's hard. He's too big. I've got to let go.

Releasing the grip I had on him, he ran out of the class right into the arms of Mr. Cobb and Mrs. Smith.

Ms. Axel stayed with my class for the rest of the afternoon as I sat in Mrs. Smith's office, explaining everything from the spitball to the closet door.

This little bastard needs to be in juvenile detention, I thought while sneaking a rub on my stomach when Mrs. Smith turned her head. *He probably knocked one of my intestines loose. Awe, my stomach hurts.*

"Duncan." Mrs. Smith placed the phone on the receiver after her third attempt to contact Mrs. Rogers. "I'm suspending him until we can get both parents in for a conference."

"This is justifiable cause to suspend him with or without a conference. I will not tolerate this type of abuse from any student. I'm also requesting that he's taken out of my class. He's not only a threat to me, but to the other students as well."

"Point well taken Duncan. We'll have an emergency meeting to make the appropriate decision."

The embarrassment I felt from the incident kept me in the teachers' lounge until I knew my last student had left.

Stepping back into my classroom only to retrieve my purse, I slipped out the back to avoid questions from other inquisitive teachers and headed for my car.

*   *   *   *   *

The detour off I-75 North to I-285 West took me straight to Hartsfield to pick up a piece of luggage it took the airline three weeks to locate.

The walk through the terminals gave me an eerie feeling when I thought about the plane that crashed earlier today. It killed everyone on board.

What a tragedy, I thought. *I would be very reluctant to fly so soon... but God has a plan for everybody. When it's your time you've got to go. Just hope that your final resting-place is in heaven and not hell.*

The sight of Marlon suddenly demolished all thoughts in my mind about Sean, my aching stomach, and the earlier plane crash. He walked right pass me, holding the hand of a familiar looking female.

Is that lil cunning dog up to his old tricks again, or is it over between he and Priscilla for good?

Oblivious to the lost luggage, I trailed the happy couple and sort of did my own PI Check.

Why am I doing this? I haven't spoken to Priscilla in two years. Anything could've happened within that span of time. What difference does it make, I still care about her despite what happened between us. If he's cheating, she needs to know. Maybe if I could get just a little closer without him recognizing me, I can eye his finger for a wedding band. They're moving a little too swift for me, and besides, I'll feel more comfortable keeping my distance. Can I build up enough courage to call her?

Finally reaching their flight terminal, I hung around until he loaded, just to have 'proof in the pudding'. But why, it's not like I was really going to call her.

After writing the flight number just in case it was needed, I headed back to my original destination, picked up my luggage, and was on the road back to Marietta.

* * * * *

The heat met me at the door as soon as I entered my apartment. I walked toward the thermostat to adjust it; still able to smell the aroma left behind from the 'Swiss Army Cologne' Aaron wore. That quickly reminded me of why the heat blasted. I showered this morning. Normally I showered at night and sponged off in the morning. 'Washing up' was mandatory in my home while growing up. I can still hear Momma now, "I don't care if you took a bath last night. You sweat when you sleep. You better always wash under your arms and twix your legs in the mornings." A smile slowly stretched across my face as I continued my stroll down the hall, thinking about Momma.

My Caller ID revealed two calls from Crestview Elementary. I knew it was nobody but Mrs. Smith. I wasn't in the mood to hear anymore news about Sean.

After kicking off my shoes, I sat on the bed and propped my head upon two pillows. My stomach continued to ache.

I can't stand that little twerp.... I took a sigh, releasing some stress. *I wish I could talk to Priscilla and Rashondra. Not just because I have some 'dirt' on Marlon, but because I miss them. I should have handled things differently two years ago. I'm the blame for losing two wonderful friends. I'm also the blame for losing the love of my life. Tony, please call me. I need to hear your voice.*

* * * * *

Awakening me from a deep sleep I had fallen into, my phone rang loud and clear. *I bet it's no one but Mrs. Smith again,* I thought while leaning over to check my Caller ID before answering. *Tony? Oh my God. I don't believe this.*

The Way We Were

Chapter 8

Rashondra

One of the most difficult decisions I had to make in my life was leaving for college. It's not because I wasn't ready to make the change; it was just the thought of leaving Grandma with no one to care for her. It really saddened me.

Physically, I was not prepared for the long ride Trailway Bus had to offer me, but mentally, I was ready for the challenge of a new beginning. My memories traveled with me.

* * * * *

During my senior year of high school, I was overjoyed when my counselor told me that I'd received a four-year academic scholarship to a college in a small rural area in Georgia.

I was not financially able to attend the senior prom and senior trip, but needless to say, I was ready for the senior dance. It was held the evening of the last day of school. I had work very hard selling huck-a-bucks and popcorn balls for twenty-five cents on Grandma's back porch. I had earned enough money to purchase a *bad* dress and a *sharp* pair of shoes.

Looks were not deceiving that evening because I had it going on. My dress was black with white polk-a-dots. It fitted my body like a rubber glove clinging to your hand. It had thin spaghetti straps across the shoulders and barely reached the middle of my thighs. I wet my hair to create more waves and brushed it behind my ears, allowing it to drop down the center of my back. Make-up would've caused my natural beauty more harm than good, therefore it was not needed.

I bet so many boys are gonna look at my ass when I walk through the cafeteria. But they better not grab it, I thought, sliding my hand along my wide, curvy hips as I looked in the mirror. *I'm saving this for one boy tonight. Whew! Goodness! That Jeff know he can have some good sex.*

"Grandma, I'm about to leave," I yelled as I walked through the living room, on my way out the front door. She didn't respond.

"Grandma," I said again, coming to a halt as I awaited her response. Still no answer.

As soon as I headed back down the hall, I found her standing in the doorway, leaning toward the left.

Barely able to understand her slurred speech, she indistinctly mumbled a feeling of numbness. Hurriedly, I assisted her to the bed she shared with Nayla. There I noticed a small amount of blood trickling from her nose.

"Grandma, are you dying?"

"Call the doctor Shondra," she murmured.

"Nayla! Go next door! Call 911! Tell them Grandma is fixing to die!" I yelled in a very panicky voice, not able to completely grasp the sight before me.

Well of course I missed the senior party because Grandma was hospitalized. She suffered a mini stroke.

Her week stay in the hospital didn't prompt one visit from Mama. I was able to find Zach in 'the cut', his usual hanging spot, and notified him of Grandma's hospitalization. He knew exactly where to find Mama because he'd inherited her drug habits and normally they kept the same company.

Zach surprisingly showed up at the hospital three days later with two dollars sent by Mama to purchase Grandma a card.

"This is an insult!" I snorted before allowing him in to visit Grandma. "Give me this damn money and don't you dare tell Grandma that this was all *your* trifling Mama could do!" I snatched the damp and wrinkled bills out of his hand and shoved him through the door of Grandma's room.

Grandma was released from the hospital with medication called Heparin. "This is to thin her blood," the doctor said, handing the prescription to me.

There was no other family member around to help care for Grandma. Granddad left her twice, taking Uncle Richard, their only son with him the second time. Besides Mama, who's not even fit to care for herself, Aunt Ethel was the only one left. She was diagnosed with Schizophrenia years ago and placed in a mental institution. I called great Uncle Dave; Grandma's only living sibling, who resided in Wyoming. Cousin Bertha informed me of his recent release from the hospital, secondary to complications of diabetes and gallstones.

After being home for two months, Grandma still displayed unsuitable behaviors. I often found her eating foods she was forbidden. On occasion, I'd snatch cigarettes from her mouth. These continued mishaps caused me to miss my freshman year at college.

* * * * *

Exhausted from cooking, cleaning, and pampering, I'll never forget the day I sat on the back porch and prayed for Zach.

We used to be closer than bread and butter. We were all Mama had for ten years. We were inseparable, so I thought.

Remembering the day Ms. Louise pierced my ears, Zach was right there with me. At the age of six, Mama felt I was old enough to wear earrings. I was scared to death of knowing a hole had to be placed in both of my ears, so I begged Mama to allow Zach to come along.

Ms. Louise sat me on a stool in her kitchen. Zach sat on the floor, directly in front of me. She must have weighed about three hundred pounds. With her big hips snapping from one side to the other, she walked over to the stove and turned it off.

The little fan she had sitting in the window did no justice for the heat stirring in the kitchen. She was perspiring heavily, leaving a trail of sweat wherever she walked. She always complained about being hot, even on the days when it was cool enough to wear sweaters. She kept a church fan in her hand at all times.

With her index finger and thumb, she rubbed the lower tip of my left ear for quite some time.

"I'm gonna pinch yo ear baby, ya hear me?"

I nodded.

"Tell me if ya feel somethin, okay."

After confirming that my ear was numb, she dipped the already threaded needle into a cup of alcohol. The thread was still loose on the ends.

"Hold yo head over sugar." She assisted by pushing my head to the side.

Peeping out the corner of my eyes, I saw the sharp point coming toward my ear. "Zach! Help me!" I shrieked, holding out my hands for comfort.

He sprang up off the floor and grabbed my straying hands. "Miss Louise, will that hurt Shondra? She's scared."

She laughed at us before replying, "Naw baby. Yo sista gonna be all right. Yall show is funny to me." She pinched my ear again. "Ya feel somethin Shondra?"

"No ma'am," I trembled.

"Now hold yo head over chile and be still. I'on wanna have to pop you in the head with this here comb like I have to do some of the other chillums coming over here, sittin in my chair, acting like they ain't got no sense," she said, flashing the black comb she'd just retrieved from the counter in my face.

"Now let Miss Louise gone put this hole in yo ear like yo Mama want me to."

Zach continued to hold my hand while I squeezed his. Tightly closing my eyes, tears rolled down my cheeks.

"She did it Shondra!" Zach yelled while shaking me as if I had drifted off into some kind of trance.

"Didn't feel a thang did ya?" said Miss Louise, tying a knot at the end of the thread.

Without delay, she finished my second ear, dabbed more alcohol on both, and added some vaseline.

"You tell Betty to buy you some alcohol and grease for them ears, okay. You 'pose to pull on them strings everyday. Use yo alcohol and grease so they don't get stuck. When you come back next Sunday, I'm gonna put you some straws in yo ears," she added, plucking one from the broom to show me what she was talking about.

"Y'all chillums been so sweet. Here, y'all go down the street to the stoe to buy y'all selves some ice cream." She handed both of us a quarter.

"Thank you Miss Louise," we said in unison as we grabbed hands and skipped down the street singing 'Milkshake, milkshake, cream of tartar, tell me the name of your sweetheart, A, B, C, D, E...'" We continued to sing until we reached the Handy Andy on the corner.

We put our left over change together after we both purchased a sixteen ounce bottle of Cola and bought one bag of salty peanuts. After pouring peanuts into our soda pop bottles, we walked back home, kicking objects on the ground and drinking our sodas.

By the time Zach had turned fourteen, Grandma could not control him. I knew he had indulged seriously into smoking reefer. I couldn't confess his wrongdoing because I smoked it on occasions myself. Not only did he pick up this bad drug habit, but he also engaged in school fights at least once a week, which always led to his suspension.

By fifteen, he quit school and moved out. I knew he was lying when he claimed to be going to live with Mama because she migrated from pillar to post herself. It wasn't long before he became a full-fledged user of all kinds of drugs.

* * * * *

Don't get me wrong, I wasn't a little 'goody-two-shoe' myself, but evil never took control over my life like it did Zach's.

My first visit to the office was when I was in the third grade. I had a serious crush on my teacher, Mr. Jacobs. He was cute and fine just like this wrestler Zach and his friends used to always watch on television.

"That's him. That's the wrestler that looks like Mr. Jacobs," I said excitedly while watching a match with Zach and some of his friends one Saturday afternoon. "What's his name?"

They began laughing and horseplaying around. I didn't find any humor in the question I asked.

"Umm, his name is umm, Abdullah the Butcher," Zach responded. He and his friends burst into laughter.

What they laughing at? They must think I like that wrestler too. They can laugh all they want to cause I know who I like. I rolled my eyes, popped my lips, and twisted my head after that thought.

The next day in class, I raised my hand and boldly said with a smile, "Mr. Jacobs, you look just like Abdullah the Butcher."

The entire class was filled with laughter. *What they laughing at? Abdullah the Butcher is real fine. They must don't know him. All of them need to just shet up.*

Well, only after a trip to the office for disrespecting the teacher and a phone call made to Mama did I realize I had the wrong name.

The cute, fine wrestler I had been watching was really named Tony Atlas. As wrong as Zach was with the name, he may as well had said Ric Flair or Dusty Rhodes. I was mad at Zach for days for getting me in trouble.

* * * * *

My first fight took place when I was ten years old, right in our own front yard. This little dried-up, snotty-nosed, nappy-headed boy had the nerves to be teasing Zach just because he was sick.

Zach had the mumps. When we came home from school, Mama placed sardines behind both of his ears. She took an old diaper and tied it around his face, securing the sardines and knotted it on the top of his head. She made him sit on the porch to keep the odor out of the house. Zach and I sat out there, did our homework, and played cards together.

I had only left the porch for two minutes for a trip the restroom. Upon my return, I heard some unusual noises outside and Zach was crying.

"What's da matter Zach?" I inquired.

Sniffing, crying, and pointing at T-Boo, Zach said, "He, he, he up there talkin 'bout I smell like Moby Dick and, and, and that's why ain got no daddy."

Putting my left hand on my hip, I leaned forward, rolled my neck in the same rhythm of my straying right index finger and said," Yo mama ain't got no daddy and that's why you smell like Jaws."

Before I realized it, my fingers bawled into a fist and popped T-Boo right in the eye. When he hit me back, as weak as Zach was, he jumped in to assist and the fight was on.

From that point on, Zach and I fought in pairs, which was seldom because nobody wanted a piece of the Hernandezes.

* * * * *

The first time I experienced sexual intercourse was at the age of thirteen. Although we had been living with Grandma, it was Mama's desire to give me a 'sweet-teen' birthday party to celebrate me becoming a teenager.

"You is almost a woman now gul," she said, leaning so close that her lips grazed my jaw. She held a joint in one hand and a bottle of whiskey in the other. She staggered away from me, swaying with every footstep.

When Miss Louise's nephew, who was visiting from Brooklyn, walked through the door, my skipping heart seemed to run away from me. He was light-skinned, with a big, round Afro. The tattoo of a dragon displayed perfectly well from underneath the muscle shirt he wore. He was an exact image of Foster Sylver.

A good hour of being indulged in conversation had not passed before he grabbed my hand and led me across the street to an abandoned building. After sitting on a tree stump smoking a joint together, he pulled me up and pushed me against the wall. He planted juicy kisses all over my face, leaving slobber everywhere. *Damn! I like his lips.*

"Look at what you did to me girl," he said, slightly pushing himself away from me. He placed my hand on the hardness that bulged from underneath his gym shorts.

This must be what they call a 'hard-on'. It sho' is much bigger hard than it is soft.

"Ooh wee. You got a hard on don't you?"

"Yeah girl cause you is so fine, you know what I mean. Come here." He pulled my body close to his and wrapped his arms around my back. "You know what I got to do now don't you?"

I nodded my head, hoping he was referring to having sex.

"It's got to go in your cat so I can shoot-off. You see what I'm saying? That's the only way it's gonna go back down."

Ooh, he wants to have sex with me. I heard it stings a little at first but then it's real good once he gets it in. Now I can finally stop lying to my friends about being a virgin. I'm getting ready to have sex. I can't wait to tell everybody.

Before I knew it, he was standing before me totally naked. His erection curved slightly upward as he lifted my sundress.

"Take your panties off sweet thang and lay over here on the grass." I did exactly as I was told. *Yes! I'm getting ready to have sex for real.* I smiled.

"Ooh! Awww! Your thang too big!" Every attempt I made to squirm my body from beneath his was of no use because he continued maneuvering until his 'thing' finally went in. *Them girls lied. This sex do hurt.*

"Yeah, I like this girly," he said while rapidly moving in and out of my rigid body as the pain slowly started to ease.

.   As soon as I began to enjoy it, his wavering movement came to a halt. Ejecting his limped organ from my body, he leaned back on his knees and said, "See, I told you it would go down."

Sneaking over to Mama's house for the next four weeks was a joy within itself. Having sex with Ant was better than eating Grandma's sweet potato pie and I thought nothing could top that.

About three months later, I discovered I was pregnant. It nearly broke Grandma's heart when I told her.

"Forgive her Lord for she know not what she has done. The devil is a mighty powerful ole thang. Come out of her Satan in the name of Jesus." Grandma dipped her index finger into a bottle of oil that Pastor Palmer had already prayed over and compressed it in a small circular motion right in the middle of my forehead.

"Lord, bless Shondra's body so that she don't have to git rid of eight babies like her Mama did." That was the last of my grandmother's prayers before two elderly ladies took me into the basement of her doctor's office and ended the little life that was growing inside of me.

*　*　*　*　*

Sex, drugs, alcohol, and lies were part of my weekend routines for the next two years. The difference between Zach and I was the fact that he was more consistent with his habits, like on a daily basis. I only became involved on the weekends. I stayed in school and was determined to graduate.

Gratitude was highly given to Grandma for sending me away to an all girls camp during the summer of my rising junior year. It was there that I learned morals and etiquette. Through my counseling sessions I learned about the dangers of unprotected sex, and how to say no to drugs. After crying in group therapy about how I resented not having Mama in my life, I was able to forgive her for her wrong doings and except the fact that her drug addiction was a terrible disease. My self-esteem heightened, making me feel unique, which gave me a new agenda.

The begging and pleading I encountered with Zach about attending the boys camp the next summer only yielded to a more rebellious attitude toward doing the right thing.

*　*　*　*　*

"Attention passengers, we will have a thirty minute lay-over at our next stop in Jacksonville. If you are traveling beyond that point, please report back to the bus in a timely manner. If Jacksonville is your final destination, as always, thank you for traveling with Trailway," the bus driver loudly announced, interrupting my thoughts.

Settled back in my seat to continue the second half of my tiresome journey, my mind drifted, yet once again, back to my loved ones at home.

My search for Zach on my departure day to say goodbye only rendered sorrow for me. *If he could only see my bus ticket or my packed bags, just maybe it would give him a change of heart,* I thought. After wandering through 'the cut' longer than I had anticipated, Zach was no where to be found.

My next venture was to say goodbye to Mama. After numerous knocks on the door, she appeared, wrapped in a towel. She peeped out the crack of the door she had created by opening it slightly.

"Hey gul, whatcha doin over this side of town?"

"Can I come in?"

"Sorry gul, not now. Gots me a man in here. You know how I be sometimes."

"Well, I just wanted to let you know that I'm leaving for college this evening."

"Gul I just hope you is for real 'bout not messin wit them drugs no mo. Them college folks gots them some good edcation 'bout themselves. They send yo ass home you go thar messin up they name."

Unclear as to how I should accept Mama's comments, I leaned forward, with water-swelled eyes and planted a kiss on her jaw through the crack of the door.

"I love you Mama."

"Gul git way from here wit all that mushy stuff. I gots to go now," she said and closed the door. Her immense lack of concern shortened my visit to her.

In the back of the taxi, Grandma, Nayla, and I held on to each other's hands all the way to the Trailway Bus Station, releasing them alternately to wipe the dampness protruding underneath our eyes and noses.

* * * * *

Evidently I was overtaken by an intense sleep because the next thing I knew, I was getting off the bus at my destination.

Chapter 9

Indigo

Momma and Daddy perpetually debated about which car had the right-of-way, the one traveling on the ramp to enter the highway, or the one already traveling in the right lane that met the ramp.

"Honey, you are suppose to get over and let those cars that are coming down the ramp onto the highway."

"No I don't, they are suppose to slow down and wait until this lane is clear," Daddy replied as he continued to drive, never letting the ramp cars over.

Those two statements always initiated a conversation that lasted for another fifteen or twenty minutes.

That day I decided to disregard their conversation. My mind was too occupied with reflections of the past as well as anticipations of a new beginning. Settled in the backseat alone, I was ready for the three-hour drive to my college campus.

* * * * *

Being the youngest of five, I was proud of myself for breaking the 'common-folks' barrier. That's what we were, just plain, ole common folks. College was never an issue in our household.

"Y'all children will be just fine if y'all go to some trade school and pick a trade," Daddy had said numerous times.

My initial dream was to become a telephone operator. It always delighted me to hear her pleasant voice on the line.

"Operator, may I help you."

"Yes, I would like to make an emergency call," I said while patiently waiting for a yes or no response from my high school boy friend whose line had been busy for the past thirty minutes.

My oldest brother, Wayne, is a mechanic. Next there's Sharon who's a secretary. Jeffrey is a cable installer and Audrey, who is only three years older than me is a beautician. They all went to a vocational school, but I wanted to be different.

"With more technology available, time has changed. I want to attend a four-year college. I want a Bachelor's Degree next to my title," I said to Granddaddy one afternoon while eating dinner with Grandmomma and him.

"Baby girl I tell ya, it sho' would be nice to have a grandchild to graduate from one of those big colleges. You know I've been saving money in that brown shoebox in the back of my closet for decades. That money in there is just burning a hole in that box, waiting on some special occasion. I didn't spend nearly half of it on Sharon's wedding. So with the good grades you're making, you just go on and apply. Now don't be trying to go all over the country. Granddaddy got to come see you graduate, and you know I'm not getting on a plane to get there." He laughed a little with his deep, hoarse sounding voice.

Soon after that discussion, Granddaddy called Daddy and told him to gather the whole family up and bring them over that evening. Along with the money Granddaddy had saved, everybody else agreed to contribute twenty dollars a month to help pay for my college tuition.

"No need to send Indy away on some kind of grant if we can pull our resources together and help her. Let somebody else who doesn't have this kind of family support get the grant," said Granddaddy.

Hesitation to complete an application was not a part of my thoughts when college recruits visited my high school during career day.

Excitedly running up the steps months later with the news of my acceptance into college was suddenly put to a halt by the grief stricken faces of Momma, Jeffrey, and Audrey that met me at the door. My instincts told me something was terribly wrong. I stopped with only one foot in the front door and returned an appalled look.

"What's wrong?" I walked right into Momma's extended arms.

"Your Granddaddy Jessie died this morning," Momma said in a soft whimpered voice. "He had a heart attack."

"Nooo! Nooo! Oh God, this can't be true! Not Granddaddy!" I wailed as my head slid from Momma's chest with the drop of my weakening knees.

* * * * * *

For as long as I could remember, Granddaddy had always been the foundation of this family. After his two oldest sons were killed by an unsolved hit-and-run accident back in the early 1950s, he, Grandmomma, and Daddy left Mississippi and moved to Georgia to start a new life. His new life consisted of accepting Jesus Christ as his Savior as he began ministering to the sinful world.

Not a Sunday went by that we didn't take our seats on the front pews of Granddaddy's church. As a kid, my favorite part of the service was watching the grown-ups receive the Holy Ghost. The Sisters and Brothers would strut up and down the aisles shouting for the Lord.

Grandmomma had her favorite Holy Ghost dance. Audrey and I called it the 'bend and strut'. Whenever she felt happy, she would stand, raise her right hand with a vigorous shake yelling, 'Hallelujah' at the same time. Placing her left hand on her hip, she would bend her knees and bounce back to an upright position three times before she would strut from the A-men corner with her left and right hands still in position. She never made it down the aisle; she danced and shouted right in front of the altar. Sometimes Audrey and I would pretend we had the Holy Ghost by mimicking some of the adults.

It was Granddaddy who baptized me at the age of five. That event is still memorable to me as if it just happened yesterday.

Momma dressed me in a white robe and tied a white towel around my head. All of the church members parked their cars on the side of a long, winding, country road in the middle of the wilderness. We walked down an embankment until we reached a swamp. With the members standing around the edge, Granddaddy and Deacon Mays slowly walked into the swamp.

As each candidate for baptism were being escorted into the swamp, the members began to sing, 'Take me to the water. Take me to the water. Take me the water. To be baptized'.

After a fragile kiss on the cheek, Daddy pushed me toward the edge of the swamp. "It's your turn Indy. Go on baby, God is with you."

Watching Granddaddy and Deacon Mays extend their arms in my direction, my body stiffened as I imagined the Loch Ness Monster leaping up, swallowing Granddaddy in one gulp. I continued to stand there as tears dribbled down my cheeks. Then I started the quick inhaling and sniffing that goes on when you've just gotten a whipping. I couldn't even hear my own voice due to the angelic voices of the church members carried away in the spirit as they continued to sing.

"What's the matter Indy?" Daddy asked.

"I'm scared Daddy. I think I see something in the water." I reached up for him to carry me as I continued the sniffing and quick, deep inhaling.

Daddy quickly grabbed my heightened left hand and pulled me into the swamp. "That's nobody but the Devil trying to get in your way of being born again. The blood of Jesus is against you Satan." He pulled me with one hand and placed the other on my forehead as he rebuked the Devil.

By the time I reached Granddaddy and Deacon Mays, I was shivering so badly that my bones felt as if they were popping loose. They both raised their right hands to God as Granddaddy placed the palm of his left hand in the middle of my back.

"I baptize you in the name of the Father, and of the Son, and of the Holy Ghost."

He dropped his elevated hand from the air as it landed right in the middle of my face. Squeezing my nose tightly, he dipped me into the water.

My head began to spin as the water filled my ears. Being in such a panic state after I emerged, I began jumping up and down. I jolted my head in hopes of releasing the water from my clogged ears. Of course the church members thought the Holy Ghost had come upon me, therefore, they jumped around and praised the Lord with me.

While being carried out of the water by Daddy, I was able to catch a glimpse of Jeffrey and Audrey hiding behind Sister Mable's wide hips, laughing at me.

Jeffrey, Audrey, and I took pleasure in spending weekends at our grandparent's house. Jeffrey is one year older than Audrey and four years older than me.

Granddaddy would sit under the big Oak tree, rocking to a rhythmical beat he had originated on his own. It was ritual for him to sport his red Kango hat and sip on several glasses of lemonade. He'd watch us play all day long, intermittently browsing through the newspaper.

We used to play Hopscotch, Land, Red Rover, Hide-n-Seek; you name it, and we played it. Sometimes we stayed out after the streetlights came on, hearkening nervously as Granddaddy told numerous ghost stories.

As soon as we returned inside from playing all day, Grandmomma would send us straight to the bathtub, one at a time. She claimed that running around and sweating all day had us smelling like cute, little puppies. *She worded it in a much nicer manner than Momma did because she would come out and just tell us we smelled like dogs.*

By the time the clock struck eleven o'clock, we would all gather around the television set in the den to watch re-runs of our favorite night time soap, 'Dark Shadows'. Being that I was young and ignorant to the truth about the existence of vampires, Jeffrey and Audrey would scare me every night, claiming that Barnabus was going to fly through my window and bite me on the neck.

* * * * *

Grandmomma asked me to sleep with her in the same bed Granddaddy had just passed away in earlier that morning. I couldn't quite comprehend her reasoning, but I adhered to her request. That night she revealed I was Granddaddy's favorite grandchild. I had felt it all along.

"Now don't you tell nobody. This is me and your secret, okay." said Grandmomma.

Every night, before the funeral, friends, family, and church members came over for the 'Setting-Up' with plenty of food. Everybody seemed to be in good spirits, which helped Grandmomma out tremendously. Momma and Daddy joined us with an overnight stay on the evening before the funeral.

The family's entrance into the church during the prelude set the tone for the rest of the evening. There was an abundance of wails and screams as we progressively walked down the aisle. We each stopped in front of the casket to say our good byes.

With a tight grip on Grandmomma's hand, the two of us walked down the aisle first. As Grandmomma carried on with her cries, I was briefly taken away into my own little world.

Granddaddy... my precious Granddaddy. They say you are going to a better place. I want to be happy for you but it's hard. I am so sad... I rubbed my fingers through the curly gray hair on his head. *Why are your jaws so puffy?* My fingers slid down his face to press on the puffiness. I was appalled by how cold his face was. *You look nice in your white suit. You're wearing the right colors for your homegoing because you are pure, immaculate, and innocent. My heart is filled with an unthinkable kind of sadness as I stand here, viewing the last of you. This pain is so immense. I feel as if a sword has been jagged through the flesh of my heart, never to be removed, inflicting such harsh suffering within.* The tears finally began to quickly pour down my face. *I love you Granddaddy. Look in on me while I'm away in college.*

Staggering to the 'A-Men' corner reserved for the family, I took my place on the pew, right next to my grief-stricken Grandmomma.

* * * * *

Granddaddy, I said to myself, looking up at the puffy, cumulus clouds hovering across the sky as we continued our drive down the country road. *I see your smile. I know you're proud of your favorite grandchild,* I added, trying to readjust my head into a more comfortable position before I dozed off to sleep.

* * * * *

"Indy, wake up honey, we're here," Momma said as she reached from the front seat pinching me on the arm. *Ooh I hate it when she does that. She doesn't realize she has a heavy hand. That hurts.*

Without saying a word about my aching arm, I wiped the slobber away that had dribble down the side of my jaw. I sat up and noticed the crowd of young adults busily moving about the college campus. I began fingering my bob back into place to look presentable as I stepped onto the campus. *I'm at college,* I said to myself as a wide grin spread across my face.

Chapter 10

Priscilla

Father didn't totally understand the significance of me wanting to leave Bloomfield to go as far south as I can to college. A change was needed.

As I boarded the plane at the Detroit Metro Airport, I felt slightly relieved of the stress that had burdened me over the last few years. I relaxed back in my seat and prepared for take-off.

* * * * *

It was just three weeks prior to my departure when Father learned of my decision not to attend Princeton, the school of *his* choice. Mother's alma mater, located in a small rural town in Georgia, was the college I'd decided on at the beginning of my junior year.

"What the hell are you trying to do, humiliate me and all that I stand for?" yelled Father after learning of my decision. Out of anger, he smashed the cigar he'd been smoking into the marble ashtray, causing a coil of smoke to gradually dissipate into the air. "Princeton is one to the best schools in this nation and you chose to deject your acceptance for a college in some little country town in Georgia? Well I'll be damned! I never thought such a thing would even cross your mind," he continued.

"Well Father, you never gave me an option. You've always had it planned out for me, from the private elementary and high schools I attended to college. I bet you already know who I'm going to marry, don't you?"

"Listen Precious," he said, making an effort to assuage his demeanor. "I only want what's best for you. Ruby's brother is one of the deans at Princeton. He's already made arrangements for you to have your own private room. All you have to do is show up."

"I don't need Ruby to make any plans for me. I know where I want to attend college and Princeton is not the place." I sat on the edge of the sofa in the family room. "It will mean much more than you can imagine if I attend Mother's alma mater. At least grant me that one wish and give me your support." I covered my face and allowed my tears to gently flow down.

"Dammit," Father said in a soft, anguished voice. He made his way across the room positioning himself on the sofa next to me. "Okay," he added after a long sigh. "Just promise me that if you don't like it after the first quarter, you will tell me. I'll come get you without hesitation."

He pulled my dampened face into his chest as I continued to cry. "Come here Precious. Lighten up. Everything is going to be alright."

Father rocked me back and forth as we sat there stealing a moment of silence. *I wonder what's on his mind?*

* * * * *

Father was always good at apologizing and attempting to make everything all right, when in reality, everything was all wrong. He provided for our family very well, but made too many mistakes along the way.

Great-Grandfather Willard was one of the first African-American entrepreneur in Auburn Hills. He brought Willard Insurance into existence in 1915. It has been passed down for generations since. What started out as one company has now flourished into 150 companies across the United States.

Father was always able to purchase any materialistic thing I wanted, but yet unable to fulfill what I needed most, the love of a father. Mother and I spent countless days and nights alone. It was a rare occasion for Father to accompany us on vacations or even trips to the park.

During elementary school, I was awakened each morning by the aroma of maid Mamie's homemade cinnamon rolls. After slipping into my cute little uniform that was ironed and hung on the door, Mother would come in and comb my hair. She neatly placed two white bows at the end of my ponytails before the two of us gathered in the kitchen for breakfast. My soft scrambled eggs and wheat toast with honey were gobbled down quickly as my mouth salivated, awaiting to feast on one of the cinnamon rolls cooling in the baking pan.

After becoming a member of Jack and Jill, an elite organization for boys and girls, most of my summers were spent away from home. Camp Atwater, Sag Harbor Resort, Martha's Vineyard, and a host of other international vacations such as Paris, Rio de Janeiro, Nigeria, China, France, and the list goes on.

By the age of twelve, I was the best gymnast, violinist, and baton twirler in middle school. None of those activities beguiled my interest to pursue on a professional level, but of course, those were things Father wanted me to do.

Being a preteen brought on more than just excelling in those hobbies. I received my first period and flourished in wisdom. Soon I realized that the glass of tea Mother sipped on nightly was actually a glass of Meukow V.S.O.P. Superior Cognac, on the rocks. The nights I'd been awakened for a midnight ride, were actually ventures to spy on Father. A goodnight hug and kiss always ridded the excitement I'd built up to see Father after his return from out of town. I was usually escorted to bed because Mother needed to speak with him about his trip. In actuality she wanted to confront him about some Mistress he'd taken.

Two months prior to my thirteenth birthday the phone rang which awakened me from a deep sleep. Not more than fifteen minutes later, Mother entered my room. I was barely dressed before we scampered out the driveway.

"Help me God. Please give me the strength to deal with what I'm about to face," Mother said. She held on to her glass of *tea*, sipping mouthfuls at a time as we dashed down the street to Lansing.

Being that I was wiser, I knew we were headed for trouble. My inquiries to Mother about the source of her anger were never answered directly. She always responded with a prayer to God.

I never anticipated the trouble we set out for would result in meeting a brother I never knew about. Jonathon was only four months younger. The two adults conversed pleasantly for about thirty minutes before we said our good byes and walked out the door.

Burdened with too much emotional pain and alcohol, Mother pulled over and called a taxi. We spent the night at a hotel.

Mother disclosed secrets I would've rather not known. She told me that after she graduated from college, she attended a job fair in Atlanta. Willard Insurance was there recruiting potential employees. The beauty of Mother enamored Father. He had to have her. With a BA in Office Administration, she was offered a position as an Administrative Assistant in one of the Detroit offices. He was twenty-five and she was twenty-one. Nine months later, family and friends gathered to attend the most lavished, fairy-tale wedding of the century. She was very honored as she walked down the aisle as the bride.

Baring the title of Mrs. Willard, she was no longer needed as an employee. Father insisted that she travels and views the world with her sisters and friends. He was always out of town on business, so she took advantage of his suggestion to travel. Her membership with the Links kept her busy as well.

She noticed signs of infidelity only three months after they were married. She made every attempt to ignore the hang-up calls, the fresh smell of soap, the make-up on his collar, and whatever else was put before her. She believed this was a temporary phase he had to go through.

"He was the love of my life. He gave me things I never dreamed of having. I was not going to allow another woman to run me away from him" she said.

A year after the marriage, Mother actually witnessed him kissing a woman she suspected him of having an affair with. Instead of confronting him with the evidence, she decided it was time for a baby. "I thought if he knew I was pregnant, it would slow him down. I didn't know of any other way to win my husband back."

Unfortunately, my older sibling never made it into this world. Father talked her into aborting it. He claimed business was going too well for him to play father.

Mother experienced four more years of heartache before she finally decided it was time to leave. He ended his plea for her to stay by asking her to conceive. Eleven months later I was born.

"I was so happy. I thought he had really changed. I thought I had my husband back the way God intended for him to be. I had no idea he was still lying. He made me abort my first child. Why didn't he force her to do the same? Baby, mommie is hurting badly right now. I need to get some sleep."

We resided at the hotel for the rest of the week. During our return trip home on Saturday, we packed as much as we could. That evening we moved into an already furnished condo in Ann Arbor.

With his powerful connections, it only took an hour for Father to locate us. He wasn't aware of everything that had transpired because he'd been out of town for two weeks.

Poor Mother. She tried to be strong. She only stayed away for two months. We soon packed our belongings and moved back home.

* * * * *

Chanel and I became very close friends during my freshman year of high school. She too, was a member of Jack and Jill. We were the only black cheerleaders on the squad, which made our bond more instant. Befriending Chanel meant lesser time with Mother. She wasn't enthusiastic at all about my newfound friend. Chanel was a relief for me from Mother. Every time she experienced an unpleasant situation with Father, she burdened me with it. I had grown tired of hearing about it.

"Why won't you share your feelings with Aunt Frances or Aunt Judy? Don't you think they can relate and give you better guidance since they are much closer to your age?" I asked her one night after witnessing her shed a large amount of tears.

"Precious, I've tried talking to them. They want this family to fall apart just like those devilish women out there who are involved with a married man. What God has put together, let no man put asunder."

"But Mother, doesn't the bible give you permission to divorce your husband if he's committing adultery?"

"Yes, but I believe God is going to rebuke that unclean spirit that's possessing your father. Ask and it shall be given unto you. Therefore, when I fall down on my knees to pray, I ask God to deliver your father out of the Devil's hand."

"But how long are you going to ask? This has been going on for a long time."

"Remember the story about Job. He was sick for so long that flesh fell from his bones. His wife even told him to go on and curse God and die. But he was patient enough to wait on his blessing. God may not come when you want him but he's right on time. Never forget that," she said.

Chanel and I did everything together. Our favorite past time was to indulge ourselves in shopping at Fairlanes Mall on the weekends. With Mother not having me around to confide in as much, I saw more barren Cognac bottles around the house.

Mother's hurt and pain became an intolerable sight for me. It also gave me a repulsive feeling toward Father. I voiced my concerns to him one afternoon. He decided to take two weeks off work and devote it to quality family time. We were a happy family during that short time frame. Before long, things were back to normal for Mother, happy today, sad tomorrow, pray today, rejoice tomorrow.

Two days after the end of my sophomore year, I was on the cordless phone speaking with Chanel. I was invited to spend two weeks with she and her family in Hawaii. In the midst of our conversation, a call beeped in.

"Hello, may I please speak with Mrs. Willard?"

Not more than five minutes after I had released Chanel from the line, clamor flowed freely from the master bedroom.

When I rushed upstairs to inquire about the noise, I found Mother in a raging fit, knocking over everything she touch.

"Oh God, he's done it again. That bastard has done it again."

"Mother, what's wrong?" I said, attempting to yell over the booms and bangs that came from the items that landed on the floor.

"Oh God Precious, he's done it again," was all she replied. She turned the bottle of Meukow to her mouth and gulped down as much as her mouth would hold. The rest slid down both sides of her face.

"Who are you talking about? What are you talking about?"

"Pack everything. We're moving out for good," she said, as she slid her feet into her sandals. She grabbed her keys and purse with one hand and clinched tightly the Meukow in the other as she sprinted down the steps.

"I'm going to pay that bastard a visit at the office!"

"Mother, wait! Don't leave!" My screams were to no avail because she slammed the door before I could finish my sentence. The Jaguar went screeching down the street.

After about two hours of anxiety, I heard the front door unlock. I jumped up off the Futon and ran to greet Mother. Upon reaching the door, maid Mamie stood there with grief written all over her face.

"Where's Mother?" Every gut feeling within told me something terrible had happened.

Before ever reaching Father's office, Mother crashed head on into an oncoming vehicle. Being thrown through the windshield, she was killed instantly.

Father did everything he thought possible to ensure I grieved without lots of complications. He took a leave of absence for the rest of the summer to 'be there' for me. He felt it was necessary in order to help prepare for a successful junior year.

A few weeks after Mother's funeral, Father disclosed the information that she'd learned of the night she was killed. Oh yes, he'd done it again, in a really big way.

"Precious." Father paused and began to sob. "Your mother found out about your brother... Another brother named Antonio. He's two years younger than you are."

At that point, I didn't know what to think of Father. *You killed my mother,* was all I could think of.

"What else are you hiding Father? How many more children are you going to tell me about?" My hand reached for a small statue of Louis Armstrong that proudly kept its place on the mantel. I whirled it across the room at Father out of anger, slightly scraping his shoulder before shattering the glass of the sliding door that led to the deck.

Several hours of consolation went on as he explained the relationship they had. His story was quite different from Mother's. Forgiving Father was a difficult decision to make, especially after I placed the blame on him for Mother's untimely death.

Mother's habits of praying rubbed off on me. Every night I asked God to fill my heart with peace.

At the end of my junior year, Chanel's mother and father divorced, which caused her to move to her mother's hometown in California. During a very tearful departure, we promised to write each other every week.

Before graduating from high school, I was bewildered by another surprise, my stepmother, Ruby. Her physical features were almost a carbon copy of Mother's, but I never could warm up to her.   I wanted my own mother to be there, not a replacement.

* * * * *

Oh yes, I'm ready for a change.   I'm ready for a new beginning. I'm ready to leave the past behind, I thought as I viewed the crowd of people after exiting the airplane.

Father had already arranged for an associate of Williard Insurance to pick me up at Hartsfield Airport and drive me the next two hours to my college campus.

Classes don't begin for another two weeks, but it was to my advantage to arrive early due to cheerleader tryouts and freshmen orientation.

Chapter 11

Rashondra

Yes! Yes! All A's my first quarter in college. Grandma is going to be so happy when she hears the good news. Mama just knew I was going to come here and mess up, but I proved her wrong. I can't believe it's time for winter break already.

* * * * *

Remembering the day I stepped off Trailway seven weeks ago, my pink sponge rollers were still attached to my bang. I was a nervous wreck. Fortunately for me, there were four other freshmen at the bus station feeling the same anxiety. We aided each other during our 'freshman-fear' and made it to campus without complications. After receiving our dormitory assignments, we registered for classes and headed for orientation.

Very indecisive as to whether I wanted to wear my brand new Sergio Valente's, Gloria Vanderbilt's, or Bonjour's, to orientation, I asked Pamela, my roommate, for a little assistance. She chose the Vanderbilt's. I was clean to the bone.

"My, my, my, these people seem to have a lot of class. I bet all of them probably come from rich families," I said to Pamela as I viewed my peers.

At the conclusion of orientation, we were told to mix and mingle with the other freshmen. The Dean felt it was very important for us to get to know some of the people we would spend the next four years with.

* * * * *

Six weeks later, after keeping my head in my books to satisfy my
need to do the right thing, Pamela and I decided to attend a Q-Pearl
induction.

"Got-toe-mighty-moe! I've never seen so many good looking
brothers in my life!" I shrieked as soon as we walked through the front door.

"What the hell did you just say?" inquired Pamela.

*Now why is she tripping, trying to act like she ain't never heard her
grandmama or drunk uncle say that when they got excited? She's from
Napoleonville, Louisiana, right smack in the southern part of Louisiana.*

"Anyway girlfriend, pinch me! Wake me up!" I continued with my
tirade. "Dam'um! Honey child these brothas look like they are straight from
Hollywood."

As we continued our stroll through the front door, all eyes were
focused on me. There was no doubt in my mind that I had it going on. The
white tank top I wore stopped just above my navel revealing my long, slim,
waistline. My cut off blue jeans shorts clung tightly to my bulging hips.

If Mama never said anything else positive about me, she always
praised me on my nice physique.

"Gul yo ass is sho' nuff spreading pretty wide. You fine just like yo
Mama," she would say.

About thirty girls introduced themselves and told why they felt
worthy of becoming a Q-Pearl. I was one of the ten that were chosen.

"I'll see you back at the dorm," Pamela said. She had the gloomiest
expression on her face after learning she was not selected.

"Okay," I responded, having too much fun to even think about
leaving so soon.

Smooth and Hunk tailed me like I was a dog in heat the entire night
during the celebration party. For a minute I thought it was some kind of
game they were playing. But no, I was the one with all the game. Clever as
a fox, I maneuvered my time between the two of them without either
noticing it.

"Are you fresh meat around here?" asked Smooth, zigzagging with
every step as we walked toward my dormitory.

"Yeah, I'm a freshman. Sure is amazing how time flies. Finals
start on Monday. I've really been studying hard," I said in my most proper
enunciation. I wanted to sound intelligent and make a good impression on
him. *Good Gretta Day! This milk-chocolate thang looks so good. Umm!
Umm! Umm!*

"I'm a sophomore. I've been on line all quarter, playing football,
and keeping my grades up at the same time. I just went over last weekend.

AaahRoof! AaahRoof!" he yelped extending his bent elbows shoulder high. He turned his forearms outwards and allowed both hands to point in the opposite directions.

Boys were not allowed into our dorm after eleven o'clock therefore, Smooth stopped me underneath a tree just opposite the walkway that lead to the dorm.

"Are you going to sneak me in or what?"

"Sneak you in?" Instantly I thought about Mama and how she reminded me of getting kicked out of school if I messed up. "No, I'll get in trouble if I do that," I replied.

"Awww, come on girl. It happens all the time. You got to get with the program. That's the only way you're going to get a piece around here." He lifted my chin as his soggy lips met mine.

Ooh, damn! He can kiss. My body cringed as he pulled his lips away. *I bet he can 'throw-down' in the bed. I wonder if he's really worth taking a chance at getting caught. What the hell, I'm horny. Haven't had any since I've been here. I'm ready to 'git-wit-it'.* Aww man, I forgot about Pamela, I thought as I scrunched my eyes in the darkness looking for a safe tree, corner, building, or any place where we could possibly do it outside. Had we not been so close to the dorm, I would've wrapped my legs around his body behind this tree.

"Naw. I better wait until I learn a little more about how the 'sneak-in' system works. I'm just a freshman, remember," I said, pretending to be so innocent.

"Alright then girl, your call. Hey, you snooze, you loose."

After that statement, he staggered away, leaving me alone, horny as hell. *Dammit Smooth*

* * * * *

Ever since the night I became a Q-Pearl, Pamela developed an attitude with me that exemplified deep jealousy simply because she had not been chosen.

"She thinks she's so pretty and fine. She ain't black for real, I think she's got a white daddy. She just makes me so sick. It kills me to even speak to her," I overheard her say as she spoke on the telephone in the hallway.

That 'hoe got some nerves talking about me to somebody. She really don't know me that well. Just wait til she brings her frumpy looking ass back in here, I huffed, anticipating her return to the room we shared.

Pamela was confronted as soon as she walked through the door. It was a very ugly moment. I almost pulled out a can of 'whip-ass' on her. I talked down on her so bad that she ran to the dorm monitor crying like a baby.

I trailed her weeping, lumpy ass down the hall. My mind told me to whip all asses that stood around observing the scene.

Just nosey. That all, just nosey. Y'all don't know me. Don't ask me no question. Mind your own damn business before I start to swinging. I don't play, I thought as I bustled through the spectators.

After a brief counseling session, the monitor advised us that it was too late to change room assignments for winter quarter. She promised to work on it for the spring.

"Let's be mature ladies and try to focus on the reason why you are here. Stay out of each other's territory and make an attempt to get along until I can move you," she concluded.

* * * * *

After finals, the campus was nearly a ghost town. Almost everyone went home for Christmas break. Unfortunately, I didn't have the funds to travel, but I thanked God that Pamela did.

With the thought of being there two weeks alone, my first task was to go back to the frat house to track down Smooth. Smooth had already left, ironically, Hunk was there with no plans of leaving for Christmas break.

Expeditiously I learned the secret of the 'sneak-in' system and screwed Hunk almost every night. From the dorm to the frat house, we acted on the lustful feelings we both revealed. He nearly blew my mind as he allowed his solid, rhythmical flesh to move in and out of my body. His forceful, upward thrusts left a serious mark on my stuff. I had to have more. He was nothing like the immature boys I messed around with in Ft. Lauderdale. I had found a real man.

He moved like a locomotive, nonstop. He literally wore me out, leaving the softness of my womanhood feeling raw.

On the eighth night, I barely moved. My engine had run out of gas. Before he left that morning, I told him my body needed a break. I laid in bed all day long, sore and exhausted, too tired to even go to breakfast and lunch.

That delicate feeling of being in love was quickly zapped away when I went searching for him two days later. I caught him kissing another female. On top of that, she was wearing the same Member's Only jacket he'd allow me to wear a few days ago. That was the first of many lessons I had to learn about life on the college campus.

* * * * *

I know him. I've seen him at the frat house several times. He's the one who answered the door last quarter when I went looking for Smooth.

"Hi, my name is Rashondra Hernandez. I'm from Ft. Lauderdale, Florida and I'm a freshman," I said, extending my hand to the three other students I had been placed in a group with in History 101.

"I'm Priscilla Willard, freshman, from Bloomfield, Michigan."

"Indigo Duncan, freshman, from Savannah, Georgia."

"Walter Lucas, junior, from Baltimore, Maryland. Ya'll can call me Suave."

"I've seen you at the frat house a few times," I said after Walter introduced himself. I winked my eye in hopes of him understanding that my visits were not to be shared with the group. Priscilla and Indigo seemed to be two intelligent, high-classed girls. I didn't want them to think less of me knowing that I'd been in and out of the frat house like that. They probably didn't even know what a hard penis looked like, especially Miss Prissy looking Priscilla.

"Oh yeah, I thought your face looked familiar," Walter responded as he winked back and smiled. That assured me he was cool.

* * * * *

We met in the library Saturday morning to start on our report about 'The Boston Massacre'. I initiated the discussion.

"I'll research Crispus Attucks. He sort of reminds me of myself. Very strong, independent man. He didn't care anything about those Red Coats out there with those weapons. And on top of that, he was a runaway, freed slave, so you know he thought he had it going on. He stood out there on that front line and was ready to beat them down." I slammed my fist into the table as we all laughed. "But the bullet got to him first. Oh yeah, he was a strong man."

Three weeks later, the presentation of our group assignment went well. We all received a ninety-nine, one point short of a hundred simply because Dr. Turner believes only God himself is perfect.

* * * * *

"There's a party going on at the frat house tonight. Let's go check it out," I said to Indigo and Priscilla one Friday evening as we ate dinner in the cafeteria. I hadn't visited since Hunk and I broke up, if you want to call him a boyfriend. I was too embarrassed.

"Well, I don't know about that. I heard those guys over there act very ferocious and uncultivated. They try to force that hunch-punch in you so they can get you in bed with them," said Priscilla.

"I've never been over there before. I did hear they were rather wild, but they are college students too. I can't imagine them doing anything crazy to us," responded Indigo.

"Well, I would rather go to the party in the student center. At least some of the professors are in and out of there," added Priscilla. "I'm really not in the mood for dancing. Anyway, I promised my best friend that I would write her to let her know how things are going."

Lord; don't tell me I've hooked up with some nerds. These little prissy girls are too slow for me. "Okay, we can go to the student center, but I'm telling you, I've been to the frat house before and it's fun. Y'all have got to enjoy college life. Have some fun!" I retorted.

"I'm all for it. I'm willing to try something new. Let's trust Rashondra's judgement. Besides, she's a Pearl anyway. Surely she wouldn't be a part of something reckless," said Indigo.

"Okay, I'll go on and go as long as we all stay together," added Priscilla.

They just don't know. Yeah, I've been over there all right. I've slept in every room in existence over there. These slow-ass, uppity girls have a lot learn. I think I'm the perfect teacher.

Chapter 12

Priscilla

The feeling of emptiness I possessed slowly began to emerge after I met Indigo and Rashondra. They most definitely weren't the type of females Father would approve for me to associate with, especially Rashondra. But, as unique as they were, I found myself clinging to them like a magnet.

* * * * *

After my initial arrival into this small town, I had a slight feeling of regret when I realized it was totally opposite of what I was used to. The more I thought about Mother, the more I understood why I had to stay.

My slim, acrobatic physique made it easy for me to be chosen as a cheerleader. My enjoyment of the football games intensified after I developed a crush on number '51'. He was the number one running back who had the speed of a Gazelle.

Father and Ruby flew down to visit for homecoming. His look of disgust as he entered my dormitory room brought a grave feeling upon me.

"Joseph," Ruby said as she tugged at his arms trying to whisper. "Let her enjoy this day and we'll help her pack tomorrow."

Pack? I strained my ears to listen to Ruby. *So Father came down here to pack my belongings and ship me off to some place I had no interest in being. I'll just have to prove to him that I really like it here, although I do find it rather boring.*

"Father, Ruby, this is my roommate Tracey." I exploited a wide grin as I pulled her cheek to touch mine.

The look Tracey gave was enough to affirm it was time to release my hold. She and I had not become friends, but more like associates. We did talk every evening when we returned from our classes, but we never did anything else together. She was rather weird if you asked me. Sometimes she laughed in her sleep. One day I walked in on her engrossed in a full-blown conversation with herself, body language and all. She claimed she was just thinking out loud. My God, she must have been absorbed in some serious thoughts.

My attempt to make a good impression regarding my college life led me to behave as a hyperactive child. I escorted Father and Ruby around the rest of the dorm and part of the campus.

At the conclusion of the football game, we drove for what seemed like hours until we found what Father considered to be a suitable restaurant to dine at, which was miles away from campus.

"Precious, you seem to be warming up to this country place. Well, you've had your experience, so are you ready to transfer to Princeton now?" Father asked the day of their departure.

I felt somewhat relieved that he did *ask* if I was ready to go. Normally, he would've told me it was time to pack my bags, no explanation. Maybe my upbeat attitude had an affect on him. Not to mention the fact that I brought up Mother's name on occasions, despite Ruby being in our presence.

"I'm going to stay Father. I'm staying until I graduate. If I decide I no longer want to be here, I'll let you know."

"Precious, this is not the kind of college life I had planned for my baby girl."

"I'm no baby. I am eighteen years old. I have a mind of my own. Can't I make my own decision about where I want to get my education? Don't try to force me to leave because of an image you're trying to uphold. What about the image you should've upheld with your family? That didn't seem to matter to you," I said as tears swelled in my eyes.

"Come here Precious." He wrapped his arms around me as I rested my head in his chest. "Don't cry. I'm sorry. You can stay. You know I love you with all my heart don't you?" he added, tilting my head back with both hands allowing me to look him directly in the face.

"Yes Father. I love you too. Please grant me this one wish along with your support, okay."

It was a done deal. Father and Ruby left, without me of course.

Three weeks later I coerced Father into sending me a roundtrip ticket to California to visit Chanel for the Christmas holidays. He pleaded for me to come home. He even promised to purchase me a new car if I spent Christmas with he and Ruby. That didn't change my mind. I was adamant about going to California.

* * * * *

She's gorgeous, I thought after Rashondra introduced herself. Her clothes look rather vile. It was evident she had no wealth in her family.

Indigo is pretty also. I've seen them both in the dormitory. I wonder who does Indigo's hair because it's always neat.

The intellectual sides of their personalities shined during our initial discussion. That gave me a level of comfort in working with them. Walter sort of had a nonchalant attitude, but his share of information in our research was enough for a successful completion.

One evening Walter noticed I was in the library finishing up an essay for another class when the lights flashed, which meant closing time. He was gentleman enough to wait until I finished my last paragraph. He didn't want me walking across the campus in the darkness alone.

"What a nice watch you're sporting," said Walter. He lifted my wrist toward his face to get a better view of my Movado.

"Thank you."

Slowly, I pulled my arm away. I gathered my belongings before we walked out the library door.

"Sooo Miss Priscilla, are you dating anyone?"

"No I'm not. But there is someone I'm interested in. He probably has a girlfriend because he's too gorgeous to be single."

The expression Walter portrayed after my statement told me I'd given him the wrong answer. Walter is a cute young man, but my heart was set on number '51'.

* * * * *

The guys in the frat house acted like undomesticated animals. For a minute I thought we had stepped into the wilderness. Rashondra left us five minutes after we walked in, claiming she needed to spend time with the other Pearls to ease their thoughts of her acting snooty.

The brothers drank, danced, stepped, cursed, screamed, and did everything else that strayed away from the words calm and decent.

"Did you see that boy grab Rashondra's butt?" I asked Indigo, appalled at the fact that her response was a hug rather than a slap in the face. "Oh Lord, this is too much for me. I'm ready to go."

"Girl relax. These guys are just having fun. Yes, some of them are taking things a little too far, but I don't think you have to worry about them aggravating you or grabbing your butt."

"Oh they better not. I'll probably write a letter to the Dean. Rashondra should write one. That guy had no right grabbing her like that. That's her privacy."

" Priscilla, just look at Rashondra. She's wearing a black, 'skin-tight' cat suit that allows her butt to protrude perfectly. She may as well accompany her outfit with a sign that reads 'desire me'. On the other hand, you are dressed in a nice pair of 100% silk, Jones Shaw blue slacks, cuffed at the end of each leg and a nice preppy blouse to match. You may as well accompany you outfit with a sign that reads 'stuck-up'. Therefore, I doubt very seriously if one of the guys would approach you in the way they are approaching Rashondra."

So she thinks those jeans and ankle cut boots she's wearing are perfect for the occasion. Maybe they are because quite a few students are wearing jeans and sweatsuits. That just comes from a lack of class. I was always taught to dress to kill when going out.

"Are you girls having fun?" Walter said as he grabbed one of our hands. He threw his head to the side as his shoulder and body followed to the beat of 'Atomic Dog'. That unglued us from the spot we'd been stuck in since our arrival.

"Not bad at all," Indigo responded, now popping the fingers of her loose hand as she dipped her head to the side in an attempt to do 'The Worm' simultaneously with Walter.

"This is most definitely something I can not get use to. It's too hot, stuffy, and wild in here," I added.

Indigo and Walter were dancing and seemed to be having fun. Joining in on 'The Worm' with them was the furthest thing from my mind. But what appeared before my eyes next instantly threw me into a two-step or something. I had no explanation as to the dance I was performing as my body roused to the beat. The expression on Indigo's face convinced me she was totally baffled by my sudden rhythm.

Number '51' had just walked through the door with an entourage of about eight following him. Remaining in a straight line, they performed a quick step routine that concluded with yelping "AaaRoof! AaaRoof!"

"Later RIP, oops, 'IP. Where's Rashondra anyway? Never mind. I'll get up with y'all later. These boys just crossed over last quarter," Walter said as he walked over to join them.

"That's him, number '51'. Oh God, he looks even better close up."

Excitedly pointing in his direction, I bounced up and down like a child waiting to lick her favorite ice cream.

"Oh girlfriend, you'll most definitely need an attitude readjustment on your feelings about coming over here now. You didn't tell me he was Walter's frat brother," replied Indigo.

Before I responded, he seemed to have noticed the attention we gave him by the staring, pointing, and blushing. He emerged from the group of frats and slowly strolled in our direction with the cutest grin on his face.

"Oh my God Indigo, he's coming over here. What am I going to say? Tell me what to do."

Chapter 13

Indigo

"It's unbelievable. Two more weeks and we're no longer freshmen. This school year went by so fast," I said to Rashondra and Priscilla as we lingered in the library after studying.

* * * * *

When I first arrived, I had to be the proudest person on campus. I was overjoyed about being away from home and attending a big, four-year college. My dream had come true.

Tangela, my roommate, was pretty cool. We hung out at some of the parties held in the student center on the weekends. Hanging out and partying was something new to me. This was not the kind of behavior I displayed at home.

Calling my parents strict would be an inappropriate description of them. But for religious reasons, I was not allowed to frequent the dances and parties during high school. Although I occasionally tiptoed behind their backs, they were never aware of it. I fell into the paths my siblings paved for me. It was not like we were into guns and drugs, but just a little innocent bouncing to the beat of 'pop/rock' instead of the gospel that reared us.

My first visit to the frat house was very surprising to Tangela. She'd never been and was astounded the night I'd awakened her to give her an ear full.

"Girl the boys were all over Rashondra. She had on this 'stank-looking' cat suit showing every crack from front to back. As fine as I am, there is no way in this world I would've walked out of my room dressed like that." We laughed as our hands met for a quick high-five.

"You don't believe me Indigo, but I bet that girl ain't nothing but a project hoe. I bet you a dollar she's straight from the ghetto. Look at the way she cursed her roommate out last quarter. Had the girl in tears. You can't tell me she's not from the projects."

"She probably is, with her buck-wild self. But I like her. There's just this distinctive warmth about her that attracts you."

"You said Priscilla was there too, right."

"Yeah, girl. Oh, you won't believe what she did. No let me back up. Guess what she had on girl."

"What, a three-pieced suit?"

"Close. Homegirl was dressed liked she had just stepped out of Vogue."

"No she wasn't."

"Yes she was."

"She didn't know y'all were going to a frat house?"

"Yes, but you know she dresses like she's being snapshot for the cover of Jet or Right-On or something."

"Honey both of your friends need a make-over on how to dress. One overdresses and the other underdresses."

"I'll have to work on that. But anyway, guess what Priscilla did?"

"Lay it on me sister."

"Okay, she had been complaining about the frat house not being her ideal place to hang out and how she was so ready to go. So all of a sudden, her entire persona changed because this guy on the football team, whom she happens to have a huge crush on, walked in with some of the other frat brothers. He noticed her pointing at him and came in our direction."

"For real?"

"Yes girl. But that's not all. When he approached us, she was gone, just disappeared, just like that," I said, popping my finger.

"Whaaaattt? Disappeared? Where in the hell did she go?"

"I don't know. She just vanished. But anyway, he assumed she left me there so that the two of us can talk."

"No he didn't girl."

"Oh yes he did. When he walked over he said, 'I noticed you were eyeing a brotha from afar. What's up with that?' Then had the nerves to rub his hand down the side of my face."

"Oh Lordy, what did you do then?"

"Girl, even with his good looks, I had to put him in check. So I said, What makes you think I was looking at you?"

"Instincts baby," he said as he pointed to his head. "My instincts tell me you've got the hots for me. I know you're embarrassed because I noticed it," he sarcastically added.

"You need to check your neurological system. Evidently there's a dent in one of your nerves because you've just processed the wrong piece of information," I said to him.

"Damn girl, what did he say when you threw that line on him," inquired an excited Tangela.

"He just said I was a 'smart honey' and would change my mind one day. I'm glad she didn't hang around to meet him with that conceited personality."

We laughed so hard our sides ached about the events that night. I promised to include her the next time we decided to go. Before long, we'd drifted off to sleep.

* * * * *

Rashondra and Priscilla decided to spend spring break in Savannah. Tangela showed a bit of jealously at the thought of them going home with me. Although she was invited, she couldn't join us due to her sister's wedding. In a way, I was pleased with the outcome because she and Rashondra really didn't care for each other. The truth would have come out had they spent an entire week together.

Daddy's arrival in the church van ensured there would be plenty of room for the three of us. Priscilla packed very lightly because she anticipated shopping. She felt it was time to purchase a few 'dress-down' pieces. Both Rashondra and I agreed.

Audrey had recently purchased a brand new Maxima. I took advantage of my opportunity to use it during my visit. We cruised up and down all the major highways including Montgomery, Abercorn, and Liberty. We made a stop at Tybee Island, visited Hilton Head, and frequented River Street. Our fun concluded with church service on Sunday morning.

While Priscilla and Rashondra packed for the return trip to college, I slipped away for a brief visit to Granddaddy. I said a short prayer and placed a single rose near his head stone. *I miss you so much.*

* * * * *

Rashondra was given a job spring quarter through the college work-study program. She was very excited at knowing she would now have the money to purchase a roundtrip ticket for her summer visit home.

She revealed to us one night how poverty stricken her family was. When she described her living conditions, it was difficult for me to fathom the thought of it. Initially I believed she was over-exaggerating, but what reason did she have to lie?

* * * * *

We all finished our finals by Tuesday and decided to elongate our stay throughout the weekend. We wanted to attend the end of the year parties.

Tangela went home Thursday, so we decided to dwell in my dorm room until our departure.

As we waited around in my room for nightfall, I reached into my mini refrigerator and pulled out three wine coolers. Rashondra accepted, but Priscilla declined. She had vowed to never take a drink after witnessing the affects alcohol had on her mother.

"Rashondra, what was that confrontation all about a few days ago between you, Hunk, and Gary?"

"Oh honey child I can't even believe I forgot to tell y'all. Okay, Hunk used to like me fall quarter. But that fetish ended by winter quarter. *I'll spare the gory details of the relationship.* Well, when we started hanging at the frat house, he became interested again. So we hooked up for a little while, you know, keeping it on the 'down-low', no commitments made. Y'all know I started seeing Gary this quarter. *Not to mention Chris, Red, and Stanley that I had a slight involvement with also.* Now I like him for real. So the other day, Gary walked up on me and Hunk talking. Hunk was trying to get me to sneak him into my room, trying to apologize for what happened between us and claiming he missed me so much."

"What? Missed you? That lil lying dog. I've seen him around here with so many women. I hope you didn't go for that," I said.

"Are you crazy? I know better. I told him he must have lost his damn mind thinking I'm about to give him another piece of this," said Rashondra pointing to her crotch. " But guess what he had the nerves to say to Gary," she added.

"I can't wait to hear this one."

"He said, 'She ain't all that in bed man, you can have her', and just walked off. That ole punk."

"You are kidding me right?" I said.

"Are you for real Rashondra?" added Priscilla, speaking for the first time since Rashondra started on her story. "That wasn't a nice thing to say. I hope he didn't hurt Gary's feelings, " she continued.

"Don't get me wrong, I really like Gary and all, but who gives a damn about how men feel. They don't think twice about hurting our feelings. Trust me, I've been there and that pain can make you feel like you're down for the last count."

"I know that's right," I added. "Men can be as trifling as they come. They are all up to no good. Even Walter tried to flirt with me."

"Oh hold up, wait a minute, you are holding back some real juice now. I can't believe you and Walter used to swing it," Rashondra excitedly interrupted.

"We never had anything going on. He just flirted with me one night with the intentions of taking it a little further, but you know I handled it."

What did he do honey child? Squeeze the juice on us," inquired Rashondra.

"Well, actually it was the first night we were at the frat house, the night that Priscilla disappeared." While recollecting that episode, we began to laugh. "I asked him had he seen her. He seductively told me no, but he wouldn't mind seeing me later on. I called him crazy and walked off. He apologized when I saw him on campus Monday morning, claiming it was the liquor."

"Umm. Y'all would've made a cute couple," said Rashondra as she placed her index finger on her temple as if she had just come up with some great invention. "The brotha does look good. I also heard he's 'packing' at least nine inches," she added, giving Priscilla hi-five, who really didn't see any humor in what she was saying.

"You *heard* he was packing? Are you sure you don't know first hand?" I inquired.

"Now what the hell are you trying to say honey child?" Rashondra snapped.

"Nothing really. I'm just thinking back on the day we introduced ourselves in that History class. I saw you wink your eye at Walter."

"Girl please. I've never messed around with him. That wink meant nothing but hey, what's up, I've seen you before." *My goodness, she watches everything.*

"Let's go to the frat house tonight," Priscilla said, interrupting what she thought was a very irrelevant conversation.

"*You* want to go to the frat house?" I said to her in amazement. "I thought you were too embarrassed to ever return there again."

"That was about two months ago. I'm sure no one remembers that scene anymore." *But the truth of the matter is, I remember it all too well.*

"What actually happened that night? I'm tired of hearing 'I don't want to talk about it'. Like you said, that was two months ago. You are over it now so spill the beans," demanded Rashondra.

"I don't even know how to explain what could've altered my way of thinking that night. I felt very perplexed when I saw him walking toward me. My stomach started churning and I literally freaked out. Since I didn't have the nerves to face him, I stumbled my way to the front door, bumping into several students before reaching the porch. 'Watch where you're going drunk-ass' was one of the many things yelled at me. Although I hadn't had a single item to drink, I felt light-headed and confused. I stood on the porch for a few seconds to allow my unsteady heartbeat to catch up with the rest of my body. As I gained my composure, I sprinted across the lawn, tripping over the shrubbery before I reached the street. I bawled like a baby, mostly due to the embarrassment. I stood up and attempted to brush the soil from my stained clothes. One of the guys said, 'Man, she must have gotten a hold of some bad stuff', and they all just laughed at me. Oh God, I never want to relive that moment."

"At least they thought you were drunk or high or something. Suppose they really knew you were running from a dude you had a crush on. That's so elementary. Now that would've been embarrassing to the utmost," said Rashondra. "I'll be glad when I see this guy that temporarily drove you insane."

* * * * *

We continued on with our conversations, while laughing... drinking...more laughing... drinking ... until we were finally exhausted.

Chapter 14

RIP

"It's still hard to believe we slept right through the parties last night," said Indigo as they left the cafeteria after brunch.

"I know that's right. Gary's probably really pissed at me right about now. We were suppose to hook up last night," Rashondra responded.

"Well Priscilla, I guess it'll be just you and me hanging out. You know Rashondra isn't going to risk not seeing her man on her last night here."

"Honey child you better call Charles. You know he's got a thang for you. Priscilla might just have to go solo tonight."

"I'm not interested in seeing him. Our relationship never escalated. He's probably somewhere catching grasshoppers and frogs. You know how he is about nature. Like I said, it's going to be me and Priscilla tonight."

"Both of you should go on and spend time with your significant others" said Priscilla. "I wish I could cuddle with my man tonight, excuse me, I mean my dream man. Under no circumstances am I implying a passion for sex. I just desire to be embraced by someone special," she added.

"Go ahead girlfriend. Claim him as your man. I don't know about this Indigo. Priscilla might be the one sneaking in tomorrow morning."

"Rashondra please. I would never become sexually involved on the first night. That's not my character. How dare you!"

"Just a joke honey. Look at you, getting all sensitive about a man who doesn't even know you exist," retorted Rashondra.

"If he's still around, he'll know she exists tonight if I have anything to do with it." Priscilla caught a glimpse of Indigo as she winked at Rashondra. She didn't say anything, but allowed a flustered expression to appear on her face.

"Don't give me that look," Indigo continued. "If he's here, you will meet him tonight. Those fantasies you've held on to all year are about to become reality. I just hope he's worth it." Indigo unlocked the door to her room. *It's unnecessary to mention how he flirted with me last quarter. It's very minor and in the past,* thought Indigo.

"Okay, here's the plan. We'll all go to the step-show at seven. Afterwards, we will party in the student center for a short moment, and then, I'm hooking up with Gary. You two will be on your own."

"That sounds like a winner."

"Sounds wonderful to me also," added Priscilla. She felt very anxious about the pending encounter that was to take place that night.

* * * * *

"There are more students lingering around than I anticipated," said Priscilla as they took a seat on the second bench in the middle of the gymnasium.

"Girl college life is the bomb, who's ready to go home," responded Rashondra. She danced a few moves to the 'Cabbage Patch' then slung her right arm around and began 'Prepping' before taking her seat next to them.

That girl acts so frantic sometimes, thought Priscilla as she watched Rashondra, who happened to be the only one standing there dancing.

They waited idly about fifteen minutes before the step-show began. When the first fraternity made an entrance into the gym, the students roared with excitement.

Several sororities and fraternities stepped on and off the floor before the fraternity Priscilla anxiously awaited was about to commence.

"Rashondra, Indigo, look, Walter's on his way in," Priscilla said as she pointed in his direction.

Walter and two other frats leisurely sauntered onto the floor with a quick trio performance before the others followed, imitating the same steps.

* * * * *

Within two hours, the step-show was over. RIP squeezed their way through the crowd of students and headed back to Indigo's room.

Still amazed by the events that had just taken place, Priscilla chattered every step of the way.

"I'm still stunned Walter called the cheerleaders to the floor while they performed. I had no intentions of going out there."

"Lucky for you, he took the initiative and pulled you out there anyway," said Indigo, giving Rashondra that slick wink again.

"Oh my God, pinch me, pinch me. Tell me it was just a dream," Priscilla continued,as they entered the dormitory."At first I was embarrassed, but when Smooth chose me to dance with over the other five cheerleaders, I felt ecstatic. The excitement I felt about being so close to him was phenomenal. I could barely keep up with the hip-shaking routine we performed. Then he whispered in my ear, 'I've been checking you out for a long time and I like what I see.' Before I could respond, he stomped and dipped to the floor with the rest of the frats."

"Honey child please! Calm your excited ass down," interrupted Rashondra.

"I'm trying to keep my composure. Okay, just let me finish my story. After I told him my name and agreed to be present at the frat house tonight, he pecked me on my cheek and walked off. Oh my God, I thought I was going to melt inside."

"Girl you better be ready to give up the stuff tonight. I've heard about Smooth, he'll most definitely want to saddle you up and take you for a ride," said Rashondra. *I had no idea she'd been mesmerized by Smooth all of this time. I almost had a piece of him fall quarter. But why bring that up now. I didn't even know her then. Like Mama always says, let sleeping dogs lie,* thought Rashondra.

"You need to stop it Rashondra, he may really like Priscilla. You never know."

"She can say what she wants to, I can handle myself. I will not be indulging in sexual intercourse tonight, " retorted Priscilla.

"Yeah, yeah, yeah," snapped Rashondra, immediately downing a mixed drink Indigo had prepared as soon as they walked into her room. "Hey Priscilla," Rashondra continued, feeling a little woozy after taking a large gulp from her second drink. "Why don't you teach the cheerleaders this cheer. We used to do it in my neighborhood all the time."

Rashondra placed the plastic cup on the dresser as Indigo and Priscilla looked on, wondering what ghetto cheer she had to share with them this time. Rashondra was most definitely one who couldn't hold her liquor well and always clowned around when drinking.

After a short repetition of claps and stomps, Rashondra began chanting the cheer. "Yo Ma. Yo Pa. Yo greedy, greedy Grandma."

Indigo was so tickled by Rashondra's entertainment that she almost dropped her drink. Surprisingly, Priscilla saw some humor in Rashondra's performance as well.

"She's ninety-nine. She drank that wine. She's the first one there in the welfare line," concluded Rashondra as their voices bellowed across the room with laugher.

Three Fuzzy Navels were enough for Indigo and Rashondra to feel very lightheaded as they departed for the party. Although Priscilla was tempted, she kept her vow not to drink.

An hour of dancing in the student center was enough for them to agree that it was time for a change in scenery.

They briefly held hands in a close huddle and conformed to meet in Indigo's room at ten o'clock sharp tomorrow morning.

Rashondra left with Gary, while Indigo and Priscilla strolled across the campus in the direction of the frat house.

* * * * *

"Okay, you go first Rashondra. We're use to your drama spills anyway," said Indigo.

"There really isn't much to tell. Gary and I went back to his room because his roommate had already left. Can y'all believe I drank two Malt Liquors on top of the gin and juice we already had? I was toe-up! I mean toe-up from the flo up!" Rashondra continued as she gave Indigo hi-five. "I can't hardly remember what happened last night. I know we had sex because I remember the slobbery kisses he put all over my wet kitty-cat. When I woke up this morning, butt naked, and smelling like funk, I wanted something to think about on my long ride home. I jerked on his thang, while he was still asleep, until it was hard. Then I jumped on it. Girlfriends, y'all don't hear me. I straddled my man and rode him until we both came. I had him whimpering like a baby."

"You don't play. You just take what you want. I'm surprised the men don't run from you. Girl if you're throwing it on men like that, I'm surprised they are not sniffing around for you all the time," responded Indigo.

Umm, you just don't know. I have more sniffers than you can imagine, thought Rashondra.

"You are rather bold if you ask me. You really shouldn't be that aggressive with men. It sort of gives you a bad name," added Priscilla.

"Comes with experience honey," Rashondra said. She pinched Priscilla on the cheek. "I can't help it if y'all are still virgins. It's time to pop those bubbles." She snapped her fingers for emphasis.

"Hold up now Rashondra. Priscilla is the only virgin around here. I told y'all about my high school boyfriend."

"You only slept with him twice, right? That's a shame, dated a year and a half and you only gave that poor boy some two times. Two times, that's nothing. You're still a virgin. Nexxxxt!"

"You are very amazing Rashondra," said Priscilla, shaking her head in disgust. *Sometimes I have to wonder how in the world I took a liking to her. She is so obnoxious sometimes. Just no class,* Priscilla said to herself.

"I'm not even thinking about what Rashondra is saying. Let me tell my story. Well of course, Priscilla disappeared at the frat house again."

"No she didn't. I just know she didn't give it up on the first night," Rashondra interrupted. "That's not her style remember." *Knowing Smooth, he got it. I don't care how prim and proper she thinks she is. She still has the same body parts as any other woman and I know her stuff tingles sometimes.*

"Darn Rashondra, let me finish my story," Indigo cut in before Priscilla had a chance to rebut. "But anyway, after dancing with Walter and a few other brothas, I decided to head back to the dorm. Guess who I ran into, sitting on the steps of the library, with a backpack on?"

"Oh wow! That's a hard one, let's see here. It couldn't have been Charles because he hates studying," said Rashondra with a 'trying to be smart' look on her face.

"Yes it was him. He invited me to sit with him. I didn't even want to know why he was at the library on a Saturday night with no classes to attend. We chatted for awhile, mostly about our plans for summer break and academics, of course. He ranted a bit about his 4.0 GPA."

"Big damn deal! Did you tell him you have a 4.0 also? Did you tell him that we all have 4.0 GPAs? He hadn't said a thang," said Rashondra, slinging her hair back into place after seeming to have 'lost it' for a moment.

"Girl let me finish my story, okay. Darn! Aaanny way, he escorted me back to the dorm and I was able to sneak him up with ease. Old Lady Mable was snoring. We ran right past her."

"Did he stay all night?" asked Priscilla with an expression that told she would be highly disappointed if he did.

"Yes."

"Did you give him some girl?" asked Rashondra, now standing.

"Ummm. Sort of. I mean, yeah we did it," Indigo said, holding her head down feeling slightly embarrassed now.

"Yes! Yes! You go girl!" Rashondra yelled, diving on the bed. Indigo rolled over in just enough time to escape her impact. "Was it good girlfriend? Did he do it to you right?"

"Oh my goodness girl, it was good."

"That's what I'm talking about. Pop those bubbles. Open yourself up. Your stuff needs to breathe. Can't do that if it's still crammed with cobwebs," said Rashondra.

Priscilla sat on the opposite bed and watched in awe as Indigo and Rashondra continued to horseplay around. She didn't know whether she should be happy or sad for Indigo.

Rashondra reached out and pinched Priscilla on the cheek again and said, "Okay Priscilla, it's your turn."

"Let me get something straight right now. I did not have sex with Smooth."

"Party-pooper! Party-pooper!" yelled Rashondra.

"I'm not going to respond to that comment," said Priscilla as she waved Rashondra off. "As soon as I walked into the frat house, he spotted me. We went outside and talked for a long time. He told me that out of the two years he'd been here, he'd never met someone he was so taken away with as myself. He noticed me at the first football game and knew he had to get himself together before he approached me. He said a lot of sweet things to me."

"Did you tell him how you freaked out the first night you saw him at the frat house?" asked Rashondra.

"No, I didn't even mention that night. Later on, he walked me back to the dorm and we stood outside for a while and talked. What really impressed me about him was he asked if he could have a kiss. He didn't just tilt his head assuming I wanted to kiss him, he asked me."

"Well, did you at least do that?" asked Rashondra.

Blushing before she could respond, she said, "Yes, when he kissed me, my knees buckled. We kissed and hugged repeatedly for the next fifteen minutes before he admitted to not wanting to keep me out too late. What a gentleman. We exchanged addresses and phone numbers and promised to call as soon as we can. This is the man for me. I know he's the one. I'm in love."

* * * * *

"Priscilla Willard, will you please report to the lobby," was announced over the intercom, which interrupted the deep conversation they were embedded in.

Realizing it was already twelve o'clock, their faces saddened for they knew it was time for their summer departures. Indigo's father was due to arrive at one o'clock. Rashondra's bus was to leave at twelve forty-five. An associate from Willard Insurance was already waiting for Priscilla in the lobby.

Indigo held out her hands as Priscilla and Rashondra were drawn to her. They stood in a small huddle and allowed a brief moment of silence. Soon the tears, hugs, and kisses took their course.

"I'm going to miss you. I'll write. I'll call. I love you. " They all departed their separate ways with vast anticipation of reuniting after the summer.

Chapter 15

Priscilla

It didn't take much effort for me to convince Indigo and Rashondra to share an off-campus three bedroom apartment with me. The dilemma was trying to influence Indigo's father that we would still live by the rules of the college campus and not fall behind. After Indigo promised to move back on campus if her grades fell below 'C' average, the dissenting feeling her father had began to ease.

* * * * *

Summer was an exhilarating intermission for me. I spent two weeks in San Francisco with Chanel and one week in Savannah with Indigo. Every attempt made to visit Rashondra yielded some excuse as to why timing was bad, therefore, I eventually relinquished that idea.

The most enjoyable occasions of all were the times I spent with Smooth. He resided in Cleveland, which was less than two hundred miles away. Each time I stepped off the airplane at Hopkins, my heart skipped numerous beats due to the overexertion of excitement I'd built up. The smile shone on his face each time I greeted him with a kiss assured me he was just as excited.

During Smooth's third visit to Bloomfield, I acceded to his plea to share my love with him. The delicate movement of his hands as he caressed my body brought an ecstatic feeling upon me. He knew I was a virgin and took pride in being the one to enter me for the first time. Foreplay was so intense that I only felt a slight pinch as he penetrated me. He repetitiously stroked my inside with his rigid manhood in a precarious, rhythmical way. A tingle continued to nab at my flesh as an after shock of the spurting vibrations I'd felt. With a tight grip, I wrapped my arms around his shoulders. Tears trickled down my cheeks. These tears were not present due to pain, but due to a newfound love and happiness. *I want you in my life forever. I'm so in love,* I thought as I continued to hold him in my arms.

Smooth understood completely after I explained my preference to call him by his birth name, Marlon. It gave me more of a personal connection with him.

Father eventually gave up on trying to convince me to attend Princeton. There was no way I would change colleges after I'd fallen in love with Marlon.

Three weeks prior to the end of summer break, Father, Ruby, and I flew back to Atlanta en route to my college. While they searched for the perfect items to furnish the apartment, I occupied myself with cheerleading camp.

A week later as I peered out the living room window, Father pulled up in a rental car. Ruby trailed him driving a candy apple red Camero, my new car.

Chapter 16

Rashondra

"There ain't no tellin what that boy might do if he get a hold of this here ticket. He done been over here and stole pictures off the wall, clothes out my closet, and meat from my freegirator. Just last week that joker done come in here and took the TV out from the livin room right while Nayla was watching it. He even told her I said it need some fixin done to it. Won nothin wrong wit it either. That ole lying, roguish, hoodlum. Just makes me sick to my stomach," was what Grandma greeted me with as soon as I walked through the front door.

"And hello to you too Grandma," I responded, kissing her on the cheek. *She's lost about fifteen pounds. I guess she's following the doctor's orders after all.*

Grandma took the second half of my round-trip bus ticket and placed it in an old empty can of white hominy that she securely kept other important papers. She returned the can to its original hiding place, which camouflaged well in the back of the pantry with the other canned goods.

Despite the cynical things Grandma said about Zach, I was still eager to see him. *I just want him to change his life and try to be somebody. I hope that by him seeing me he'll realize there's still a chance.*

As soon as I finished dinner that evening, I headed for 'the cut'. When I finally tracked him down, I barely recognized his face. The female he resided with looked just as shabby.

"Who the hell are you?" she said as she snatched the screen door open before I could finish my first round of knocks.

"I'm Rashondra. I'm looking for Zach. I was told he lives here." *This heifer better thank the Lord I got a lil education about myself because I can easily see my right hand slipping from the control of my brain, landing right in the middle of her face.*

"Doobaby, go git Mama piece. Zach done been out thar messin round agin." Doobaby or whatever his name was looked every bit of five years old. He ran to the back of the apartment wearing a soiled looking pamper.

"I'm not messing around with him, he's my..."

"He yo nothing bitch. He my man," she snapped as she stepped out on the porch. She appeared to be about seven or eight months pregnant. *I wonder if it's Zach's child. I hope not.*

"You mighty bold steppin up in my crib tryin to come after my man. Last woman did that kinda mess got her ass stabbed. Now you fixin to git yo ass shot." She yanked the pistol out of Doobaby's hand.

There I stood, face to face, with this outraged female simply because I wanted to visit my brother. As I watched her take the gun from Doobaby, my life flashed before my very own eyes. I forced my stiffened feet to take tiny steps backwards wondering how to handle this true victim of drugs that stood in front of me.

Before she had a chance to elevate the hand clutching the pistol, Zach grabbed her by the back of the neck and shove her to the side.

"This my damn sista fool. I done told you to stop thanking every woman that walks by is gittin some of this here," he said groping his crotch.

What was I to say to him? I was at a lost for words. He looked so bad. My heart began to long for the Zach I used to frequent the corner Handy Andy with, purchasing our favorite past time snack, Cola and salty peanuts.

After a brief conversation, I hugged and kissed my brother goodbye. Tears swelled in my eyes as I walked away. *Have I lost my brother forever?*

There was no way I was going to allow Priscilla to come visit this hell hole. She would get the culture shock of her life. She wouldn't be able to survive one day in the projects. It's rough. Too much drama.

The news Priscilla presented about living off campus couldn't have made me happier. With that in mind, I felt a need to return early to settle in. With the rebate money left over from my financial assistance, the work-study job I had was no longer needed. All of my concentration can now be placed on studying. *And of course screwing from time to time.*

Every attempt I made to locate Mama over the summer was unsuccessful. No one knew where she was, not even Zach. That really troubled me.

Before leaving, I gave Nayla my college address. I felt a third grader should be able to write a complete letter. Well at least I did in Mr. Jacob's class.

The day I departed, Grandma and Nayla stood on the front porch crying. They waved goodbye as the taxi pulled off. *I'll be glad when I graduate and start making some money. I'm getting them out of the ghetto.*

* * * * *

With the free time I had after returning to school early, I decided to audition for a 'Dancing-Doll'. After I performed a last minute routine I composed, I was chosen without hesitation.

Chapter 17

Indigo

Summer was not as exciting as I had anticipated. The fun I predicted to have after reuniting with high school friends was very limited. Instead, I spent a lot of time with Grandmomma. That bonding time really lifted her spirits.

It was sort of neat when Priscilla came to visit. I had a new friend to show off. Rashondra and I wrote each other once a week. Walter and I conversed over the telephone a few times. Tangela wrote me a letter stating she would not be returning to campus because she was four months pregnant. She didn't reveal the father.

Charles called a few times before her left for some kind of spiritual retreat. At that point, we communicated by letter. He shared with me his two weeks experience in the North Carolina Mountains. He drank only spring water and ate fresh fruits and vegetables.

"You'll see a big difference in me when I return," he had warned me.

* * * * *

Daddy was not thrilled at all about the news of his baby girl moving off campus. He claimed that too much freedom would cause too many problems. I convinced him that I'd always been a responsible and trustworthy person. I also promised to move back on campus if my grades started to fall.

* * * * *

Being the last of the trio to return to college, I was amazed to learn that the red Camero parked in front of the apartment belonged to Priscilla.

But nothing surprised me more than to see Rashondra on the football field, shaking her big rump as a 'Dancing Doll'. She most definitely had no shame in her game.

Chapter 18

RIP

The sight of Charles for the first time after summer break took Indigo by surprise. She couldn't believe her eyes. He walked into their biology class styling a lustrous Jheri curl. His wide-spread nose was a good perch for the glasses resting upon it. His anorexic appearance put his weigh at about one hundred twenty pounds. He was a total resemblance of J.J. from 'Good Times', but looked just a tad bit classier. What a big turn off it was to see such a drastic change. She knew it was time to end their so-called relationship.

Well this nerd took revenge of their break-up. He slipped cash to Erika, a struggling female, who was in their biology class. The plan was for her to copy from Indigo's test. Before turning it in, she was to write a note on her test claiming she'd witnessed Indigo eyeing her paper on several occasions.

After the completion of grading the papers, they both scored ninety-twos and had the same wrong answers. It was obvious Charles's plan was a success.

Indigo was faced with the possibility of being kicked out of school. She and Erika had to meet with the school board for a decision.

I wonder why Erika lied on me like that? Indigo thought as her brain kicked into full speed. She carefully assessed the occurrences prior to the test. Her analysis led to the assumed culprit...Charles. *I just know he had something to do with this.*

* * * * *

"I was accused of copying off Erika's test. Now we have to meet with the school board," Indigo said in a very frustrated tone. She walked right over to the refrigerator in hopes of finding a wine cooler.

Priscilla jumped up from the kitchen table and Rashondra made her way over from the stove before Indigo could take another step.

"Oh no, how could something so ridiculous like this happen? Everybody knows by now your are a very brilliant student who would never result to cheating," said Priscilla.

"You mean Erika? Dumb ass, still-taking-developmental-studies-as-a-sophomore Erika?" inquired Rashondra.

"Yes," replied Indigo. She explained the whole ordeal and her suspicion of Charles. An angry Rashondra was ready for war.

"That lil frizzle headed toothpick has some nerves. Girl let's go kick his ass," said an infuriating Rashondra. She pulled her hair back into a ponytail and grabbed a rubber band from the counter to hold it in place. "He can't get mad at you because you don't want his ugly ass anymore. Does he know how he looks? Seriously, has he looked in a mirror? He is 'thru' with a capital T! You had the nerves to say he looks like a classy J.J. Girl, J.J. looks like Billy Dee Williams when compared to Charles. Honey child, I'm so pissed. I hate it when men try to dog you out just because you don't want them. They dump us all the time. That's why I don't stay with one man too long. They ain't hitting on nothing."

"Rashondra, please. Get off your soapbox and let's help her in a rational way. Fighting is not going to solve the problem. Just suppose Charles really had nothing to do with this at all. Indigo you need to go back to Dr. Adams and tell her the truth."

"What do you think I did the first time?" said Indigo abruptly.

"Take the Bible with you this time. Ask her if she believes in God. Place your hand on it and tell your side again. God will work it out."

"Oh just shut up Mother Teresa. Why don't you know that the truth ain't worth a damn sometimes? She told the truth and still has to go before the board. Okay. My goodness, sometimes I just don't know what to say about you honey."

"You don't have to get an attitude with me Rashondra. You and your foul mouth think violence will solve it all. There is a much better way to handle this. If it was up to you, Charles, Erika, and Dr. Adams would probably have a few slashes in them."

"Hold up a damn minute. You ain't never seen me cut nobody up. You are going a little too far Miss Perfect."

"Girls please. Both of y'all are taking this too far. This is my problem. Can I please have my time? I need you all to be here for me, not fight against one another," said Indigo as she extended her hands.

Rashondra and Priscilla both felt guilty about their inconsiderate behavior. They joined hands and apologized.

"Awe man, look at my bologna. They're burnt." Rashondra quickly broke the group hold and ran toward the stove. She lifted the three blackened, withered-looking pieces of bologna with a fork as smoke began to disperse throughout the kitchen.

"Oops, I'm sorry. My intentions were to tell you I saw the meat rising in the middle, but we were so engrossed in our own little spat that it just slipped mind," responded Priscilla as she lifted the window to give the smoke an outlet.

"Dog gone it Priscilla! You still should've told me they had puffed up. You knew they were ready then."

"Pardon me Rashondra, I told you it slipped my mind. You act as if I wanted the little meat to burn on purpose."

"Knowing you, you probably did. You always frown at the fact that I eat bologna anyway. I'm sorry I didn't grow up rich like you did. Yes I eat bologna, spam, vienna sausages, potted meat..., need I go on?"

"There you two go again. Please stop it. We have some mind boggling decisions to make," interrupted Indigo.

The steam from their brawl finally diffused as the smoked faded away also. After a second apology, they brainstormed a plan to help prove Indigo's case and to get back at Charles.

* * * * *

A new boyfriend almost every month was habitual for Rashondra. "Out with the old, in with the new," she said. That was a motto every time she decided to dismiss another so-called boyfriend.

As long as her grades were top notched, Rashondra had no problem placing her 'fun' on a pedestal. One night as she partied at the frat house, she completely lost her self-control. Too many cups of 'hunch-punch' coerced her to strip, in front of everybody. She sang along with Salt and Pepa and unbuttoned her shirt at the same time. "Push it good. Push, push it real good." Off came her shirt. A cotton bra held her 32B's in place. She gyrated her hips with every beat of the song. The guys cheered and screeched as they chanted, "Take it off! Take it off! Take it off!"

Feeling hyped from the chant, she popped the button on her jeans. Then she unzipped her pants preparing to go all the way. With a sudden jerk on her arm, Walter franticly snatched her away from the center of attraction. He pulled her out the door and across the street to chastise her.

* * * * *

"What am I going to say?" asked Rashondra as she paced the living room floor in circles. She received a letter from the Dean who requested a meeting in his office.

"I'm going to get kicked out of school just like Mama said. It's just hereditary to do wrong. I'm a failure," she continued almost in a state of panic.

"Come here," Indigo said as she placed her arm around Rashondra's shoulder for comfort. "Stop crying please. Everything is going to be all right, just listen to me. Tell Dean Rozier we all went out to celebrate passing the Regents Test. Go on and tell him that you had one drink and got carried away because you're really not a drinker. I can't think of any sane excuse you can give as to why you took your shirt off. At that point, let your academic achievements work for you."

"I agree with Indigo. At least you won't be lying. Be strong okay. We'll pray for you," added Priscilla.

They both embraced Rashondra as she continued to sob. *I can't get suspended. I can't go back home. I may not make it back out if I do,* Rashondra thought as she continued to cry in the arms of her two best friends.

Her trip to the Dean's office and three months of probation kept Rashondra on a low profile for the rest of her sophomore year.

* * * * *

"Busted! Ohh I'm telling," Rashondra said to Smooth when she saw him walk out of the girls' dorm with one of the cheerleaders. "You should be ashamed of yourself," now addressing her conversation to the female. "You know Smooth is Priscilla's man."

It had become customary for Marlon to have a few female friends on the side. He most definitely was not the charming little prince that he portrayed over the summer. He had a craving for women like a chocolate fiend.

"Great guggle-muggle. Honey child let me tell you what I saw," Rashondra said as soon as she dashed through the front door. Indigo and Priscilla had already settled in the living room.

God, not Marlon again, please not Marlon again, Priscilla thought.

"What happened?" asked Indigo. She left the beanbag chair and placed herself right next to Priscilla on the love sofa. She had a gut feeling it was bad news about Marlon.

"Girl, I caught Smooth, I meant Marlon, with Faye. They were walking out the back door of the dorm together."

"Well, what did he say? Were they studying?" Priscilla inquired, feeling uneasy about where this was leading.

"Priscilla, didn't we tell you that's a lame excuse he gives you," said Indigo, now appearing somewhat angry at the statement that just flowed from Priscilla's mouth. She walked away from the sofa and continued, "How many excuses are you going to except from him? This is the fourth woman we've found out about this year and you've allowed him to tell you some mess like, 'Baby you know I have a lot of study groups. Don't listen to your single friends, they're just jealous.' What makes it so bad is, you actually believe it."

"In all honesty, Marlon does have a lot of study groups. He's probably not exactly truthful about when he studies, but he does study a lot. I love you and Rashondra just like sisters. I know you are not jealous of me. I know you all wouldn't do anything to purposely hurt me. I resent that statement."

"Child you need some liberation about yourself. There is no way in the world I'll let one man dog me out like that. They mess up, they're gone. Take a look around. There are too many brothers out there that looks just as good as Marlon. Look a Rick, he's been asking about you since the day he saw us confront Marlon about Melissa. But naw, you don't want to give anybody a chance but the man who breaks your heart every month," added Rashondra.

"I'm sorry. I can't help it. I love Marlon so much," Priscilla said hesitantly.

That was usually her plea as to the reason why she accepted so much from the man of her dreams. The man that had a habit of shattering her heart to pieces.

* * * * *

Walter took on a 'big brother' role and established a tight bond with RIP throughout their first two years of college. As their sophomore year came to an end, their hearts saddened at the realization of his departure.

After his graduation ceremony, they hurried home to finish the preparations for a surprise party for him.

During a tearful farewell on his final day, Walter pledged to keep in touch with them for life.

Chapter 19

RIP

By their junior year of college, RIP had become a very popular trio. Priscilla continued to cheer, yet enduring much heartache from Marlon. Rashondra was still a 'Dancing Doll', but became very low key with her social life. Indigo was on the debate team with plans of running for president of the Student Government Association her senior year.

Walter came to visit during homecoming week. They had a blast, partying and entertaining. Each night they stayed up until the wee hours of the morning, reminiscing. That Sunday morning they said goodbye as Walter headed up Interstate 75 north en route to Hartsfield Airport. RIP anxiously anticipated Walter's next visit.

* * * * *

Marlon graduated at the end of RIP's junior year. His football career had fallen short due to his obsessive drinking habits. By his senior year, he'd become a binge drinker and wanted to party with his frat brothers all the time. His superstar reputation descended.

Priscilla blamed herself for the sudden inclination of his drinking. She felt the questions and pressure about other women had a major effect on him. The guilt she possessed led her to persuade Mr. Willard into offering Marlon an executive position at one of the Atlanta based companies. When he learned of his nearly six figure income, Marlon accepted without hesitation.

With the thought of Marlon not returning, along with her own insecurity, Priscilla decided it would be in her best interest to transfer to a college in Atlanta. It took Rashondra and Indigo hours of lecturing to finally convince Priscilla how unwise her decision was. With the influence of her best friends and a promise from Marlon to marry her upon graduation, she felt secure enough to stay her last year.

Chapter 20

RIP

"RIP is in the house! Oo'ah! Oo'ah! RIP is in the house!" they shouted in unison. That particular party in the student center was to be the last of their dances as college students. Graduation was to take place the following morning.

"Oh no he didn't go there!" Rashondra yelled. She bent her arms and danced a few moves to the Robot as the song 'Flashlight' blasted the building. Within seconds, she was in the middle of the dance floor.

"The roof, the roof, the roof is on fire!"the crowd of students roared. "We don't need no water let the mothersucker burn! Burn mothersucker, burn!" they continued, daring not to use the 'F' word. Dean Rozier had taught them better.

At the same time, Priscilla and Indigo coerced the crowd of students to form a soul train line. Rashondra 'robotted' her way to the end as Priscilla trailed.

"Go Priscilla! Go Priscilla!" Rashondra initiated the chant as the students joined in. Priscilla proceeded down the soul train line doing the Electric Boogaloo. Her dance was evidence of her excitement because they had never seen her wiggle and get loose like that.

As Indigo approached the front of the line, she allured Todd along. They singled and doubled bumped their way to the end.

* * * * *

Never in Indigo's wildest imagination did she think she would meet a guy like Todd. He left such a powerful mark of lust on her.

She had noticed him on campus numerous times. They even had two classes together. But they never had any detailed one-on-one contact. Basically just hi and bye.

Toward the end of fall quarter, there was a surprise knock on RIP's back door. Todd had come over to borrow a cup of flour for their neighbor.

Initially, Indigo thought it was the aroma seeping through the air from the fried chicken she was cooking that led to his next question. But as the conversation continued, she realized her error in thought.

"What's for dessert?" he had asked.

"I don't know. I hadn't planned on preparing dessert. Do you have any suggestions?"

"Yeah...me. Ten o'clock."

Oh my goodness. He's coming on pretty strong. What should I say? I'll go on and test the water. I like a challenge, she thought.

"Umm, ten o'clock. That's cool. I'll see you then."

What have I gotten myself into? Rashondra is rubbing off on me big time.

"Priscilla, Rashondra, come here!" she shouted from the kitchen hardly able to put a hold on her excitement.

"What's up honey child with your loud self?" said Rashondra.

"Guess whose coming to see me tonight?" Indigo said enthusiastically.

"Well I hope it's Ed, although I've never seen you this thrilled about a visit from him before," replied Priscilla.

"Wrong. It's Todd."

"What, Todd?" Rashondra said. Her excitement was so intense that the push she gave Indigo on the shoulder landed her back into the refrigerator. "You mean Todd with the big 'thang'?"

"Oh yes girl," Indigo responded after regaining her balance.

"Lord have mercy. Indigo, please don't tell me you are about to cheat on Ed. It will break his heart if he knew you were even thinking about another man," said Priscilla. She shook her head with a disappointed expression on her face.

"Well, it's not like Ed has been all that faithful to me. I just caught him at the movies with Roni two weeks ago. Remember?"

"He told you he went alone and she just happened to be there. He even tried to get you to accompany him but you turned him down. Besides, doesn't Todd have a girlfriend?" said Priscilla this time with a curious expression.

Not responding to what Priscilla just asked, Rashondra added, "I say go for it honey child. Everybody wants a piece of him. It's not like Ed is talking about marriage or anything. He's already told you he's not coming back winter quarter. I wouldn't lock myself down with a man whose about to walk out of my life soon."

"Don't listen to Rashondra. She's already had too many females knocking on our door about their men. I just don't want any more trouble around here," added Priscilla.

"Well Priscilla since you are so scared, you just go to bed early. On top of that, cover your head with your pillow. That way you won't see or hear anything. Indigo, honey, you handle your business, okay girlfriend. I'll cover for you if needed," said Rashondra.

*　*　*　*　*

When Todd first walked into Indigo's bedroom, she had an eerie feeling in regards to what was about to transpire. After he placed his tongue into her mouth and their lips locked, that eerie feeling quickly vanished.

He slowly removed her nightgown while making small compression on her face with his colossal lips. He continued with the compressions as his elongated tongue slithered from her neck to her rigid nipples. He alternated soft, juicy suctions from breast to breast before progressing to her abdomen. His tongue twirled as his head moved in circular motions. Not stopping the flow of his lips, he lifted her lower body and removed her silk panties.

"Oh yes baby," he said with his deep sexy voice before smothering his face into her womanhood.

Oh my goodness. He's going down on the first time Ooohh, aaahh, this feels soooo good.

He licked and sucked, sending shock waves throughout her body. His tongue slowly penetrated her opening. The amazing rhythm he created forced her to wail his name in ecstasy. Elevating her body a little higher, he gently kissed her buttocks, gradually allowing his tongue to slide in between. Todd wasted no time. He did the ultimate. His tongue traveled up her walls as far as it could go. Her body began to vibrate, non-stop, repeatedly.

She assimilated all of his love as he gave it to her. Her teeth grind tightly, attempting to hold in the cries that needed to come out. *Oh yes, yes, yes, this feels so good. Uhh, aah, help me, um, um, um. I can't handle it.* She made every effort to withdraw the sounds that lingered at the tip of her tongue. *Oh my God! I'm whipped.*

"How are you feeling baby?" he asked as he sighed and panted.

"Ooooh baby, please don't stop. I want all of you," she replied with a very weakened tone. Her body quivered as those previously muted uhhs, oohs, and aahs escaped.

He raised his head and knelt in an upright position. He looked down at the 'I'm whipped' expression she wore on her face and said, "I'm ready for mine now."

Oh no, no, no, Indigo thought. *He can't possibly expect for me to go down on him. I've never done that before. I most definitely can't do it the first time.*

He reached into his pocket and pulled out a condom. He slipped in on like an expert and entered her.

Whew! thought Indigo, relieved that her suspicion was incorrect.

The rotation of his hips allowed him to gently sway in and out. She felt the pleasure of her muscles contract with his enlarged manhood. He worked until he became limp.

Tonight my mind ventured to a world unknown. How does a twenty-year old man know so much about a female's mind and body? Yes indeed, he is truly blessed with a total sex package. What a wonderful feeling he gave me. I've never felt so good before.

This erotic scenario continued whenever they needed it. Indigo dropped Ed like hotcakes. She didn't want anybody else after experiencing Todd.

* * * * *

While taking a break from dancing, Priscilla sat in a chair, wiping away the perspiration that had formed on her forehead. She reminisced about the senior year she was leaving behind.

"Ladies and gentlemen, may I have your attention please as I introduce the homecoming queen and her court... This year's homecoming queen is Miss Priscilla Dillard, from Bloomfield, Michigan."

The fans applauded as Priscilla stood, holding the arm of Marlon. She gave a Miss America wave as she exited the field. Her hand elevated slightly higher when she spotted her father and Ruby sitting amongst the crowd. She winked at Rashondra who was kneeling on the football field with the other Dancing Dolls waiting patiently for the homecoming court to exit for the conclusion of their dance routine. As she continued her stroll, she caught a glimpse of Indigo, Todd, and Walter. They received a special wave as well.

RIP, family, and friends assembled at the apartment for a small celebration after the football game. Mr. Willard had already hired a caterer who provided fancy Hors D'oeuvres and several bottles of Moet. Around nine o'clock, Mr. Willard and Ruby were headed back to Atlanta for the next flight out to Michigan.

Marlon and Walter awakened early Sunday morning for their drive back to Atlanta where Walter would fly out to Washington, D.C. Before Marlon left, he placed a special envelope in Priscilla's hand.

"It's a surprise. Don't open it until I'm gone. Keep it under lock and key because you will need it when you arrive in Atlanta for Christmas break," Marlon had said.

Marlon and Walter said their good-byes and departed back to Atlanta. As soon as the car disappeared down the street, Priscilla anxiously opened the envelope. He left her with two roundtrip tickets to Aspen, Colorado for a week vacation during Christmas break.

Marlon and Priscilla had an extravagant time on the ski slopes. Each night they cuddled by the fireplace in attempts to thaw their frozen bodies. They made love countless times which drew them closer.

Before Priscilla drove back to campus two weeks later, Marlon gave her another surprise envelope. He instructed her to open it when she returned to her apartment.

Curiosity got the best of Priscilla. Before she made it to the Lakewood Freeway exit off of I-75 south, she'd pulled over and tore open the envelope. Inside were a key and a note that read, "This key to my condo is the key to my heart".

I love you so much baby, thought Priscilla as she held the key to her heart and took a long sigh before continuing to drive back to school.

*   *   *   *   *

"Do you girls want to ride to Atlanta with me this weekend. I'm going up to surprise my baby," Priscilla said two weeks later, flashing the key in front of Indigo and Rashondra's faces.

"That was very sweet of Marlon to give you that key, but just keep in mind it doesn't mean he won't do anything wrong," said Indigo.

"I know that. I've gone through so much with Marlon. He was just a totally different person over the Christmas break."

"People do change and I hope Marlon has, but always keep your guard up," added Indigo.

"Do you all think I should call first, I mean, maybe he's working overtime or will have an out of town business trip?"

"He gave you the key, right?" said Rashondra bluntly.

"Yes, but I don't know, I just want things to continue to work out for us."

"Well, use it. Call his bluff. Let's go. If he gets busted, then that's good for you. You'll know that key was just another front," continued Rashondra.

*   *   *   *   *

The music blasting from Marlon's condo was so loud that it gave Priscilla flashbacks of the frat house.

"Sounds like he's home," Priscilla said, developing an uncanny feeling. *Oh God, I just don't feel right about this. I should have called first. I know I should have.*

"Where's the key? Let's go in." Rashondra attempted to snatch the key from Priscilla's feeble hands.

"Wait, I would rather ring the doorbell. I just don't feel good about this."

"I agree, please ring the doorbell first." *Maybe the ding-dong would give Marlon a little time to regroup just incase he is inside with some woman,* thought Indigo.

"Girl you are crazy. He gave you the key, so use it. If he's got a woman in there, hey, you handle Marlon and I'll beat her down," said Rashondra as she smacked her right fist into her left palm.

Priscilla felt a little daring and placed the key into the hole despite the advice from Indigo. The sight of what she witnessed as she cautiously pushed open the door gave her a feeling of fragility.

The coil of smoke emanating from the cigar Marlon smoked met them at the door. He seemed very relaxed on the sofa, enjoying the scene. Two females dressed in only red thongs provided him with erotic entertainment. One female stood directly in front of him. She gradually forced her rotating hips closer to his face. The other female had already place one knee on the sofa as she tilted her dangling breasts toward his face. Marlon leaned forward and projected his lips in an attempt to grasp one of her nipples.

"Marlon! No!" Priscilla shrieked before the feeling of torment compelled her to the floor.

With her back against the wall, she slowly emerged from the floor and made an effort to regain her composure. Rashondra grabbed one the females by the arm and pulled her to the floor. She threatened to whip her ass if she and her friend didn't get out of there with the quickness. Priscilla's limp body slid to the floor again as great drops of tears exuded down her cheeks.

Marlon placed himself on the floor next to her and said in panic, "Priscilla baby, let me explain please. See,what happened was..."

"You have nothing to say to her," said an angry Indigo. "Come on Priscilla, get up and let's get the hell out of here." She grabbed Priscilla by the arm and attempted to lift her off the floor. Priscilla knew she had to be angry because she'd never heard Indigo swear before.

"Get your hands off of my woman. I love her. Baby, please let me explain what happened. It's not what you think."

"Marlon, who in the hell do you think is going to believe anything that comes out of that trifling mouth of yours? You ole dirty, low-down dog. Let's jump his ass," Rashondra said sticking her finger in his face as the two females scampered out the front door.

"Stop it! Please!" Priscilla yelled. "Just wait for me in the car. I'm coming. Let me hear what he has to say. It's only fair."

"Honey child you are a straight up fool. I can't help but to dog you out this time. You are acting really stupid Priscilla. You should be slapping his ass in the face but instead 'Let me hear what sweetie has to say'," said Rashondra as she mimicked Priscilla. She walked out the door trailed by Indigo.

It was hard for Priscilla to believe that an elite organization Marlon wanted to become a member of would initiate him with such degrading acts. Marlon promised he wouldn't join because he realized how much it hurt her.

The tears he shed as they talked had her yearning to stay and cry on his shoulders. She didn't. She had to be strong. She left.

As they drove back to college, Priscilla discussed with Indigo and Rashondra the conversation that took place between she and Marlon. They assisted in her realization that it was just another one of his lies.

I wonder what would have happened had we not walked in at the right time. Thank you God for intervening. Just the thought of him in the bed with those two females make me feel despondent, thought Priscilla as she laid her head on the back, leaving Indigo in charge of driving.

Along with the phone calls and letters, Priscilla received roses, candy, clothes, shoes, and any materialistic thing a man could think of to regain his lost love. That reminded her so much of her father's quest to get back into her mother's life. She did cherish his efforts, but couldn't allow herself to give in.

A month later Marlon did the unexpected. A surprise visit led to a proposal. On one knee, Marlon presented her with a ravishing two carat Marquise. *If this isn't true love, what else could it be?* How could she say no?

* * * * *

Zach came to visit Rashondra in an attempt to turn his life around. He had served four months in jail for drug charges. As part of his probation, he wasn't supposed to leave town. He insisted that his visit would be the turning point in his life. Without a second thought, Rashondra withdrew the money from her bank account and purchased him a ticket. She would do anything to get her family out of that hell hole.

"Girl you didn't tell me Zach looked that good," Indigo said when she saw him. "I might have to sneak a little flirt on while he's here."

"Indigo, pulleeze. He ain't all of that. Besides, I thought Todd was all you wanted and needed. He'll drop you in a heart beat if he found out you had a piece of my brother?"

"Who said anything about having sex with Zach. All I said is I might flirt with him a little."

"Yeah, right. He's staying in the same house with a woman flirting with him; you can't tell me he won't make any moves. Like I said, Todd will leave you without hesitation. Women forgive, men leave."

"What Todd don't know, won't hurt," responded Indigo.

"Watch yourself honey, you're trying to compete with me. I'm suppose to be the only 'hoe' is this house," she said as they laughed. *My brother does look kinda of good I must say. Being locked up for four months cleaned his body of those drugs that had taken over. He looks so much better.*

At first Zach seemed to blend well with college life. He made new friends and even got kind of close to Indigo. Rashondra often laughed as she reminisced the day he came into their apartment to fill them in on his so-called new discovery.

"Hey y'all, them boys are bad out there," Zach said.

"Boy what are you talking about?" inquired Rashondra.

"Them boys were just out there in the front of the student center doing some kind of dance together. Kinda reminds me of New Edition but it's a lot more of them." He retrieved the broomstick from the corner of the kitchen and attempted to imitate what he'd seen. He swung his arm forward simultaneously tapping the handle on the floor.

"Are you referring to a male fraternity?" said Priscilla, slightly disturbed that Zach had been there a whole quarter and was not aware of the group's proper name.

"Yea, I guess. I'on know. I thank they call themselves Kappa Apple Dapple or something like that. All I know is them boys were smooth as hell out there. Hey, whatcha got to do to be one of them?"

"Well for starters, you have to enroll in college. If you can keep your GPA up to at least a 2.7, then you can pledge," explained Indigo.

But before long, Zach was back on drugs again. Rashondra had a gut feeling he hadn't stopped anyway. When she caught him smoking marijuana, she didn't make a big deal out of it because quite a few college students got high as well. But the day she saw him with a crack pipe, which also happened to be the same day she witnessed a somewhat passionate kiss between he and Indigo, she knew it was time to send him back.

Indigo was saddened by the news of Zach's departure back to Ft. Lauderdale. Not so much because she wanted a relationship with him, but because she felt he had potential. She never talked about the kiss they shared nor any feelings she had behind it. All she ever revealed about that night was she had had a fight with Todd. That's how she ended up having a drink with Zach.

"It's in God's hands now," said Priscilla the day he left.

They knew all about Zach and the drug habits he'd taken on. Rashondra even revealed the few years she shared that same drug world with him but was fortunate enough to get out.

"Just don't give up on him. Pray that the spirit of the Lord will fill his heart and lead him to the path of righteousness. That's what I had to do with Marlon. It gives you a better feeling about the future."

Poor thing, Rashondra thought in reference to Priscilla.

*   *   *   *   *

The party in the student center was still going strong when Marlon and Walter walked in. Walter must have changed his flight because they were both expected to arrive early Saturday morning. Priscilla was ecstatic to see her fiancée beforehand.

They danced until they were worn out. Soon they headed back to the apartment where Rashondra's Grandmother and Nayla were already asleep.

Mr. Willard and Ruby arrived Saturday morning along with Indigo's family. Mr. and Mrs. Duncan, Grandmama Duncan, Sharon and her husband, Dale, their boys, Demmerick and Demaria, Wayne, his wife Jennifer, and Jeffrey, and Audrey.

*   *   *   *   *

On Saturday, twelve noon, their families assembled themselves together to observe this special occasion.

They took pride in their steps as they marched across the stage, shook the president's hand, and received their diplomas.

"Indigo Duncan, Magna cum Laude."

"Priscilla Willard, Magna cum Laude."

"Rashondra Hernandez, Summa cum Laude."

Chapter 21

Priscilla

After graduation, Marlon insisted that I move in with him and start preparing for our wedding. His condo was perfect for the two of us, but I anticipated children in the very near future and knew we would need more space.

The wedding in Buckhead was the largest affair to eventuate that weekend. Father's family attended. Most of them flew down from Michigan. Even my two brothers, Jonathon and Antonio came along. I decided to bury the resentment I had and welcomed them with open arms.

Several relatives from Mother's side of the family drove in from Alabama. It delighted me to mingle with kin people I hadn't seen in years.

Business associates of Willard Insurance from all over the country were present. They felt it was a privilege to be invited as a guest of the chief director of the company.

Although Marlon's father and mother were divorced, they both were at the wedding along with other relatives.

Marlon's parents divorced when he was eleven years old. Three years later, his mother was in a car accident that left her crippled for several years. As a result of the accident, Marlon moved to Ohio with his father in hopes of a speedy recovery. In an agreement by both parents, Marlon moved in with his father and visited his mother in Griffin, Georgia over the summer.

The wedding party was small. Indigo, Rashondra, Chanel, and Marlon's oldest sister were my bridesmaids. Walter, Marlon's brother, and two of his frat brothers were groomsmen. After we said our "I do's", the wedding party trotted down Peachtree Street in carriages drawn by horses to the Marquis for the grand reception.

Father's gift to us was a five-bedroom, Victorian style house located in North Cobb. Although it would be another three months before the builders completed the project, Marlon was in awe as he feasted his eyes upon what he considered his prize possession.

The lifestyle Father exposed Marlon to was beyond his wildest dreams. In other words, he had the 'big head' and thought he was 'all of that'.

Marlon possessed too much pride to allow me to work, so I stayed at home as he insisted. I shopped every weekend and remodeled every time a new issue of <u>Better Homes and Garden</u> arrived in the mail. Eight months later, I was pregnant with Marlon III.

* * * * *

The announcement of my pregnancy didn't set off sparks between Marlon and I like I had anticipated. He was a 'big-time' businessman as he claimed it, and spent most of his time away from his wife and child to be.

Two months into my pregnancy I made preparations to attend Chanel's wedding in Los Angeles. After hours of pleading with Marlon to accompany me, he refused to go. He allegedly had an important business meeting that same weekend, therefore he purchased round-trip tickets for Indigo and Rashondra to travel along with me instead.

Being such loyal friends, they packed their luggage and were ready for flight. They didn't want me to travel alone.

Even after the baby was born, Marlon always concocted justifiable reasons to be out of the house. If he wasn't working out at the gym, he was working late hours at the office. If he wasn't playing golf with business associates, he was playing basketball with friends.

One Saturday morning I was fortunate enough to catch Marlon at home before he had a chance to walk out the door. I began to express the loneliness I felt with him being away so much.

"Marlon, it's been six weeks since we've spent a weekend together. Do you have to go in this morning? It's Saturday for God's sakes. I want you to visit the circus with Marlon III and me."

"So you've been counting the weekends I haven't stayed at home, huh? Why are you doing this? You know I'm a busy man."

"But playing basketball with Tyronne doesn't consist of business. I would like for you to spend the day with us...please."

"Who do I come home to every night? You, not my friends or business associates. We may not spend a lot of *day* time together, but I'm here every night unless I'm out of town on business."

"You're right sweetie, but I'm tired of having to call on Indigo and Rashondra every time I want companionship. I want and need the companionship of my husband sometimes."

"Baby you know I give you all the companionship you need in the bed at night anytime you want it. I take care of you and you know it. You don't' be screaming and crying for nothing."

"It's not all about satisfying from a sexual point of view, I want to spend some quality time with you. We have a child. I want to do family things."

"You're always complaining about something. Do I ever do anything right?"

No, not much is what I need to say if I'm going to be truthful about it. I just won't answer that question. "You do come home every night, sometimes at four and five in the morning, but you are here. But is that supposed to be good enough for me? Your business trips are becoming more frequent. Am I not supposed to concern myself with that? I'm seeing a pattern here. This is the same kind of thing my mother went through with my father."

"How dare you compare me to your father? I don't have kids spread across the country like he does. I would never ask you to abort our precious child just because I'm not home often. I know you need help with the baby, that's why I hired Karla as a part time nanny."

"How could you throw the wrongdoing of my father up in my face after all he's done for you? All I'm trying to say is I can relate to the loneliness Mother experienced."

"You're the one insinuating some kind of pattern going on with your father and me. That seems just like comparing to me. I'm sorry but my personality is nothing like Mr. Willard," retorted Marlon.

"You should be thankful that he had a pleasant enough personality to hire you with no experience. He is the one who ensured you'd get the proper training necessary so that you would be the success that you are today."

"Yes your father has done a lot for me and I do thank him for it, but I am not like him. When I'm not home on the weekends, I'm still taking care of business. I have to frequent with my employees to show my appreciation. Although Tyronne is a pretty cool brother outside of Willard, he does work for me, remember? Don't you know that the employees working for me recruited more clients to Willard Insurance last year than any office across the nation? I'm bringing in big bank for your family."

"Marlon, you don't have to work at all and you know it. My family has plenty of money. We can live the same lifestyle without you having to ever clock in again," pleaded Priscilla.

"What kind of man do you think I am? I'm not about to sit up on my ass and not work. Is that what you want me to do, just sit around and take handouts from your family? I have too much dignity about myself. I like the job I have. I don't plan on giving it up to sit at home with you all day. Maybe that was a point your father tried to make to your mother, but she couldn't understand it. Within the next year or so, I plan to be the director of the whole southeast region, not just the Atlanta region."

"But it's not fair Marlon. Why can't you see what it's doing to me?"

"Listen, I'm not about to sit here and argue with you about family time. It will come sooner or later. You are just gonna have to accept that."

"Well I don't understand it. I'm so lonely. I just want to spend some time with my husband. What's wrong with you? Why can't you see my pain?" inquired Priscilla. Tears fell from her eyes as she used the palms of her hands to wipe them away.

"Baby, you're making a big deal out of nothing. Call Indigo and Rashondra. That's what you do all the time anyway."

"That's because you don't give me any other choice. If it weren't for their frequent visits I would be like a hermit sitting here all the time."

"Well maybe if you hadn't gotten pregnant so quick, you would still be able to hang out with them sometime. I love Marlon III, but business is business."

"When Marlon?" I asked, purposefully ignoring the comment he'd just made about me becoming pregnant. "When can we have a family outing? What is it going to take?"

"Call my secretary and make an appointment if you feel we need to have an outing that damn bad. If she can find an open spot on a Saturday, then it's on. Let me get the hell up out of here. This ain't nothing but a bunch of bullshit. I've got to go."

He walked right out the door before I could utter another word to him. "Damn you Marlon!" I screamed as I threw a glass vase into the fireplace.

* * * * *

Only about a year later I received the dreadful phone call from Rashondra which led Indigo and I on a PI Check to Cartersville. Even after I asked him to leave and refused to respond to any of his attempted contacts, the pain didn't go away.

Two months after his departure, his mistress, Sarita called questioning me about my relationship with Marlon. *Oh my God, what nerves she have calling me about my 'own' husband,* I thought, ready to hang up on her. But I stayed on the phone instead because I felt we needed to have a woman to woman to talk. My plan of what needed to be said was curtailed by the news she delivered about Marlon.

"I had a vaginal exam yesterday and was told I have chlamydia. Marlon is the only man I've been with for the last year," said Sarita.

My goodness Lord, help me. She's been sleeping with my husband for a year. Chlamydia? I can't believe this. My chest swelled with uncontrollable pain. I listened to her go on and on about Marlon and how she only put up with our marriage because he'd planned to leave me as soon as Marlon III turned two. Her continued blathering led me to believe she really loved *my* husband.

"Yes, I was patient when it came to you, but I'll be damned if I deal with some other nasty whore he's sleeping around with who's spreading her foul infection to me," she added.

Just minutes after the phone call, I left the house en route to Griffin. I knew I would see Marlon and pondered over how to approach *my* husband, whom I've been separated from, about sleeping with another woman, *other* than Sarita.

How many more women are there? What do these women have to offer him that I don't? I love Marlon and would've done anything for him. He knows that. Why can't he love me back? What did I do wrong? Oh God, I miss him so much. Tears fell as I continued my drive.

* * * * *

When Marlon returned home eight months later, he admitted to his weakness, which is *women*. He promised to seek counseling because his family was more important to him than anything else in this world.

Two months of therapy was all Marlon could endeavor. I objected his decision to terminate his involvement and pleaded for his continuance. He was adamant about his choice; therefore, I didn't put anymore pressure on him. He deserved credit for the admittance of his problem and to seek help from the beginning.

Three months after the termination of Marlon's counseling sessions, he continued to spend more time at home with his family. I'd noticed a big change in his character and was pleased with the results.

* * * * *

The same evening I shared with Marlon the news about my second pregnancy, was the same evening he made plans for a sixth year anniversary party. That was enough to assure me he was ready for a new beginning.

The decision to keep my pregnancy a secret until the celebration was rather difficult. It taunted the tip of my tongue many times when Indigo and Rashondra were present. I had to hold back for I knew my announcement would be the highlight of the evening.

* * * * *

Indigo and Rashondra came over to assist with the guest list. Rashondra felt Marlon had really made a change and was very excited. Indigo admitted that she'd observed a slight shift in his persona, but with his history, she wouldn't put her total faith in him.

* * * * *

After five years of marital bliss and blues, which included a son, several affairs on Marlon's behalf, and eight months of separation, I initially didn't know what to expect from this relationship. Oh yes, I've been through hell and back in attempts to appreciate the love I have for Marlon. My sweetie has prevailed this time. Marlon has proven that time brings about a change. All things are possible if you only believe.

Chapter 22

Rashondra

Upon graduating from college, my residential dwelling was not a difficult decision to make. I migrated to the metro Atlanta area and called it my home.

No love was lost when Indigo and I decided not to live together. We both landed careers in our fields of study and were financially able to start on our own.

For a while, our weekends consisted of habitually hanging out at every nightclub brought to our attention. We even nabbed Priscilla a few times on our hangouts. Before long, I grew tired of dealing with the commute back to College Park after a few drinks. That put a halt to the *every-weekend-partying* routine I'd indulged myself in.

* * * * *

Reggie and I began dating not long after I moved to the Atlanta area. I met him at 'The Phoenix' nightclub, the same night I won a mini skirt contest.

The attraction was very strong and over a short period of time, I'd fallen for him. Being in love was an enormous change for me. During my college days I dropped men with the quickness at the slightest inkling of misdeed.

One of my most memorable moments with Reggie was a night after we finished a round of invigorating lovemaking. I grabbed an empty beer bottle off the nightstand and stood in the middle of his bed, naked. I placed the bottle to my mouth pretending it was a microphone and began to sing powerfully, "Ooh, boy, I love you so, never ever ever gonna let you go, once I get my hands on you-oo. Ooh, boy, I love you so, never ever ever gonna let you go, I hope you feel the same way too-oo." My long, wavy hair swayed from side to side as I twitched my body to place emphasis on my singing.

He grabbed my legs from below, causing me to tumble over on the bed. We wrestled around for a few minutes before lust struck again. It wasn't long before we surrendered, yet again, into lovemaking. Oh yes, I thought he was the one.

It didn't take long before the lies started to kick in. After about a year of dating, his lies became so unbearable that I had to cut him loose. He was one of the first guys to really hurt me.

Not wanting to deal with the Friday night gunshot victims at the hospital, I called in sick. As I sat at home with nothing to do, I realized how lonely I was. Within thirty minutes, I'd packed an overnight bag and jumped in my brand new Saab and headed to Decatur. I wanted to pay my man a surprise visit. Indigo considered surprise visits as semi PI Checks because you never knew who would get the surprise.

When I saw his car in the parking lot and his roommate's car gone, I really hoped not to find any unwarranted situations. I just wanted to have that time alone with my man.

I rang the doorbell and knocked several time, but they both went unanswered. *Maybe he and Dave are hanging out tonight, or maybe he's in there with another woman.* That thought stayed on my mind as I strolled to the back of the complex because curiosity got the best of me.

As I approached his bedroom window, which happened to be on the first floor, the vibrations of Phyllis Hyman's strong alto voice emanated through the windowsill. My eyes scrunched tightly as I tried to get a clear view of a shadow that had just walked into his bedroom.

"Reggie, open the door. I see you. What are you doing?" I said after I realized there were more than one shadow creeping about.

There was still no answer. *How could he do this to me? This bastard is really tripping. He told me he loved me and now he's got some heifer tiptoeing around in there as if this is some kind of game. Oh hell no! I'm not going for this.*

After my continuous knocks and cries at his window went un-answered, I decided to take matters in my own hands.

These dummies don't even have the kitchen window locked. Once I squeeze myself through, I'm whipping every ass I see.

"Reggie!" I yelled as I climbed out of the kitchen sink. "This ain't no damn game! I saw your ass and you need to fess up! I want to see the hoe you got up in here!" *Here goes. I feel it coming. The 'ghetto' in me is coming out.*

When I turned the corner to where his room was, the door was locked. *Okay, he's gone above and beyond trying to hide this 'project hoe' from me.* Without hesitation, I kicked the door. "Reggie, if you don't open this god damn door right now I will kick this mutha down and you know I ain't playing!" *Damn! It's so hard for me to not act like I'm straight from the projects when I'm mad.*

A trying-to-pretend-to-be-sleepy look appeared on Reggie's face through the crack of the door as he slowly pulled it open.

"Damn Rashondra. What in the hell are you in tripping about? Awe man my head hurts. I was trying to get some sleep. How did you get in here?" he whispered.

"Don't worry about all of that. Where the hell is she?" I pushed him aside to enter his bedroom.

"Where's who?" he inquired as he walked over to the stereo and muted the volume.

"Don't try to play me for no damn fool. I saw you in here with that hoe, so where is she?" I rambled through the closet, looked under the bed, and check every spot in his bedroom I thought he would've hidden her.

"Baby, what are you talking about? Who are you looking for? I was in here trying to sleep."

"Trying to sleep where Reggie?"

"In my bed, where do you think?'

"Stop lying to me dammit! I stood out there and banged on your window several times. You don't sleep that hard. I know you. I've slept with you many nights," I retorted.

"That was you? I thought I heard some knocking but it stopped, so I figured I was dreaming."

"Who does these earrings belong to?" I interrogated. There was a pair of gold loop earrings resting on his nightstand. I picked them up and flung them at his face.

"Damn Rashondra you need to watch yourself in here slanging stuff around. Those earrings belong to one of Dave's women. She was over here earlier and I saw her taking them off because she said her ears were hurting. When they left, I noticed she had left them on the coffee table in the living room."

"What the hell that's got to do with you?"

"Well I just decided to bring them in here so that no one will steal them."

"Why do you think I'm stupid? You have really hurt me Reggie."

It only took a few minutes for me to notice that the same window I'd just banged on numerous times, was slightly opened. *Okay, I really need to regroup now because I'm starting to cry. He is lying through his teeth. That opened window is all the proof I need.*

"You better be glad I'm an educated black woman because the mess you pulled tonight is some mess that would've gotten your ass sliced up if I hadn't tried to better myself."

"Why you tripping babe? I'm not messing around. Do you see anybody in here?"

"Save it Reggie. You ain't worth it."

I walked out his door that night, torn apart and broken hearted, but I never went back. Of course several phone calls were made by him attempting to rekindle. After I finally cursed him out 'ghetto-style', his phone calls ceased.

Never will I allow myself to fall that deeply for a man again. Damn, I can truly say this has given me a taste of what Priscilla goes through with Marlon. How in the hell does she have the strength to deal with it everyday?

* * * * *

Getting to know a man long enough for a good screw was not a difficult task to accomplish at all. At one point my phone rang so much that I changed the number and went private with it. That calling six and seven times a day didn't set well with me at all. It's never the man you really want calling, but always some bad experience guy working your nerves, like Tom for example.

Tom and I met about three months after my ridiculous caper with Reggie. He was nice looking and everything, but I wanted to kick his ass after the first sexual encounter we had.

Playing on what he considered his romantic ego, he brought whip cream to bed. Okay, that was cool. Been there. Done that. Liked it. He shook the can as he gnawed on my erected nipples. *Umm, so far, so good*, I thought as I anticipated the whip cream melting as it spread across my steamy womanhood.

He gave the can a final shake before tilting it with his finger in position. Unaware of his plans, the damn fool sprayed the whip cream down my ear. My eardrum tingled as he inserted his tongue down the canal before I could jerk my head away.

"Yeah baby. Good ain't it," he said as he sucked and slurped at my ear.

"Have you lost your damn mind, fool!"

Adrenaline rushed through my body as I forced him off me. I hastily ousted myself from his bed and snatched the cover from my body. My hand reached for a bottle of Jovan Musk that was displayed on his dresser, along with his Brute and All Spice. Country ass! I violently hurled the Jovan at him. I was totally pissed off. Oh, it was on.

"Girl you're crazy. Coming up in here throwing my own stuff at me. Get the hell out of here before I kick your ass."

"You kick my ass you stupid fool. Come on, I'm ready."

Standing in the nude, I balled my fingers and swung at him. He stepped back just in time to miss my oncoming fist.

"You better be glad I'm a damn decent man cause girl I'll break every bone in your body."

Lucky for him, he walked out after that statement. I couldn't put my clothes on fast enough. *This psychopathic dunce has a serious problem. Oh I can't believe he just sprayed whip cream down my ear. I was ready to get 'real' ghetto on him and kick his ass. They say you can take a person out of the projects but you can't take the projects out of that person. Boy I tell ya, I've had several 'ghetto' relapses lately. I wish Walter were here. I'd tell him to kick Tom's ass. He probably wouldn't though. Naw, better yet, I should call Zach and have him come up here and beat him down. I know he would do it.*

"Don't call me anymore," I said to Tom as I sashayed out the door.

The next day my ear continued to bother me. *After I finish this aerosol treatment on this patient, I need to go see a doctor. Awe man, my ear is killing me.*

The hospital's clinic confirmed I had a middle ear infection along with a fever of one hundred and three. When I picked up my prescription for Amoxicillin and Tylenol, my mind wandered back to yesterday. *That no-classed, ignorant-ass fool gave me a damn ear infection.*

After I walked through my front door feeling every bit of exhaustion, I was thankful that my supervisor permitted me to depart from work early.

No he didn't. No he didn't have the nerve to call me. Four times at that. His mind is really bad, I thought as I listened to his rugged voice on my answering machine. He apologized and wanted to make amends.

As soon as his last message was heard, the phone rang. Ingeniously, I glimpsed at the Caller ID before answering. *Out of area, umm, I wonder who that could be.*

"Hello," I said in a very monotonous voice, which was evident of my mood.

"Hello, my I please speak with the person in charge of the phone bill?"

"This is she and I'm not interested," I snapped.

"Umm, your aren't?"

"That's what I just said isn't it? Now take my name out of your database?"

"Ma'am, you mean to tell me you are not interested in saving money?"

"No! I'm rich!" I yelped. CLICK! I slammed the phone on the receiver.

On that note, I called the respiratory department to inform them of my plans to take the doctor's advice and not come in for the next two days.

Those sick days merged with my two off days, which gave me a four-day break. I packed my bags and called Indigo and Priscilla for a quick good bye before leaving for Ft. Lauderdale.

"Pray that I have a safe trip. I'll call tomorrow to confirm I've made it safely," I said to them after releasing my three-way call connection.

After hours of driving and several coffee stops, I finally exited the turnpike, took a right onto Sunrise Boulevard, and headed to Grandma's.

* * * * *

"Who that knocking on my doe this time in da morning?" Grandma asked. She peeked out the living room window before releasing the latch on the door.

"It's me, Shondra."

"Shondra, baby that you fo real? What you doing on the road like that and it's three in da morning. Baby you know that's dangerous."

"I know Grandma. I promise not to do it again."

Nothing had change around Grandma's apartment. She still slept with old underwear clinging to her head. She probably wouldn't wear a scarf even if I bought one for her.

Nayla had taken my old bedroom and slept like an angel when I peeped in on her. What a difference two years will make in an adolescent. By the shape that bulged from underneath the sheet, she'd really grown.

I prepared a pallet for myself on the living room floor with some old blankets Grandma had stored away. I denied her request to take the sofa because several coils of springs stuck out.

The aroma that bounced off the bacon, eggs, cheese, and homemade biscuits Grandma stirred up in the kitchen awakened me earlier than I anticipated. Umm, breakfast smelled so good. She sure knows how to make you feel at home. After breakfast I decided to go visit Mama.

It's not that I think I'm 'all-that' or anything, but it troubles me to know that things don't change in the projects. I have pleaded with Grandma to pack she and Nayla's bags and move to Atlanta with me. She refused to do so claiming she needed to keep an eye on Mama and Zach. Is she crazy? Why would she subject herself to all of the foolishness that goes on in the ghetto? But, Grandma is set in her ways. I stopped nagging her about it. She became complacent with the one hundred dollars I mail her monthly.

* * * * * *

My visit with Mama was short and rather unpleasant, as always. She used to be very nice looking. She paraded an hour glass figure like a model for <u>Vogue</u>. Not anymore, she looked more like an old victim of anorexia. I almost didn't recognize her.

"Come in gul. Been a long time since cha been by to see yo Mama. You stopped lovin me gul, huh, huh?"

With a cigarette in one hand, she cupped my chin with her other and vivaciously jolted my face from side to side as I walked through the door.

Oh goodness, did she spill a bottle of whiskey in here or what? Whew! It smells terrible. Roaches crawled around as if they paid half the rent. They didn't even bother to scramble from the chair when I attempted to sit down.

"How are you doing Mama?"

"Gul, you know yo Mama is always doin right in spirits. I'ma lil low on bread though. You is up thar in big Lanta wit that good payin job. You s'pose you can you break yo Mama off a lil somethin-somethin?"

"How much money do you need?"

"Umm, let's see. Bout five big ones. Can you do that for me gul?"

"Five thousands dollars?" I asked, instantly having a flashback of the day she and Harold had used up thousands of dollars of drugs he was suppose to sell which led to his death.

That must have tickled Mama to death because she laughed so hard, her frail looking body fell back on the sofa.

"Naw gul. Is you crazy? Who in the world got that kinda money? I'on even thank the president got that kinda of money. Five dollars gul. One, two, three, foe, five," she said as she demonstrated with each finger on one hand. "Damn you is crazy. I'on thank you rich or nothin," she added.

Poor man's mentality. She thinks I have to be rich to have five thousand dollars. Thank you God for Grandmama sending me to camp that summer. I would probably still be here, a splitting image of Mama, begging for five dollars, I thought as I fingered through my wallet. I pulled out a fifty-dollar bill and gave it to her.

"Holy shit gul. You done hit the jackpot up thar. Whoa doggy! My gul didn't give me a slice of bread, she done gave me the whole damn bakery," she shrieked while doing some kind of old fashioned dance. Her hips shifted from side to side as she kissed the bill as if it were her key to heaven.

* * * * *

On Saturday evening Zach came by to grab a bite to eat. With a giddy expression and persona, he only stayed a few minutes. I was happy to see him, but sad to know he was still caught up in the drug zone. I really didn't foresee a problem when he asked to borrow my Saab for a quick drive down the street to the store for a pack of cigarettes.

Well, Saturday night came, no Zach. Sunday, still no Zach. Knowing I'd plan to leave Monday morning only made matters worse. After nearly panicking around eight o'clock, I did what I had to do. I left

Grandma's house on foot and set off for my venture to 'the cut'. Even after Grandma begged me not to go, I continued my stroll right out the door. At that point, I was pissed off to the highest point of pisstivity. I was on a mission.

As I turned down 13th Avenue, I noticed my black Saab parked on the side of the road with both the driver and passenger doors opened. To the left of me I detected a bit of commotion. I took a few steps closer and was able to hear Zach's voice, loud and clear. After forcing my way through the small crowd, I witnessed Zach clinging his hands tightly around the neck of a timorous teenager.

"You going to hell tonight!" he hollered as he pounded the poor child's head into the wall. The jumping around and laughter displayed by the small group convinced me that they seemed to enjoy the incident.

"Zach," I said pulling him by the back of his shirt. "What are you trying to do, kill this boy? Let him go."

"God dammit Shondra, git out from round here. You crazy or something? This ain't no place for you." He released the chokehold he had on the teenager and pushed me backwards.

"No, you're the one whose crazy taking my car and keeping it like you're paying the note. Where are my damn keys?" Zach knew I was highly pissed because I've never cursed at him before. To my surprise, that didn't phase him.

"You want your keys, then take them dammit." He jingled the keys in my face before jogging back toward my abandoned car.

"Eeeyyy baabeee wit yo fine self," said T-boo as he followed Zach. He plopped his long, lanky looking self into the passenger side of my car and closed the door. *Ugh, he looks so disgusting. He's still got that same ole, nasty looking, crusty nose I punched him in twelve years ago when he teased Zach about wearing the sardines behind his ears.*

He was instantly ignored as I directed my attention to Zach. "What do you think you're doing? Do you know you're in somebody else's car? How the hell do you think you can just stay gone all night and the next day in *my* car?" *I feel it coming. I feel it coming on strong. Oh yes I am officially speaking loud and ghetto now, with the neck rolling and pointing finger and all. I don't give a damn. I want my car.*

"Give me my damn car!" I reached over him in an attempt to snatch the keys out of the ignition.

"You ain't gitting nothing Niggaaaah!" he retorted. Without delay he pressed the accelerator to the floor and sped off down the road. There I stood, pissed and helpless.

Too ashamed to face me after eluding in my car, Zach left it parked in Grandma's driveway later that night. He did have enough sense to leave the keys under the car mat.

Around five o'clock Monday morning, after kissing Grandma and Nayla goodbye, I began my journey back to Atlanta. Right after I turned out of the driveway, about five houses down, Dinky stood on the curve next to the mailbox, awaiting my arrival.

Dinky had to be about fifteen years old. He had one eye and walked with a limp. Being that I was the only car on the block at such an early hour, he patiently waited for me to pass. As soon as I was within about fifty feet, he sprinted toward the driver's side of my car and yelped a hoarse sounding, "Roof! Roof! Roof! Roof!"

That damn dog is still chasing cars after all of these years. You would think he'd be used to seeing four-wheeled vehicles as old as he is, I thought, deciding this time not to accelerate and permit him to chase me like I've always done. This time I stopped my car, allowing him to catch up.

"Roof! Roof! Roof!" he grunted simultaneously with a low snarl.

"Go to hell!" I shrieked back, taking the anger I had with Zach out on Dinky. It was about time somebody put an end to the unnecessary car chases he'd gotten a joy out of doing.

The hoarse sounding barks Dinky had yapped only seconds ago instantly turned into soft whimpers as he tucked his head between his front legs, made an about face, and crawled on his belly back to his original destination.

Bet that'll end his barking career! Lord I'm ready to leave this place.

Next, I stopped at the corner service station to gas up before getting back on the road. After paying the cashier for the fill up and a can of orange juice and ranch flavored nachos; I headed back toward my car.

A weird looking, familiar face stood near the front fender of my Saab. He was dressed in 'bum' attire. His hands were positioned in his pockets as a cigarette butt dangled from the corner of his mouth.

That looks just like Stank-Bottom who lived on the other side of Miss Louise, I thought as I walked closer to my car. *It is him. I hope he doesn't recognize my face. Ugh, I don't even want to think about how he got his neighborhood nickname. I just knew he was going to grow up and be somebody. His momma was saved and they went to church every Sunday morning and Friday night. I'm not about to give him any money. That's all these bums do that hang around this service station, beg for money.*

Before I could place my key into the lock on the door, he walked up to me, pointed a small pistol to the side of my face and said, "Give me yo keys so I can git yo car." The cigarette butt clinched by his teeth dropped to the ground.

"Excuse me?" I inquired, wondering if my suspicion of what seemed to be transpiring was factual.

"You heard me hoe, give me yo keys."

"Stank-Bottom, do you know who I am? Do you know this ain't your car? Do you know you don't pay the car note every month?"

"I'on care who you is. Give me yo car fore somebody pull up, dammit, stupid gul," he retorted appearing to be somewhat agitated by my dauntless demeanor. He gripped the pistol tighter and took two steps closer, placing the gun within inches of my face.

"You are crazy if you think I'm about to give you *my* car. *I* left the projects and went to college so that *I* can get a good education to be able to buy myself a brand new car like this. I bought it for *me* to drive, not to just give it to somebody just because they ask for it. And get that damn gun out of my face!" I said angrily, slapping his wrist with my orange juice bottle.

"I'ma kill you now hoe. You stupid as hell," he stuttered as he went to retrieve the gun from the other side of the gas tank.

As soon as he walked off, two cars entered the service station. I quickly jumped into my car and sped off. I watched him dip down to pick up the gun as he continued to run.

Oh Lordy, that was a close one. But that's what you have to do to these ole slum ass thugs. You have to let them know that you are just as crazy as they are. I don't think I would have done that had I not known him though.

Getting a ticket punched at the tollbooth was the first time I ever felt excited about paying to drive on the turnpike. *I don't know when I'm coming back down this way. Damn, all of this drama replaced the thoughts I had about the ear infection I came here with.*

* * * * *

One gloomy Saturday morning, Indigo called, extending an invitation for me to visit the Martin Luther King, Jr. Historic Center with her, Priscilla, and Marlon III. My hesitation to answer gave her an instant edgy feeling toward me. I mean my goodness, she had already detailed her plans for us to do a little history touring when we fly out to D.C. in two months for Walter's birthday party.

"Oh girl we've got to go visit the homes of Frederick Douglas and George Washington when we go see Walter," she had said.

I'm not into all of that history stuff. I mean, yes, I know about slavery and the struggles African-Americans went through, but who gives a damn about where someone used to live.

With them being my girls and all, I didn't turn Indigo down. We toured the center during black history month. Our visit happened to be the same day 'The 100 Black Men of Atlanta' were on tour also. Just as I positioned my physique for a pose in front of Dr. King's tomb, this fine, dark-chocolate guy strolled by. *Umm, umm, umm,* was all I could say as my head turned in the direction he walked.

My maneuvering techniques landed me his phone number and a date for the weekend. One date led to another as we began a wonderful relationship together. I had only known him three months before he took me home to meet his mother. I was a bit concerned about leaving a bad impression because that happened to be same evening I saw Marlon's Mercedes parked a few houses down. My cunning personality handled the situation in an honest way, which left no questions asked.

Oh yes, I was slowly falling in love. I couldn't believe it, but it was true. I no longer desired another man. Derrick was my satisfaction.

* * * * *

Two years later, Grandma called and shared some good news with me. First, Mama had just returned home from rehabilitation after two months. She was forced to go after passing out in the middle of the road as she attempted to cross Sunrise Boulevard. When the paramedics realized she was sloppy drunk, they took her straight to a rehabilitation center.

Second, Zach was on his way to that same clinic. After she revealed his last major episode with 'the cut' crowd, you'd think he was ready to give himself to Christ instead of a rehabilitation center.

Grandma tiresomely told me of the night he ran into her apartment, picked up her telephone, and dialed 911.

"Neighbor shooting neighbor! Neighbor shooting neighbor!" He slammed the phone on the receiver and walked out the door, without any explanation.

A minute later, he walked back in, picked up the phone, dialed 911 again and said, "I just shot me a niggah and I hope he's dead." Slamming the phone down for the second time, he walked out the door without explaining his behavior.

Those calls alerted all of the service workers and before long, the police, an ambulance, the fire department, and news reporters swarmed Grandma's yard seeking the action.

Minutes later, T-Boo sprinted across the street yelling and pointing in the direction of 'the cut'. He informed the crew that Zach was on the ground unconscious.

Grandma and the rest of the crew followed T-Boo's lead to the destination where Zach laid. He bled helplessly. The paramedics loaded him into the ambulance and prepared to pull off. Without warning, the back doors of the ambulance flew open. A very conscious Zach jumped out with an oxygen mask still covering his face and muttered, "Let me git that punk! You dead niggah! You dead!"

After he was released from the hospital wearing a brace for a fractured rib, he was ready to go into hiding to conceal the thirty-two stitches he wore for the incisions on his face. The 911 calls indicating a shooting had taken place were all fabrications by Zach. Later Grandma learned that T-Boo and two other guys had jumped him.

* * * * *

The relationship between Derrick and I blossomed as the seasons changed. I didn't think anything else could happen that would give me the elated feeling I had with Derrick in my life, until I received a phone call from Zach.

After three months of jail and two months of rehabilitation, he wanted to come visit. He even mentioned the possibility of making Atlanta his home.

My heart was titillated at the thought of having a chance to reunite with my brother. I was happy to know that he was ready for a different scenario, something much better than what he'd experienced all of his life in the 'hood'.

I'll do whatever it takes to help him start a new life. No news could top this. Well, I'll take that back, Derrick asking me to marry him would. It's going on three years now, what is he waiting on? It's time to make a move.

* * * * *

After two hours of writing, stuffing, and licking invitations, I was ready to get out of Priscilla's stuffy house. Besides, Derrick promised he would come by and help organize the extra bedroom for Zach.

Chapter 23

Indigo

Initially, Daddy wasn't pleased with the idea of me living in Atlanta. He felt Savannah had enough teaching opportunities for me to start a career. I eventually persuaded him to change his mind by reminding him of the good upbringing I received which will assist me in making the right choices in life. He gave in but vowed to keep an eye on me.

Todd and I continued to date off and on, but there were no serious efforts made in securing a committed relationship. I had no plans of moving to Columbus and he had no plans of departing. I'd been there numerous times and couldn't understand why he chose Columbus over Atlanta. But nonetheless, I enjoyed our weekend rendezvous.

Just the thought of how he used his massive tongue to provide me with illustrious pleasure, made me wonder how he held it all in his mouth. His enormous, luscious lips gave him a very captivating look. I loved hearing the juicy, passionate, smacks they made when he licked me up and down.

The weekends I wasn't clubbing with Rashondra, I was working up a nice sweat in efforts to keep up with Todd's sexual maneuvers. After about a year of driving up and down I-85, the weekly visits became monthly, soon bimonthly. Eventually our relationship became an 'every now and then' thing. He didn't mind the drive up I-85 whenever my body needed a fix. My goodness, he really made it hard for the next man.

* * * * *

After my very first interview, I was offered a second grade position in Cobb County. It was quite a difficult adjustment for me because I was the only African-American teacher in the school.

"Duncan, we have to get you some friends in here," said the principal, Mrs. Smith, after she passed me in the hall one day.

What is she trying to say? She needs to hire some black teachers. I don't need any friends. I'm here to do a job, not build a friendship circle. The nerves of her, I had thought.

I would've never guessed that being a new teacher meant having the most precarious class. Out of the twenty-three students within my class, I had fourteen whites, five blacks, and three others. Eleven of them performed below grade level, five were gifted, and the other seven were average, so they said. Along with intelligence levels, I had three that took medications for Attention Deficit Hyperactivity Disorder, two that had been diagnosed by the school psychiatrist with an Emotional Behavior Disorder, two had a speech impediment, and three who were serviced for English as a Second Language. It was a challenge, but I took the class with pride and proved that all students were educable.

My prize possession was Quandrarick. Poor child. He was pitiful. I'll never forget the day I had him read to me a paragraph from a book he'd chosen for reading time. The four-sentence paragraph contained information about a ship carrying oil that accidentally hit an iceberg. The oil spilled into the ocean, causing massive pollution.

So I said to him, "Quandrarick, what does 'accidentally' mean in this paragraph?"

He placed his index finger on his cheek and pondered before he responded with, "In a car".

Okay, this child does not understand, let me try another approach, I thought before saying, "The ship hit the iceberg by accident. What does 'accident' mean?"

He pondered again, this time looking at the ceiling before responding; "Umm... it hurt?"

My Lord, how could you read every word in a paragraph and have no clue as to what you've just read. This is unbelievable. My college instructors never taught me how to deal with this.

"Okay Quandrarick honey, listen to me carefully." *All I want him to say is 'by mistake' or 'didn't mean to do it'.* "If you spill your milk on another student by accident, what does that mean?"

He looked at me and smiled as if a light bulb had just come on and excitedly responded, "I'm sorry?"

I worked overtime with him. I even volunteered to tutor him at no charge two days a week. Initially I had very negative thoughts about his capability. I pulled out all of my resources to assist him. I went from recorded books to colored overlays. Miraculously his reading comprehension heightened from a Pre-Primer level to second grade, first month. I did not allow the fact that he should've been reading at a second grade, ninth-month level by June discourage me. A two-grade level jump in one year was enough satisfaction for me.

By the end of the school year, Mrs. Smith was so impressed with my overall test scores, she chose me as a member of 'The Model School' committee. That didn't set well at all with some of the veteran teachers.

Five other selected teachers and myself spent the next two years meeting with board members, attending seminars, and visiting other schools before we started what was to be a three year process to become a model school of reading. This landed me out of town on the weekends at least once a month.

My life for a while consisted of work, very few dates, and minimum family time.

* * * * *

One weekend while en route to a water park with my two nephews, I detoured to the nearest mall to pick up a pair of swimming shorts. The drive up the highway became unbearable when the ten minutes it should have taken turned into an hour and thirty-five minutes.

As I continued to gradually move along, I was amazed at the deadlock in traffic. We were idle for five minutes before we moved up a few feet.

What in the world was going on? I peered through the rearview mirror and noticed the agitated looks on Demaria and Demmerick's faces.

When I moved a little closer, a tall, blonde female walked by my car with tears rolling down her cheeks. She held the hands of two small children.

"Excuse me Ms. Do you mind me asking what's wrong?"

She looked at me and nodded her head. She released the hand of one of the children and pointed toward the sky. "Look! Can you believe it? Can you believe what they've done?"

Before I could respond, she quickly grabbed the child's loose hand and ran off. *Did a plane crash or something? Why are all these people walking around in the middle of the street?*

My decision to pull over to the side as many others had already done gave me a quick explanation as to what was going on. Demaria and Demmerick followed as we wiggled our way through the crowd.

"Keep the piece of history! Keep the piece of history!" A large group of people walked around and chanted loudly in protest.

It was unbelievable. Those half-witted simpletons had nothing better to do on a Saturday afternoon than to be out there, holding up traffic for miles, crying over a freaking wooden bird. For whatever reasons, who cares, somebody decided to remodel this landmark duck, chicken, turkey or whatever it was, because it had become too old and raggedy to stand. Those people were actually crying, crocodile tears, because it was going to be remodeled.

Rashondra thought I was over exaggerating when I described the events I saw. "What makes it so bad girl, this man was arrested for stealing the beak of the old bird, claiming he wanted a souvenir," I added.

"Ooh honey child, that's too funny to me. He is worst than that foolish tree lady, " Rashondra said as she laughed.

"Naw, he's not worst than the tree lady. Now her mind is extremely bad. Why does she thinks it's normal to live in a tree for three months and depend on other protesters for food and clothes, just because she feels it's her earthly duty to save this Oak tree."

"Why is the dummy trying to save that tree anyway? Damn she's crazy. She must think she's related to Tarzan."

"Well she claims her great-great-grandfather left a diary about him being in the Civil War."

"Girlfriend stop it right now," interrupted Rashondra, laughing as if she'd heard the funniest joke.

"You are so silly,"I said, laughing along with Rashondra."Any way, she said something about the three inch wide hole in the tree comes from the gun he was shooting."

"Three inch wide? What kind of gun was that? Girl that hole probably came from Woody the Woodpecker."

Rashondra had me chuckling so hard that my jaw felt heavy. We both took a moment to allow the completion of our laughs before I continued to speak. "Whether she realizes it or not, she's taken the home of some bird, monkey, raccoon or whatever animal dwelled in that tree before she moved her crazy self in it. I'm glad I don't have any type of fetish over any person or thing that would cause me react that way. Well I take that back, 'God' is the only reason I would exhibit unusual behavior," I added.

* * * * *

For a while, my social life swung very low on the pendulum. The handful of guys I met were dropped with the quickness due to a lack of what I called, 'plain old common sense'.

Jeffrey is a good example. We eyed one another several times while positioned on opposite sides of the bar listening to the live jazz band. We both sipped on what we thought was necessary to have a relaxing evening.

An hour had passed and I continued to sit alone. I realized Priscilla had stood me up. There was no reason for me to call it a night, so I stayed and enjoyed the show.

After about two hours of Jeffery and I exchanging glances, we finally said our hellos, swapped phone numbers, and called it a night.

The next evening after returning from aerobics, I checked my Caller ID and noticed he'd called. "Hi. I saw your name on my Caller ID box. How are you?" I said during my return call.

"Whew Lordy. Caller ID Box? Boy I tell ya, you women are just too much for me."

What in the world is he talking about? I think I'll be better off by not entertaining that thought. "You mentioned last night something about catching a matinee. It's after five o'clock. I know we've missed them all by now."

"Yeah, I knew that when you didn't call me back by four. Well, let's see, umm, is there a dollar movie near you?"

Am I hearing him correctly? No he didn't just ask me if there's a dollar movie theater near me. Now I've never been the one to want a man for his financial status, but this is a big turn-off for a first date.

"Dollar movie? I'm really not interested in watching an old movie," I said, using that as an excuse to not call him cheap. "We can catch a movie at the Galleria. I'll pay," I added.

"Hey, that was not what I was suggesting, but it sounds like a deal. You seem to be one of those women who got her act together in the nineties. You crossed over into the new millennium with no flaws. You got that ID box and everything. I'll be over there in about forty-five minutes."

Okay, he's rather simple-minded. He has lost some serious points already. I guess I'll go on and go out with him. It's not like I have a man anyway.

On the way to the theatre, his fourteen-year-old Maverick broke down, right in the middle traffic. Cars blew their horns as if we were purposely sitting there just to spite them. I was quite embarrassed.

He had to completely shut everything off in his car, including the radio to re-crank it. We arrived at the theater late. I was a very unhappy camper by then.

Claiming to have a taste for Mexican food, he pulled right up into Taco Bell's parking lot. As we carried on with a casual conversation, I was ready for the date to end, much sooner than later.

He was baffled that I possessed a cellular phone, a VCR, and a computer. He literally fainted when I told him that Rashondra, Priscilla and I paid $150 a night for our hotel room during a mini vacation in Cancun, Mexico. "And that was a discount. The regular price was $285 a night," I added.

"My goodness, what kind of people can pay that kind of money for a room? Whew, my God," he said as he wiped the sweat away that dripped down his forehead.

Oh yes, he lacked common sense and every thing else that was affiliated with living in the present.

Then there was Tyler, a nice looking, educated, brother. He worked part-time as a County Commissioner and attended Emory School of Law. We hung out a few times before I felt ready to share my intimate side with him.

Foreplay lasted no more than two or three minutes before he slipped on a condom and entered me. He couldn't have stroked no more than five times before he trembled and yelled my name in gratification.

What??? Oh just wait a minute! This can't be it!

He withdrew his limped organ. I popped my lips in disgust as he rested on top of me.

"What's wrong sweetie?" he said nearly out of breath.

He's serious too, asking me what's wrong as if he just did something. Oh I'm just too mad.

"What's wrong? Do you really want to know what's wrong? I'll tell you what's wrong. You *came* too quick, that's what's wrong."

"Damn babe, you sure know how to upset a man's ego."

"Ego? The type of performance you just laid on me should be embarrassing. You've got to be a virgin. Ooh, just get up off me!"

"What?" he said, baffled by my words and actions.

"Sorry if I offended you, but you asked." I pushed him off of me and crawled out of the bed.

Although I've never been the type of woman who had men galore like Rashondra, I finally got a taste of what she would call a 'minuteman'. How disgusting.

"I know you're not leaving are you?" questioned Tyler. "Don't go. I'm having a bad night. Give me about thirty minutes and I'll be ready to roll," he pleaded.

You're not rolling on me. I'm about to roll myself up out of here, I thought before responding, "I've got to go. I forgot to take my birth control pill tonight."

Now this is where common sense kicks in. Common sense should've told him that he can not become sexually involved with a woman, climax in one minute, and expect for her to ever want to sleep with him again. What's even worst, it was the first encounter.

Oh yes, I walked out his door with 'bad experience' written all over my face. My only solution at that time was Todd.

Please don't have company; I thought as I dialed Todd's number from my cellular phone. I hadn't heard from him in over three months.

"Hello," said a somnolent sounding Todd on the other end.

"Hi, umm Todd, this is Indigo."

"Indigo, hey, what's up baby," he responded with a tad bit of perk in his voice after he realized it was me on the other end. That was enough to affirm he was alone.

"Sorry to have awaken you, but I need to see you, badly."

"What's wrong? Where are you?"

"I just had a bad experience and I'm not able to sleep. I'm in Atlanta riding around the perimeter trying to clear my head."

"You want to drive all the way down here at one o'clock in the morning? That could be very dangerous."

"I'll be careful. Give me about two hours instead of one in a half, okay."

"Okay baby, I'll be waiting for you."

Yes! Yes! Yes! I sped home, took a quick shower, threw a pair of jeans and a T-shirt into my overnight bag, put my Firebird into fifth speed, and jetted down I-85 south to be with Todd.

By three, I was knocking on his door. The gleam on my face was evidence of the excitement I bared. My private section began to unravel at the sight of him. He wrapped his arms around me for comfort. Mine went around him for pleasure.

"Are you okay babe?" he asked.

"Yes, I was upset when a police office pulled me over, mistaking me for someone else," I lied.

"What happened? What did he say?"

"I really don't feel like talking about it right now. Just hold me."

"My pleasure," he whispered in a seductive tone.

As Todd held me in his arms, a very libidinous feeling overcame me. I delicately squeezed his body into mine, which was *my* nonverbal way of gesturing I wanted him to make love to me.

Todd gently pushed me back against the front door. He cupped my 34 Bs in his hands and began to gnaw at the buds protruding through the outside of my shirt. The sexy, popping noises produced from his lips had me in awe. I began to unbutton his shirt as he lifted mine over my head.

As our jaws locked in on a fiery kiss, his tongue wandered around savoring my sweet juices. I gently grabbed it with my teeth and began sucking delicately. That had him moaning with regalement.

We both stood, topless, creating friction as we rubbed, hugged, and kissed. His hands gently slid down my back and relaxed on my hips. He gripped a cheek with each hand and impelled his middle finger inside of me. I angled my hips slightly upward for comfort, wailing a low *Ooooohh* as I continued to peck at his neck.

My pants fell to the floor, his followed. He dropped to his knees and lifted me slightly. With my back still against the front door, I wrapped my legs around his shoulders. The motion of his head bobbing up and down as he brushed me with his tongue from front to back, sent convulsions through my mid-section.

"Ooh Todd, baby, baby, uh, ah, ooh, baby, you're the best, ooh yesss, yesss, don't stop, baby, oohhhhhhhh!"

After that last oohhhh, vibrations initiated in my legs and immediately launched throughout my whole body. As I grasped his head to keep my balance, I was entranced by the thought that Todd had fulfilled all of my sexual fantasies.

He raised me even higher and stood in an upright position. Strength moved within from some unknown force as I enclosed my weakened legs around his waist. He slowly entered me, inch by inch, until my walls contracted all nine inches. The tingling in my body started to rise again as I reached extremity for the second time.

Oh no. He didn't put on a condom, I thought within the split second my mind allowed me to. *Ooh this feels so good. What is he thinking? Ooh my goodness, it feels so good.*

"Do you feel me?" he asked in a low, seductive voice.

"Yessss"

"Am I hitting it right?"

"Oh my God, yesss."

"Do you like it?"

"Oh yes, yes, yes!"

"Can I have my way with you?"

"Have your way baby," I continued to moan. *Extremity number three.*

"I want you Indigo."

"You got me baby."

"I want you to be my woman."

"I want you to be my man."

Evidently my last response must have hit some unknown nerve in Todd. He moved in and out of me like never before. *Extremity number four.*

His moans increased. His movement increased. What surprised me even more was the tear I saw in his eye.

Still locked in love making position, he carried me from the door onto the sofa. He quickly withdrew his organ and pinched the tip of it to withhold his crucial period. That didn't stop the slobbery kisses he planted all over my body, while waiting for his nectar to tame itself.

Before long, he reentered my cavern. We weltered in love making, alternating positions as often as needed. I was on top, my side, my knees, and my back; oh it was on until the break of dawn.

The next morning, Todd permitted me to sleep in because he felt rest would be useful before I took the hour and a half drive back home. He arose around nine and left for the basketball camp he coached for some youths in his old neighborhood.

The things Todd said to me while we made love gave me a perplexed feeling. He asked me to move to Columbus. He said he wanted a solid relationship with me. He said he was ready to settle down and get married.

For that moment, I felt like I was in love. I wanted him just as much as he wanted me. The thought of being his woman was intriguing. It was surely something worth thinking about.

Twenty minutes after his departure, I realized I was not as restless as I'd thought. I sat on the edge of his bed still completely nude and fingered through a small stack of papers, mostly envelopes, that rested on his nightstand. My intentions were to leave him a note to thank him for the wonderful time I had and how anxious I was about discussing our future.

Angela Tolbert? Who is this? Curiosity tugged at my mind as I held the ripped envelope I'd retrieved from the stack. *She lives in Columbus. Why is she sending him a letter?* I continued to ponder as I read the self-addressed portion of the envelope. *This is none of my business. Todd and I do not have a committed relationship, not yet anyway. I should care less about what else is going on in his life. He would be totally shocked if he walked in and saw me reading this letter.* I relaxed my back against the headboard, crossed my legs Indian-style and read it anyway.

"Um, um, um," was basically all I could murmur as I refolded the letter and placed it back inside the envelope.

She misses him. She can't go on without him. She will do anything it takes to get him back. She can't breathe without him. How in the world do some women become so hooked on these men? I have to admit that Todd does have what it takes to tangle any woman into his web of love, but darn, she can't breathe without him. She has serious issues.

That one letter set the tone for me to begin a PI Check. That was something I'd never done nor anticipated to do with Todd. I couldn't help but wonder who else was getting from him what I received last night. I'm a woman. I'm supposed to have lots of emotions, so they say. My inquiring mind wanted to know.

The drawer on his nightstand was where I began. I carefully unfolded, read, and placed each piece of paper in the same manner taken. My goodness, there were notes, phone numbers, cards, pictures, letters, a drawer full of stuff he would rid himself of quickly if he ever decided to settle down. He had women galore. He can 'do' a woman every day of the week if he wanted to.

There was one sad thing about the search. As I ventured from one drawer to another, including the bathroom cabinets, not one time did I notice a condom. Just the thought of me allowing him inside without protection sent butterflies swarming through my stomach. I wondered how many other women were getting a feel of his unhooded head.

As I sat there and thought about my relationship with Todd over the years, I realized that it really wasn't true love that I felt for him, but merely a strong lust for his sex. He was simply the best. Trust me, Rashondra has had many tales about her men, but even she acknowledges that she hadn't met a Todd yet.

The realization of my feelings made it easier for me to conclude that I was not going to pursue a relationship with him. I cared about him, very deeply. I could be with him and never desire another man. But I couldn't deal with fighting off his swarm of women. I was not returning. That was the last time for Todd's warmnest to nestle me.

*   *   *   *   *

When Rashondra and I flew to Washington, D.C. for Walter's birthday party, my eyes trailed Tony the entire evening. I was too timid to allow him knowledge of my interest. It sort of reminded me of how Priscilla must have felt the night she panicked at the sight of Marlon when we visited the frat house for the first time.

Subsequently, when I returned to Marietta, I phoned Walter to inquire about the *fine* brother I'd chatted about with Rashondra during our flight back. He revealed that Tony was his cousin who resided in the metro Atlanta area also. The initial surprise instantly turned into blissfulness when Walter informed me that Tony sought information about me as well.

After a couple weeks of conversing over the telephone, Tony and I decided to set up a date. Unfortunately, the first few dates resulted in cancellation on both ends, due to our busy schedules. With him living in Peachtree City and I in Marietta, it was rather difficult to meet if we had other things going on that same day.

His job as a fireman, working twenty-four on, and forty-eight off, conflicted with my five days on, two days off. After about four months of phone conversation and cancelled dates, we finally met for lunch at 'The Cheesecake Factory' in Buckhead.

A year or so of casually dating and adapting to one another's schedules passed before we finally became a couple. Desires for Todd slowly dissipated.

*   *   *   *   *

"Is your buddy Tyronne coming to the party? I didn't see an invitation for him when we stuffed them last week," I jokingly asked Priscilla. She can barely stand the sight of him.

"Girl you know he is. That's Marlon's ace-boon-coon, however you say it."

"If you're hipped, you're hipped. If you're not, you're not. But honey child you said it right, go on with the story," interrupted Rashrondra.

"Well he's the one who used to keep my man out all times of the night. Marlon claimed it was business just because Tyronne worked for him.

I'm not stupid. I knew what they were up to. Beside, after one of his counseling sessions, Marlon admitted to me some of the things they did when he was 'out there' involved with other women. But that's a part of the past now. Marlon has redeemed his wrong doings and with the grace of God, I've forgiven my man."

"Didn't you say Tyronne and Marlon hadn't been on good terms lately, something about you walking in his office while they were in the middle of a heated argument? You never did tell us all the details," I said.

"Oh yeah, that was about two months ago. Marlon claimed it was a bad business deal but as a result of my PI Check, his secretary informed me that Tyronne and Sarita had been involved. You all know that was the disrespectful heifer that caused Marlon and I to separate. I never confronted him about it because things have been going so well between us. That's why I never mentioned it again to you all. But anyway, Tyronne called here last week and wanted Marlon to hang out. My man turned him down because we had dinner plans, " Priscilla said with a smile.

"I don't care what you say Indigo, Marlon has changed. He would've never turned down a date with one of his boys for a date with his wife," retorted Rashondra.

"Yes he has changed. This is the happiest I've been in years. Although, I still don't care too much for Tyronne because I feel he's a bad influence on Marlon, but he's forgivable also. Marlon feels that inviting Tyronne to the celebration will sort of break the ice between them. He just feels that it's good business," added Priscilla.

"Well, I'm happy for you girlfriend, just keep a strong mind. Rashondra, how's Zach adjusting to Atlanta after being here for a week?" I asked, now directing my attention to Rashondra. That was enough about Mr. Marlon.

"Oh honey child, he thinks Atlanta is the bomb. He's never home, claims he's out on interviews all the time."

"Maybe Marlon can get him an entry level job at Willard Insurance. What kind of business background does he have? I forgot to tell you he called three days ago and asked me to 'hook him up' with a job at Willard. I gave him the directions to the office and told him to ask for Sharron in human resource," said Priscilla.

"Child please. You know Zach has had a rough life. He's never had a job. I can't even believe he called about a job at Willard. Well I guess I need to look on the bright side. That does show how determined he is. I'm going to do everything I can to ensure he doesn't ever go back to that filthy lifestyle he had back home," said Rashondra.

"Is he coming to the party?" I inquired.

"I would like for him to if you don't mind," said Rashondra as she directed her attention to Priscilla.

"Well, since he's your brother, he can come. I don't mean anything bad about this but I hope he really is off of those drugs because I don't want any of that at the party."

I can tell that didn't set well with Rashondra. Normally, she would go off on Priscilla at the slightest inkling of a disagreement. But when it comes to Zach, she has a very sensitive side. After all he's been through, she really believes he's changed. Just like I tell Priscilla to keep a strong mind when it comes to Marlon, I tell Rashondra the same thing about Zach. I just don't view Marlon and Zach the way they do.

Chapter 24

RIP

Priscilla was utterly happy about the new persona Marlon portrayed. She gave him a smile that was evidence of the love she carried in her heart as they pulled into the front of the Marquis Hotel. He tilted his head downward to kiss her left cheek just before handing the keys of the Mercedes to the valet attendant. He'd insisted that their anniversary celebration be held in the same place as their wedding reception.

They hadn't been there longer than fifteen minutes before Indigo and Rashondra promenaded through the front door escorted by their significant others. Priscilla was content with her best friends' choices in men. They had finally found the right ones to love.

"Hi. I'm so grateful that you all could make it so early." Priscilla reached over to hug them.

Derrick looked tantalizing as always. His perfect, dark-chocolate complexion did wonders for his shaven head. Tony was cute also. He was more of a milk-chocolate complexion. With one more swap from the razor, he would be just as bald as Derrick.

"Where's the man of the hour?" asked Indigo as she released her body from Priscilla's hug which ended with a soft kiss on the cheek.

"He's walking around. Sort of welcoming the guests and ensuring that everybody is okay."

"Marlon always have been a big entertainer," added Rashondra after she kissed the other side of Priscilla's cheek.

"Where's Zach? Is he still coming?" Priscilla said to Rashondra.

"Yes, he's bringing my car. Claimed he had to make a stop and pick up something." *I'm sure he went to get a gift for them. He seemed to have felt a little awkward after seeing Derrick and I with a gift.* "So I told him to take my car and I'll ride with my honey." Rashondra reached backwards, smiled, and pinched Derrick on the cheek.

Unfortunately Chanel couldn't make it. Due to her eighth month of pregnancy, she felt it would be a bit much to travel. Walter was already in town. He was expected to walk through the door at anytime.

* * * * *

"Ladies and gentlemen, may I have your attention please. We're here to celebrate a deserving occasion for Mr. and Mrs. Marlon Turner. God has blessed them with six years of marital bliss," said the master of ceremony.

The crowd applauded.

"At this time, I would like to call the couple of the evening to the floor. They will lead you all with a dance to their favorite tune from years ago."

Marlon firmly held Priscilla in his arms as they danced to 'When I'm With You', by Tony Terry. Priscilla's spirit was filled with exhilaration as she placed her head on his shoulder and squeezed her eyes in effort to hold back the tears. *I haven't felt this happy since the summer we became a couple. Thank you God for bringing Marlon back to me.*

"Excuse me, may I have this dance please?" A very familiar male voice was heard echoing over the music. Priscilla lifted her head from Marlon's shoulder to identify the owner.

"Father. I didn't think you could make it. I'm so glad to see you."

"Precious, I wouldn't be able to live with myself had I missed out on such a special occasion for my baby girl."

As Priscilla and Mr. Willard continued to dance, other couples joined them. Walter winked and gave her a quick smack on the cheek before wrapping his arms around a female's shoulder to dance.

Minutes later, Marlon strolled onto the dance floor holding on to Ruby's hand. Priscilla's heart pulsated at what she thought was about to transpire. He interrupted their dance and placed Ruby's hand into Mr. Willard's. Marlon regained he and Priscilla's original position before the interference.

Thank God. I don't know how I would've handled the sight of Marlon holding Ruby in his arms, thought Priscilla after a feeling of relief. She placed her head on his shoulder and submitted her mind, body, and soul to the solace she felt.

* * * * *

The party was going well. The women sipped on Moet, while most men enjoyed Cognac with a slice of lime. The atmosphere was mellow.

"Hey Cilla girl. Looking good as ever. Where's the keg?" said Zach. He smelled as if he'd been dipped into a barrel of whisky.

"We don't have a keg here." *My God, no class at all.* "You can stop one of the servers and have them bring you a drink, or you can go over to the bar," she added. *I know he's Rashondra's brother and she loves him dearly, but there's something about Zach that just doesn't set right with me. He most definitely doesn't fit in with this crowd. He's asking me about a keg of beer. Poor thing, how pitiful. I haven't seen one of those since the parties at the frat house. Enough thoughts about that waggish character.... I guess I'll make the announcement about the little life growing inside of me in about thirty minutes. Where's Marlon?*

* * * * *

"Girl, you need to slow down. You are not a 'Dancing Doll' anymore. Tone it down girlfriend!"

"Oh shut up Indigo. You're just jealous. Now you know I've got to see if I've still got it in me," retorted Rashondra.

"Oh yes, you still got it alright. Girl you're acting just like a 'shake dancer'. Lord have mercy."

"I've got to shake what my mama gave me," responded Rashondra. She stopped and did a quick 'booty shake' one last time before they exited the dance floor.

"I'm going to the ladies room since Tony and Derrick are gone to get us drinks. Have you seen Priscilla?"

"Not since Derrick and I went to dance and you know we were out there through seven or eight songs. She was looking for Marlon. I told her he and Tyronne were walking toward the front of the room. By the way, have you seen Zach?"

"No, not since you brought him over to meet Tony about forty five minutes ago."

"Go on honey child and handle your business in the bathroom. I'm going to walk around for a minute. I'll meet you back here in about fifteen minutes."

This room is so big. You would think there are restrooms in every corner. I can't believe how far down the hall the restroom is from the main ballroom, thought Indigo.

"Hey Zach," Indigo said colliding with him as she turned the hall corner that led to the restroom.

"What's up? Yo man ain't tagging alone is he?" He peeped around the corner for assurance.

"No, he went to get me a drink. What are you doing standing over here by yourself?"

Zach's eyes were red and slightly shut. He appeared somewhat jittery. He licked his lips and vigorously rubbed his hands together before responding, "Oh, um, I'm waitin on somebody."

"Who else do you know at this party besides our little clique?" inquired Indigo.

Taking a sigh and peeping around the corner again, Zach replied, "Oh, just some fine babe I met here da night. She told me to meet her here in five minutes."

Zach glanced at his watch and muttered, "Dam'um! It's 11:15." Seeming a bit agitated about the time, he mumbled a few more words that Indigo could not make out before changing the subject. "You still lookin good. I sho' nuff wish I had did right by you when I was at college with y'all. This could've been me and you celebrating. I always wondered what woulda happened if Shondra hadn't came in that livin room, knocking our business."

"Who knows?" responded Indigo. She really didn't want to 'go there' with him. "Rashondra is looking for you. We're standing over there by the dessert table. I'll tell her I saw you," she added. She walked off and entered the restroom.

Although Indigo did have a wee crush on Zach back then, the only reason she shared a kiss with him was to have something to assuage her thoughts from Todd. Todd had her whipped like a beaten egg. For what the relationship was worth, she was too deeply driven by the sexual desires she possessed for him. She needed a little stimulation from another source. Her plan was to become intoxicated and sleep with Zach that night. But thanks to Rashondra, she came in, sat down, and in so many words, told Zach he had overstayed his welcome.

Indigo had pity for Rashondra. She was trying really hard to make Zach's life and adjustment to Atlanta run as smooth as possible. She even revealed the friction it was causing between she and Derrick. He didn't believe in Zach at all. He felt that Zach was a user. Indigo promised she would do whatever she could to assist.

Everyone deserves another chance. I guess... Okay, my hair is still laid. Let me get out of this restroom.

Indigo washed her hands and grabbed a paper towel to dry them. Daring not to touch the handle of the door with her *clean* hands, she used the damped towel to pull it open.

Those guys sure are loud in the men's restroom, she thought while propping the door open with her foot and aiming the paper towel at the trash can.

Missing the wastebasket by a long shot, Indigo went to retrieve the paper towel off the floor and placed it in the trash.

Deciding not to waste anymore time aiming, she used her pinky finger to pull the door open.

Before she could step a foot out of the restroom, an unfamiliar popping sound instantaneously blared through the hallway. *What was that? A firecracker?*

She closed the door at once and rested her back against it. She rubbed her hand across her chest in hopes of easing the palpitations. A minute passed before Indigo gradually poked her head out the door. Everything appeared to be calm. She left the restroom en route to her original location near the dessert table.

What in the world was that popping noise I heard? I'll be sure to let Marlon or Priscilla know whenever I see them. Oh well, no one is acting unusual in here, Indigo continued to think as she walked toward the table.

Tony, Derrick, and Rashondra were no where to be found. Indigo decided to wander about to search for other familiar faces.

Indigo hadn't seen Priscilla in a while. She hoped Marlon was found in good hands. She still didn't trust him wholeheartedly. He'd done too much.

* * * * *

"Hey sweetheart," Indigo said to Tony. Tiny specks of water began to filtrate down the sides of one of the drinks he held. One more swallow would consume the other. He stood there conversing with Walter.

"Were you looking for me?" Tony said as he handed the moist glass to Indigo.

"Actually I was just walking around. When are you going back to DC?" she said as she grabbed Tony's loose hand and addressed her question to Walter.

"Tomorrow. Are you having fun yet?"

"Yes, this is really nice. This room is so big. You have to walk for days before you finally run into someone you know," she said jokingly.

During the midst of their conversation, twelve police officers moved hastily through the ballroom. The music stopped unexpectedly. People started to panic.

"May I have your attention please. We have an emergency situation. Will everyone please find the nearest exit sign and evacuate the ballroom," announced the Emcee.

"What's going on here? Where's Priscilla? Where's Rashondra?"

"Come on baby, we have to leave. You heard what he said."

"But suppose something has happened to Priscilla or Rashondra. I've got to find them."

"Indigo baby, no, come on. We'll find them once we're in the lobby."

Tony convinced Indigo to walk right out of the ballroom, leaving her best friends behind. The thought of abandonment gave her an uncomfortable feeling. She was sure they were just as frenzied over the notion of not knowing where she was as well.

* * * * *

They paced the lobby for about fifteen minutes in delirium before they were all located, with the exception of Marlon and Zach.

"Where's Marlon?" Indigo asked Priscilla who stood with her father and Ruby. She wept gently.

"I don't know. There are still a few people inside. They won't let me go in to look for him."

"What in the hell is going on?" asked an infuriated Rashondra.

"I don't know that either. They won't tell us anything."

"Well they are going to tell me something. I'll be back Precious," said Mr. Willard. He walked up to the police officers that guarded the door. After a few irascible words he walked in. Three minutes later Mr. Willard came out with Marlon. He continued pass the group to check on Ruby after Walter informed him she had gone to find a seat.

"Oh my God, sweetheart, are you alright? Where have you been?" said Priscilla. She ran to meet Marlon before he reached the rest of the group.

"Damn. I don't believe this," responded Marlon in a startled tone. The group of friends gravitated toward Marlon and Priscilla.

"What is it sweetie? What's wrong?"

"I can't believe what has happened tonight. Here at our anniversary party." The redness shone in Marlon's eyes was evident he'd been crying. Priscilla stood in front of him tightly gripping his hands. She could tell by the sullen expression he wore that he was very perturbed.

"What's going on man?" questioned Walter, taking a step closer to Marlon.

"Somebody was murdered."

"Murdered!!?" they all exclaimed in unison.

"Yeah."

Priscilla wrapped her arms around Marlon as her tears resumed. They were baffled by the news he had just given them.

"Do you know who it is?" said Walter.

"Yeah," Marlon continued, allowing his head to drop.

"Please, no! Don't tell me it was Zach," Rashondra interrupted, realizing now that Zach had not been located yet.

"I identified the body. It was my partner Tyronne." The tears dropped generously as he embraced Priscilla tighter.

They all stood there too disconcerted to speak. The coroner rolled the body out on a stretcher. A bloodstained sheet covered it.

The detectives wasted no time swarming the area with pens and pads in their hands. They asked numerous questions with high hopes of solving the murder mystery.

"Does anyone over here know Tyronne Baxter?" said one of the detectives.

"Yes," replied Priscilla. She massaged Marlon's shoulders as she continued to talk. "He works with my husband at Willard Insurance."

Oh no, not now. Close your mouth please, thought Indigo. She stepped closer to Priscilla trusting that her body language would exhort her to end the conversation.

Unfortunately, the body language and facial expression went unnoticed as Priscilla continued to speak, "My husband only invited Tyronne to our celebration so that he could amend their work relationship after a bad business deal a few weeks ago."

Jesus Christ! Is she crazy? What is she doing? thought Rashondra.

"Mr. Turner, may I speak to you alone?" said the detective. He walked Marlon over to an area where there were four other detectives waiting.

Walter advised Priscilla to stay with Indigo and Rashondra while he and Tony stayed close to Marlon.

"Dammit Priscilla do you know what you've just done?" said a distressed Rashondra.

"I'm only telling the truth. Tyronne wouldn't have been here if Marlon didn't feel sorry for him. Tyronne was murdered okay. Why would someone want to kill him? There's no telling what kind of trouble he was in. I don't want them to think Marlon was a good friend to some one like that."

"You just don't get it do you?" Rashondra huffed. "I'll be back, I need to find Zach." Rashondra shook her head, popped her lips, and walked away. Derrick followed her. *Sometimes she acts just like she doesn't even have cat sense. Damn! What is it that's in her mind that makes her feels she has to tell the truth about every goddamn thing she knows? Ludicrous!* thought Rashondra.

"Priscilla, I know you meant no harm, but you shouldn't have said anything about Marlon and Tyronne having a bad business deal. You've probably just made Marlon a suspect," said Indigo as she held Priscilla's hand for comfort.

"Why would they think that? Marlon may have a history of infidelity, but he would never shoot anyone! I know he wouldn't! He's not a murderer!"

"Come here, I know you are going through a lot right now. Take a deep breath and try to calm down." Indigo placed her arm around Priscilla's shoulder. "Think about what I'm saying. Were you with Marlon at all times tonight? Will you be able to tell the detectives where Marlon was at the time of the murder?

She placed her head on Indigo's shoulder realizing she probably should've kept her mouth closed that time.

After numerous questions, Marlon returned to the area where Priscilla and Indigo waited. The detectives were close behind. He had a very rampageous look on his face as he snatched Priscilla by the arm and pulled her away.

"You have no idea what you've just done to me do you? Because of your big mouth, I've got to go to the police station for further questioning."

"Marlon, I'm sorry. I didn't mean to give them an impression that you may be involved. I thought I was helping out by telling them the truth."

"Just a second Marlon, don't treat her like that. You know she meant no harm. That's just the way Priscilla is," retorted Indigo.

"Stay out of it Indigo. This is between my wife and me."

Marlon and Priscilla walked out the door. Walter followed them. Priscilla was not allowed to ride in the police car so Walter volunteered to drive her there.

Indigo and Tony lingered around until Rashondra and Derrick returned. She explained to Rashondra what was going on with Marlon. They headed for the police station, without Zach.

Indigo's mind was so frazzled by the events that had taken place that she was unable to drive. When Marlon told them that Tyronne was murdered in the men's restroom, she couldn't help but to think about Zach and how he was lingering around, the unusually loud male voices, and the popping noise she heard.

Could it possibly be Zach? Was he really waiting on a female or was it Tyronne? He doesn't know Tyronne, does he? Oh I have the worst headache, thought Indigo as she placed her head on Tony's shoulder en route to the police station.

* * * * *

They all dawdled around at the police station until about 1:30 AM anticipating good news about Marlon. Mr. Willard insisted that they leave and get some rest. He promised to have Priscilla call as soon as Marlon was released. Walter went back to the hotel to prepare for an early morning flight. Indigo left with Tony and Rashondra left with Derrick.

The ringing of the phone at 4:45 AM awakened Indigo immediately. She knew things had turned for the worse when she heard the frail voice of Priscilla on the other end.

"Indigo, Marlon has been arrested. A gun was found behind a building near 'Underground' that was used in the murder. It's registered to

Marlon. They found blood on it that was consistent with Tyronne's DNA. You and Rashondra need to come down here please."

After Indigo explained to Tony that she and Rashondra needed to go visit Priscilla together, he understood completely.

Marlon's gun? Oh my goodness. And all of this time I'm thinking Zach may have had something to do with this.

Indigo took a sigh to release some of the stress as she headed to Rashondra's apartment.

I told Rashondra to call me if she hears from Zach. She has not called yet. This is so strange. Okay, let me calm down and think clearly. Zach is a true suspect in my mind simply because of the timing. But Marlon's gun was found. Maybe Marlon was already in the restroom. Maybe Zach witnessed something and Marlon paid him off to keep quiet. Could that be why Zach is missing? Oh, I don't know. Okay, Zach was acting very nervous. He kept peeping around the corner. No harm intended Zach, but I can't imagine what decent woman at that party would've wanted to meet you. Not the way you were looking. So Zach lied to me about the woman. Then, he was getting pissed off about the time? But still, how does he know Tyronne? Now Priscilla did mention something about Zach inquiring about a job at Willards. Maybe he met Tyronne when he went up there? Zach knows something. I don't know what , but he's involved in some way, concluded Indigo as she mounted the two flights of stairs to Rashondra's apartment.

Chapter 25

RIP

Rashondra did not want to acknowledge any validity in the news Indigo delivered about Zach. As a matter of fact, she did everything but called Indigo a liar.

"That can't be. Zach doesn't know Tyronne and he barely knows Marlon. Besides, as far as you know, he could've left with that female he was waiting on," responded Rashondra in Zach's defense.

"That's very possible, but I can't help but to think about how strange he was acting. He could hardly keep still."

"If you mention anything about Zach, he won't have a chance. With his track record, I'm sure he will get the maximum sentence no matter what he's charged with."

"I'm not pointing my finger at Zach, but I just feel he knows something. I need to let the detectives know what I saw."

"Indigo, you can't say anything about what you saw."

"Why not Rashondra? If Zach saw something, he needs to tell it," snapped Indigo, believing all along that Zach was probably more than just a witness.

"No. Let it go. It will only cause more heartache. Let's just be there for Priscilla and pray that things work out for Marlon." Rashondra grabbed her purse and headed out the door to Indigo's car.

"But Rashondra, Marlon has been charged with murder. The questioning session is over. I'm holding back some information that could possibly help this case."

"Help who in this case? Marlon? So you want to run to the police, and tell them you saw Zach in the hall, although you are not accusing him of any wrong-doings, but you just need to let them know he was in the hall. Okay, you were in the hall at the same time. Does that make you a suspect?"

"You are totally misunderstanding. It was more than just seeing him in the hall."

"Save it Indigo.   Just keep your goddamn mouth shut!" yelped Rashondra as tears rolled down her cheeks.

Stunned by Rashondra's choice of words, Indigo adhered.   They continued their ride in silence.

We are all feeling a bit anxious right now, but I don't appreciate her cursing me. Oh she will know my feelings about this once things calm down, thought Indigo.

* * * * *

The jail was filled with news reporters, scurrying about to be the first to either print or air the story.

They approached Indigo and Rashondra as soon as they walked in. "Excuses me ladies, what can you tell us about the murder that took place in the Marquis ballroom?"

"We have no comments," Indigo said. They struggled to push their way through the stirring reporters.

"Is it true that you two are friends of Mrs. Turner? Can you give us some information about the murder?"

"We said we have nothing to say dammit!" Rashondra snapped. She rammed the microphone into the reporter's nose. "Now show that on the news," she added.

By the time they reached Priscilla, she was very bewildered.   Her eyes were swollen and blood-shot red from constant crying.   She told them the detective's theory.

Besides the gun being found, one of the valet attendants was able to describe a young man that fitted Marlon's description going into their Mercedes about thirty minutes before the 911 call.   This information prompted the detectives to search Marlon's car.   There they found a jimmied car lock and a disarmed alarm; all of which they concluded Marlon had staged.

Have the detectives been able to get a statement from anyone that can give Marlon an alibi at the time of the shooting? Time of shooting... My God, what I'm holding back is more valuable than I thought. Zach looked at his watch and it was eleven-fifteen. I was only in the restroom about three or four minutes before I heard the popping noise, Indigo thought, twitching in her seat as her brain began working overtime.

Indigo was in a very awkward situation.   She loved both of her friends dearly, but was hardly able to sit still after she realized how much pain Priscilla felt.

They sat together for hours, saying very little.   Priscilla thought about Marlon and the torment he felt being locked in a jail cell.   Rashondra thought about Zach.   She wondered where he was.   Did he know Tyronne? Did he kill Tyronne? Why is he missing? Indigo thought about both Priscilla and Rashondra.   She was totally mystified about her next move.

Around noon, Indigo felt they all needed a break away from the police station to reinvigorate their minds. Priscilla refused to leave. She wanted to stay until she was able to bring her husband back home where he belonged.

When Indigo approached the front door of her apartment, she retrieved the newspaper and noticed the murder story on the front page. *'Notable black-businessman found to be the number one suspect'* was the first line of print. The heaviness she felt led her to the first seat available which was the love sofa in the living room.

These reporters hold nothing back. If I didn't know Marlon first hand, after reading this article, there would be no doubt in my mind that he's the murderer. I'm glad I missed the twelve o'clock news.

* * * * *

Her attempt to take a nap was cut short due to insomnia. She got dressed and went to visit Rashondra.

Indigo had always been the one to ruminate the perfect plan or strategy to get out of any given situation. This time she was at a standstill. She'd finally reached rock bottom.

By Sunday evening Rashondra still hadn't heard from Zach. Rashondra continued to pressure Indigo about not revealing the information she knew.

"You're being selfish. Right now this really isn't about protecting Zach or saving Marlon. This is about me having a conscious. I can't believe you want me to continue with this secret simply because you think Zach's history will result in unfair treatment. What you are asking me to do is not right?" said Indigo.

"All I asked you to do is not mention anything until I talk to Zach."

"When are you going to talk to Zach? You don't even know where he is Rashondra. I have some vital information and it needs to be told. My goodness, I should've spoken up last night at the police station. But no, I decided to walk away, avoiding the issue. How do you think Priscilla is going to feel when she finds out I didn't say anything?"

"She doesn't have to find out. You don't have to *ever* tell her. Mr. Willard is rich. He has money and power. He can get Marlon out of jail. He can even get Johnny Cochran if he needs to. Marlon is guaranteed to get a not-guilty verdict. Who or what does Zach have? Nothing. Nobody but Grandma and me."

By this time Rashondra was walking around her apartment in delirium. She felt a nervous breakdown coming on.

" If Zach is arrested, they will lock him up and throw away the key. Probably give him the death penalty. He will never see society again. How can you connect him with Tyronne anyway? Marlon's gun was found. That should tell you something. How in the world could Zach get his hands on a gun that belonged to Marlon?"

"That's true, but you need to think about the reality of this whole scenario. Where is Zach?" Indigo snapped back, feeling every bit of agitation too. "Why has he suddenly disappeared without a trace? What makes it so bad, he's in *your* car. Have you told police your car is missing? I hate to say it, but I think Zach and Marlon had something to do with this."

Rashondra placed both hands over her face and wailed. "I don't know where he is! I don't know why he's missing! Oh God, I hope he really doesn't have anything to do with this!"

Indigo enclosed her arms around Rashondra's shoulders, attempting to provide her with a little comfort. As they both took seats on the living room sofa, Rashondra rested her head upon Indigo's chest. They rocked back and forth.

I feel so bad. I just don't know what to do. Granddaddy help... I know you are probably looking down at me shaking your head in awe, wondering why I'm not doing what's right. I don't know what's right.

* * * * *

Indigo and Rashondra returned to the jail around six that evening. Priscilla was still in the same frame of mind. The three of them hugged for a long time before the silence was broken.

"Precious honey, you need to eat."

"No Father, I have no appetite. Just tell me that Marlon is on his way out."

"We're still working on it. He will be getting out on bond soon, but they still have enough evidence for a trial. No one has come forth with any additional information that will lead the detectives to the possibility of another suspect."

Indigo felt vertiginous. She immediately excused herself to the restroom. She entered the first stall and allowed her contracting stomach to release the lunch she'd barely eaten that day. She felt ill. She had to leave. Before Rashondra exited her car, she told her she couldn't hold back too much longer.

That night Indigo could not sleep. She tossed and turned for over two hours. She felt like the devil was riding her back.

"I rebuke you Satan in the name of Jesus. Leave me alone!" She yelled so loud that she heard her echo bouncing off the wall.

Indigo crawled out of the bed drenched with sweat. She took a quick shower, threw on a pair of jeans and a T-shirt and headed back to the police station at 2:00 AM, despite the fact that she had to be at work at 7:30 AM.

Priscilla was slouched over in a chair wrapped in a blanket. She was wide-awake when Indigo approached her.

My God, look at her. How could I do this to her? Please forgive me God. Please forgive me Priscilla. Please forgive me Rashondra.

"I've got something to tell you." Indigo said.

How do I start? How do I explain Rashondra's point of view? How do I expect her to understand? How is she going to take it? Here it is, almost twenty-four hours later; I should have said something last night.

Indigo carefully explained whom she'd seen and what she'd heard the night of the shooting. She attempted to explain Rashondra's point of view but was hindered by an enraged side of Priscilla that she never knew existed.

Priscilla threw the balled-up blanket into Indigo's face and yelled, "How could you do this to me and my family? What kind of friend are you? You sat here last night and earlier today and watched me suffer! You knew all this time that Zach shot Tyronne and you wouldn't tell!" Priscilla was hysterical.

"I didn't say he shot Tyronne. I said I ran into him in the hallway. I didn't even see him go into the restroom," Indigo replied in her defense.

"What happened to the promise we made to be there for each other no matter what happens?"

"Priscilla, I have been here for you, day and night," Indigo said. She reached out to embrace Priscilla, only to be rejected this time.

Priscilla grabbed Indigo by the neck, shoving her into the wall. She screamed and cried, "This is the worst thing you and Rashondra could've ever done to me! Oh my God! I hate you! Get out of my damn sight! Get out of my damn life!"

Releasing her grip, Priscilla stormed out the waiting area leaving Indigo in isolation. She reported the new information to the first available police officer.

Priscilla immediately called Rashondra, having nothing but harsh words for her. "You betrayed our friendship! Why did you pressure Indigo into withholding information that could've saved my family a lot of grief? How could you not see the pain I was going through for something my husband did not do? You're nothing but an evil-thinking, self-centered, conniver! I hate you! I don't need a friend like you in my life!"

After about an hour worth of questioning for something that took less than a minute for Indigo to say initially, she went home, without saying goodbye to Priscilla.

Indigo's Caller ID displayed Rashondra's name five times. She phoned her back, hoping she would understand why she did what she did.

"You told! You promised me you wouldn't say anything!"

"Rashondra, listen, please try to understand," begged Indigo.

"No, you listen to me dammit! You have gotten my brother involved in a murder he probably knows nothing about. Why couldn't you have waited? Why did you have to tell on him?"

"I only told the detectives what I saw. Marlon is in jail..."

"The hell with Marlon!" Rashondra interrupted. "He's got money, power, all the right resources. Why didn't you listen to me? Oh my God. My brother, my poor brother. They are going to kill him. I know they are. I know what they do to people from the ghetto. We are nobodies to them. Why Indigo? Why?"

Indigo sat in silence. She was at a lost for words. She held the phone to her ear and cried. She wanted so badly to hold out her hands like she'd done many times before. She wanted so badly to huddle with her friends for comfort. Her silence was broken by a clamorous click from the other end. Rashondra had hung up on her.

Indigo phoned back. Rashondra slammed the phone on its receiver. Indigo phoned back a third time. CLICK!

A few hours later, Indigo called in sick. She hadn't slept in twenty-four hours. She phoned Tony at the fire station, although he wouldn't have a day off again until Tuesday. His voice assured her that at least he was on her side.

After a warm cup of milk didn't work, she jogged across the street to the Amoco service station and purchased a box of Sominex for sleep.

* * * * *

Detectives were at Rashondra's apartment first thing Monday morning questioning Zach's whereabouts. She felt a need to advise them that her car was missing also. She didn't want to be connected in any kind of way just in case he did have something to do with the murder.

Within two hours, Marlon was released from jail. The charges against him were dropped due to evidence found that linked Zach to the murder of Tyronne.

Rashondra's car was found, abandoned on I-75 south in Macon at the Eisenhower Parkway exit. Inside they found the jacket Zach had worn with bloodstains on it. There was also a cellular phone registered to Marlon on the back seat.

Chapter 26

Priscilla

Two years after the cataclysmic events of our anniversary celebration, my emotions are still shattered from the pain it left behind. Barring the title 'Mother' of twin girls and a six-year-old son is all the reason I need to grasp hold of my sanity, for their sakes.

* * * * *

Forty-eight hours after Marlon's hideous stay in jail, the accusations against him were dropped. Only moments after we'd walked through the front door, Indigo called. As soon as I made out the words, 'Hi Priscilla" from her bewildered voice, she was stopped in mid-sentence.

"Don't ever call my house again, betrayer," I hooted and slammed the phone on the receiver. I was too engrossed with the excitement of my husband's return home to give that evil-thinking, so-called, used-to-be-friend of mine second thoughts.

On that same evening Walter called from Washington, DC. He was ecstatic about the news of Marlon's release as well as my pregnancy. What really startled him was the information I shared about RIP being literally ripped apart. Although he showed compassion in reference to my feelings of anguish, he still couldn't believe I wanted nothing more to do with Indigo and Rashondra.

"You girls have always been there for each other through the good and bad times. This is unbelievable," he had said.

* * * * *

It wasn't long after our anniversary celebration that Marlon's frequent out of town business trips and late hours at the office became habitual again, two months later to be exact.

As the weeks passed, that excitement soon diminished and sadness slowly crept upon me. I began to have regrets about the heartless words I shouted at Indigo and Rashondra. Would they understand that those words were spoken out of anger? Probably not, because at that point in time, I couldn't acknowledge their reasoning.

The selfishness Rashondra portrayed in wanting Indigo to keep the secret about Zach seemed unforgivable at that time. She had a love for her brother that could move mountains. Sort of like the love I have for Marlon. I now empathize with Rashondra, understanding completely the pain she must have endured.

Then there's Indigo. I continue to have flashbacks about the look of torment on her face when I rejected her embrace. That was the first time ever. Seeing the tears swell in her eyes when I told her I hated her makes my body cower. Even after that, she still called the next day to make amends. I wouldn't even listen. It's my fault. It's my entire fault.

* * * * *

The trial started six months after Zach's arrest. I eased my way into the back of the courtroom the day Indigo had to testify. Disguising myself was in my best interest because we hadn't spoken since that horrid day. I wore a silk scarf tied around my head, knotted underneath my chin, and a pair of black Ray-Bans.

Indigo looked very dignified as she gave the prosecutors her ingenuous replies. I was only able to observe a glimpse of Rashondra from the side, but it was easy to conclude the disconsolation she must have been feeling.

* * * * *

The announcement of my pregnancy was never revealed to them due to the turning of events.

Marlon's secretary gave me a baby shower, but it just wasn't the same without my best friends around. I envisioned Indigo just taking over, making all the plans, and doing all of the decorating. Rashondra would've been assisting. Every thing would've been just perfect.

I've often wondered if ending our friendship was the right thing. I miss them dearly. I miss Rashondra's scurrilous personality, telling me precisely how she felt, about anything, especially when it came to some type of contrary behavior Marlon had indulged himself in. She always told me exactly what I needed to hear, straightforward, no additives. I miss Indigo's embrace; the sound advice she gave me. I miss the good times we shared just being RIP.

* * * * *

A month ago, to my surprise, a florist delivered five dozen of pink roses to my front door. Minutes after the florist pulled away, Marlon walked in snuggling two bottles of Moet.

He retrieved two large pillows from the basement. They were the same pillows we'd cuddled on during our first skiing trip to Aspen. We found a nice little cozy spot by the fireplace. You would think the weather would begin to warm up being that the first day of spring was only three weeks away.

For the first time in three weeks he'd arrived home before nine o'clock. The kids were already asleep and it felt good to have that anticipated quality time with my husband.

While relishing the moment we shared, I cautiously took my first sip of alcohol. Two sips later, I felt slightly lightheaded.

"You know what sweetie?" I said, positioning my head on Marlon's chest. He began stroking his hand up and down my arm. It felt so good.

"What's up baby?"

" I've been thinking about Indigo and Rashondra a lot lately. I really miss them."

"I don't miss those instigators. That loud-mouth-ass Rashondra and know-it-all Indigo got on my nerves anyway. They always kept a bunch of mess going on between us. You know that's true."

"Now Marlon, you have to be honest here. They never deliberately lied on you. They always had my best interests at heart."

"Well, I disagree. I think they had their *own* interests at heart. They stayed in our business too much. That's probably why we had as many problems as we did. You allowed them to persuade you from your true feelings."

Maybe Marlon is right to a certain degree. They were very involved in my marriage. Marlon is no angel, and I still have my suspicions about him... but when I think about it, I haven't been able to place my finger on any evidence that suggests an affair since they have been out of my life. The longevity of my marriage is very important to me, therefore, I need to convince Marlon of their sincerity.

"No I didn't," I responded, removing my head from his chest. I looked him directly in the face and continued, "No matter what they said, I always told them I love you. They knew that. They just felt like you were bringing me down emotionally, physically, and mentally. In a way, you were. I've been through a lot with you."

"I know it baby. I'm sorry," he said as he kissed me on the cheek. He handed me the glass of Moet I'd placed on the marble flooring around the fireplace. "I love you. You know I do. Life is just a challenge and sometimes it's very difficult for me to say no."

"It's difficult for you to say no to what? Women? Are you having another affair?" I said after taking another sip of Moet.

"No, baby, what I mean is with me being a top executive at Willard's, I'm always faced with challenges at work. It's hard for me to say, 'No I can't meet because I have to get home to my family'. That's why I'm returning home at late hours and working some weekends. Life is extremely hard for a successful, African-American male..."

"I love you so much," I interrupted, ready to take control of the romantic evening Marlon had planned for us. Feeling a little woozy, I gave him the flute I'd been sipping from and crawled on top of him. We hadn't made love in three weeks and my body was craving for his touch.

Whew! thought Marlon.

Chapter 27

Rashondra

"Derrick, are you ready? Their plane arrives in thirty minutes. You know they've never flown before. We need to be at the door when they step off the plane."

"I'm coming. Where did you put my black, leather coat?"

"It's in the hall closet."

This was like a miracle transpiring. Grandma, Mama, and Nayla were coming to visit for Christmas. I hadn't seen Grandma and Nayla since Zach's trial a year and a half ago. At that time Mama was so heavily indulged in drugs that she was not capable of going anywhere but back to rehabilitation.

When Zach was found guilty of second-degree murder, Mama placed the bulk of the blame on herself. Months of continued drug use went on before she finally went back into rehab. There she stayed for nine months. Since her departure five months ago, she's been drug free and ready for a new life.

When Derrick notified me of a special he'd found while browsing through the Sunday's paper, I quickly pulled out my Visa and confirmed a flight for three.

Tension built as we approached the flight gate. My anticipation slightly decreased when we were informed of a twenty-minute delay.

As I sat in the area near the gate awaiting Derrick's return with a cup of coffee, I began to think back on the awful calamity that entered my life over a year and a half ago.

* * * * *

The morning Priscilla called me at 3:00 A.M. to put an end to our friendship, I knew my life was about to become more complicated. At that moment, I felt so much hatred for Indigo.

It didn't get any better because I called Indigo five times and she still didn't have the decency to pickup and answer. By the time she finally called back, I was so irate I could've literally kicked her ass. I couldn't believe she'd turned her back on me. I didn't want to hear a damn thing she had to say. I just wanted her to know how hurt I was and how I wanted nothing more to do with her.

It didn't take long for the detectives to track Zach down. They raided Grandma's apartment three days after he became the main suspect in Tyronne's murder.

When the bangs blared through Grandma's front door preceding the voices of several FBI Agents, Zach advised her and Nayla to stay in the back room while he handled the situation. Grandma refused to abide by his request. The begging and pleading that tolled from their frail voices helped Zach to realize he could no longer hide.

Too distraught and embarrassed by the media leading the public to assume my brother was a dangerous, drug-dealing, murderer, I took a two weeks leave of absent from my job in an attempt to regain sanity.

* * * * *

Zach was jailed without bail while he awaited trial. My attempted visits were denied for weeks due to him not placing me on the visitation list. His demeanor was tearing me apart. Although Derrick stood by my side, I thought about the comfort I would've received had Indigo and Priscilla been around.

Two weeks prior to his trial, I received a long letter from Zach. He revealed secrets I would have never guessed he'd kept.

He started off by apologizing for not allowing me to visit. He didn't know how to face me after what he'd done. He felt a need to explain everything before the trial started.

He became involved with the Cuban Drug Lords in Miami, claiming it felt right to him because he's half Cuban. *"The money was flowin good and Juan treated me like a brotha. He the big-man in the gang,"* he wrote.

He met Tyronne two years ago while making a drop in Valdosta, which continued to be their meeting point. Tyronne picked up the drugs, and Zach collected the money. *"Tyronne didn't have all the money for the last drop so I dialed Juan up and asked how to handle it. He told me Tyronne was good business so take the half he had to offer and set up a second pick up date."*

The following week, which was an agreed time to pick up the other five hundred thousand dollars, Tyronne was a no-show. That set Juan off so he contacted Tyronne himself. Tyronne lied and said he had indeed given the other half of the money to Zach. Juan began to question Zach about the missing money.

"I told him I ain't got no money cause Tyronne just didn't show up, I swear." As a result of that, Juan sent Zach to Atlanta to look for Tyronne.

"Bring back my half of million dollars or a news paper clipping of his dead body is exactly what Juan told me. No money, no news clipping, yo dead body will be in the paper. And then Nayla's and Grandma's."

Saddened by the information I was gathering from his letter, I reflected for a moment on the reason why I *thought* Zach had come to Atlanta. I truly felt he was trying to make a change in his life. If only I knew he was involved in such a predicament, maybe I could have helped him. I'm sure Priscilla would have assisted financially.

My stomach began to knot up as I continued to read. Zach explained the threat of death hanging over his head if he didn't follow through with one of the two orders given to him. Zach tracked Tyronne down at Willard Insurance. After a heated argument and an apology for a misunderstanding, Tyronne assured Zach he would receive the money at the anniversary party.

Zach pulled up right behind Tyronne. When he saw Tyronne reach into his glove compartment and place a gun into his jacket, he knew he was headed for trouble. *"I panicked Shondra. I didn't have no gun and I didn't know what to do. All I could think about was what Juan would do to Grandma and Nayla if he didn't get his money. I didn't care about myself."*

Realizing he had to be the better man, he used his street-sense to silence the alarm in Marlon's Mercedes and opened the door.

"I took a gun and some other stuff. I wasn't planning to kill nobody, but wanted to protect myself. Please believe me. Of all the trouble I've been in, I ain't never shot nobody," he continued to explain in his letter.

When Zach confronted Tyronne about the money, he said he didn't have it. Zach warned him of Juan's death threat if he didn't give up the money this time. *"Then he pulled out his gun and said 'You bad, shoot me!'"*

"When I was pulling out Marlon's gun, he hit me in the head with his gun two times. That knocked me into the wall and I fell on the floor. He stood up there pointing his gun at me so I started pointing back. I didn't think he wanted to kill me for real cause he would've already shot me. Then he said there was no way he would be brought down by a bunch of Hispanics and put the gun to my head. When he did that, I pulled the trigger. I only shot him cause I thought I was about to die."

His admittance to shooting Tyronne instantly brought the food I thought I'd digested back to surface. I jetted to the bathroom, praying that the contraction of my stomach would stop. After I finished vomiting, I fixed myself a glass of room temperature water before taking my seat back on the sofa. Somberly, I continued to read.

"I must have lost my mind or something," Zach wrote. *"Cause when he fell to the floor, I took his gun. I slipped out a side door and left. I stopped your car on the side of the road downtown Atlanta and dipped behind a building to throw away Marlon's gun. I kept driving down the interstate for about an hour and a half before I ran out of gas. I was so scared Shondra I mean I was scared as hell. I took off my jacket cause it had blood all over it and jumped out your car and left it there. When I went to this gas station off the road, I caught a ride to Valdosta. That's where I hooked up with one of my partners and rode to Miami with him the next morning. I sold Tyronne's gun on the streets in Miami. I know that was messed-up. I just wasn't in my right mind. Please tell me you believe me. I never wanted to kill him. I was trying to protect myself. My lawyer said it was going to be hard to prove self-defense but he was going to try."*

* * * * *

The trial went on for three weeks. Grandma and Nayla sat on one side of me; Derrick was on the other. I clenched his hand throughout the trial.

The day Indigo approached the stand, I rotated my hand into hard circles around my stomach, trying to relieve some of the queasiness. She was nervous. I heard it in her voice. Although I was tormented with pain, I was proud that she stuck with her story. With all the twisting and turning of words the prosecutor threw at her, she sat there with stride and only told what she saw. When she walked out of the courtroom that day, I never saw her again.

I wish I could've said something to her. I wish I could've told her how sorry I was for accusing her of lying on Zach. I soon began to realize that she only did what was right. I must have been a fool to curse her out the way that I did.

During the preliminary hearing, the prosecutors wanted to charge Zach with second-degree murder, and the defense claimed it was justifiable homicide because Zach was attacked. He'd taken pictures of the almost healed wounds on Zach's forehead the day he was appointed as his attorney. After bickering back and forth about Zach's charges, the judge decided that second-degree murder, along with a few other charges, would suffice. As a result of the three days the jurors deliberated, they found Zach guilty of all charges, giving him the maximum of twenty-five years in prison.

* * * * *

Three weeks after the trial, Derrick proposed to me. He wanted to have a small wedding, inviting only family and a few friends. I was totally against it and lured him to the courthouse.

"Who am I going to invite, Grandma and Nayla? I have no papa to give me away, I have no sister nor friends to be bridesmaids, I have no mama to be walked down the aisle by the usher, so who's coming?" I had said to him, sobbing deeply from the hurt and pain of missing my family and friends. His embrace assured me he understood.

* * * * *

Derrick has truly been a blessing to me. I don't know how I would've made it through the trials and tribulations I've encountered had he not been by my side. I can honestly say that those unwanted changes that have transpired in my life have altered my demeanor a great deal. That beat-you-down attitude has emotionally beaten me down.

At one time, due to the influences of Derrick, I seriously considered calling Indigo and Priscilla to bury the hatchet. I guess I was still left with too much pride. That lead to my refusal. I couldn't do it. I didn't know how to do it.

The times I'd spoken with Walter only made me miss them even more. He always brought up RIP in one way or another. I admitted to him my desire to reunite with them, but I just didn't think it would ever be the way it used to be.

Chapter 28

Indigo

Sean's resistance to my discipline after he shoved a kindergarten at the water fountain caused the slight headache I had to escalate. That led me to call my HMO for a same day appointment.

As I waited in the sitting area, a young man walked in, resembling Zach from head to toe. Seeing that similarity led me back to something that has dominated my mind time and time again...the trial.

* * * * *

Look at my friend, I thought at the same time I was settling into the witness chair. Rashondra's long, black, silky hair ascended down both sides of her shoulder. She had the perfect visage for a glamour shot. Her Grandmother and sister were positioned on one side of her and Derrick was on the other.

Our eyes locked only for a split second. Immediately I felt nervous. I couldn't bare it. *If only I could reach out and touch her. What is she thinking about me right now?*

My eyes sauntered around the courtroom to place my focus elsewhere. On the last row of seats, one particular female caught my attention. *Oh my God. That's Priscilla. I know it's her. She can't hide under that scarf and those sunglasses. That's her.*

Great masses of saliva agitated my throat as I attempted to swallow. Before my swallow was complete, the prosecutor asked me to state my full name. Forcing the lump down ended in a hideous round of coughs.

Although I was a witness for the prosecutors, I did not allow them to assuage me from the actual facts I'd seen the night of the murder. I was pleased to hear the defense lawyer clarify that I did not see Zach enter the restroom.

I left the witness stand with stride glowing from my outer appearance. I walked straight up the aisle not turning to view neither Rashondra nor Priscilla. I went right through the double doors that led to the hallway. Tony was already waiting for me. We embraced. I wept. The feeling I bared was almost worst than that of Granddaddy's funeral.

Tony had been such an understanding and supportive better half throughout the whole ordeal. He only spoke encouraging words and promised to be at my side.

A week after the trial, the oppressive feelings lingered. In an attempt to lift my spirits, Tony surprised me with two round trip tickets to the Bahamas. We were to leave as soon as school ended. A vacation was needed.

We had such a remarkable time during our visit to Nassau. I'd never been on a *real* vacation with a man before. We did everything from snorkeling, to deep-sea fishing; candle light dinner, to making love on the beach. *This is the man I want to marry,* I thought as we walked hand in hand from the beach after experiencing love making at its highest peak.

It never occurred to me that Tony had completely replaced every desire I had for Todd's touch until our Bahamas experience. I hated comparing the two because Todd did have a slight edge over Tony. But love conquered all. The fact that I was in love made it all better.

*   *   *   *   *

My thoughts of the past were slightly deterred after I noticed I'd been sitting in the waiting room for twenty-five minutes. In an effort to make the patients feel a little at ease, there was a sign posted that advised them to let the receptionist know if their wait was more than fifteen minutes. I guess I wasn't the only patient who'd complained before.

"Excuse me," I said to the receptionist. "I've been sitting out here for twenty-five. Is there a problem?"

"Wait a minute. Let me go check." She left the receptionist area and returned within seconds. "She's a little backed up. If you are not called back in ten minutes, let me know."

Settled back in my seat, not happy about having to wait another ten minutes, my mind drifted again.

*   *   *   *   *

Tony left for work one morning as I continued on with my deep sleep. The ringing of the phone awakened me. Although Tony had no problem with me answering his telephone simply because our relationship had reached that level, I didn't make it a habit because it was never for me. If he needed to call from the fire station, I would know it's him by the special ring. So that morning the phone went unanswered. What caught my attention was the female's voice I heard on the answering machine.

"Hi Tony," she took a sigh. "This is Brandi. I know the letter I sent last week must have really surprised you. I need to hear from you. Please call me."

What is she talking about? What letter? Tony never mentioned anything about a letter.

Brandi is his ex-girlfriend. They dated about three years before he ended their relationship due to an affair she was involved in. He told me she'd called a few times afterwards, but he made it clear that there was no turning back. He never went into details about their relationship. I just felt he held a lot of bitterness towards her for what she'd done.

Just thinking back, when I came over two days ago, Tony was not acting his normal self. When I questioned him about his demeanor, he said it was stress from the job. We didn't make love last night nor the night before and I hadn't seen him all week. Something had to be going on.

With my brain functioning at full force, my heart rate increased with each breath of air I inhaled. It was extremely hard for me to wipe out what I'd just heard and return to my deep sleep.

Reaching for the phone, I hesitated a moment before dialing it. *Why can't I just shake this feeling and let it go until I see Tony. Although he won't be off work for another twenty-four hours, I did promise him I would prepare a big dinner and bring it out there. Maybe I could question him then.* I placed the phone back on the receiver.

Even after I took a shower, I still felt troubled about what I'd heard. I sat on the edge of the bed and viewed the Caller ID just to see where she was calling from. I pressed play on the answering machine to reassure myself of what I thought I'd heard earlier. *Yes, I heard it right the first time. What is going on? What did she write to him that could have surprised him after three years?*

I picked up the phone again, this time dialing without hesitation. *What am I going to say? How do I begin this conversation?*

"Clayton County Fire Department, may I help you?"

"Yes, may I please speak with Tony Palmer."

"Sorry ma'am, he and the crew left about fifteen minutes ago. There's a terrible fire downtown. He'll be gone for a while. Can I take a message?"

"Yes, tell him that Indigo called and I'll bring dinner down around seven."

"Oh, hey Indigo. I hope you're bringing some of that good ole, southern-style macaroni and cheese. I'll tell him you called. See ya."

What do I do in the meantime? I'm not going to call her, but I have to know what's going on. I can remember telling Priscilla and Rashondra that there comes a time when a woman has to have a PI Check for her own personal satisfaction. I'm too anxious, I need to know now. Sorry Tony, I tried to call you first.

It didn't take much rambling to find the letter Brandi sent him. There it rested, fresh and crisp, in the top drawer of his dresser. Remembering that I'd taken it from the right corner, I sat on the edge of the bed, opened it, and began to read.

A son named JaQuez, two and a half years old. Tony left Brandi because she told him she was pregnant and it wasn't his child. He never told me that, I thought. *She recently had a DNA test, proving the man she'd been with for the past three years is not the father. "Terry was the only other person I was sleeping around with. It's your child Tony,"* she had written. *Why didn't he tell me about this letter? I thought we were open and honest about everything. When did he think the timing would be right, after he took a paternity test? I can't believe this. He already has a seven-year old daughter from a previous relationship. Now I don't have a problem with that. But another child? My goodness. And fact that he's withholding this information from me is absurd. I can not believe this.*

After vigilantly placing the letter back into its proper place, I laid across the bed and cried. *I can't believe this is happening to me. I love him but I don't think I can deal with this. If I never needed Priscilla and Rashondra before, I sure do need them now. Who do I vent to about my feelings?*

After I spent a great deal sobbing, I decided I needed to leave his apartment. I stared at a picture we'd taken in the Bahamas once more before walking out the door. Tears refill my eyes.

Finally answering Tony's third phone call, he wanted to know why I didn't show up at the fire station with dinner as planned, and why was I at home.

"Did you check your messages on the answering machine?"

"No. You left me a message?"

No response from me, only a sigh.

"I dialed my other line a few times. When you didn't answer, I thought maybe you were at the grocery store or something. What's going on?"

"Brandi called."

"Oh, really," he said, instantaneously changing his voice range from semi-anger to despondent.

"Yes she did."

He hesitated before responding, "I was going to tell you what was going on. You know I would never hold anything as serious as this from you." Tony automatically assumed I'd spoken with Brandi.

"You were going to tell me when?"

"After I had a chance to absorb it."

"How long was that going to take?"

"I don't know baby, but you know I was going to tell you," he answered ruefully. I imagined Tony on the other end of the line, dressed in uniform, holding the phone to his ear with his right hand, caressing his forehead with the other. He was probably looking toward the floor, wearing a somber expression.

"What I thought was so unique about our relationship was the fact that we could open up and talk about anything. Things we couldn't share with family and friends. You stripped that away from us when you held back what was going on," I said, still not telling exactly what I heard.

"Baby, I'm so sorry you had to find out the way you did. I was going to tell you about JaQuez on my time." His statement was evident that he thought Brandi had spilled the beans to me.

"Your time. Huh. Finding out you have a son is a serious issue, not something you are supposed to place on hold."

"You are not being reasonable Indigo. You know we still have a special kind of relationship. I'm sorry I didn't tell you what was going on when *you* felt like I should've. I just found out five days ago, okay. Is it wrong for me to have my own personal time to think this over before babbling about it?" Tony retorted. I detected a bit of unbalanced emotions in his response.

"What ever happened to needing me to talk to and getting it off your chest? I'm always venting to you about difficult situations with me."

"Well that's a big difference between you and me. I don't always *need* someone to talk to about what's going on in my life."

"So you were not planning on telling me, huh?"

"I'm not saying I wasn't going to tell you. All I'm saying is that I didn't need you or anybody else to talk to about the situation. I was going to tell you out of respect, not because I needed to vent."

Was I being unreasonable like Tony had expressed or was I acting on my emotions?

"I just can't handle this. You go on and take your time to think. In the meantime, I'm going to do some thinking myself. I need some time alone," I uttered.

"What? I know you're not about to walk out on our relationship because I didn't tell you at your convenience," Tony inquired.

"I just don't understand when you thought the timing was going to be right to share that with me."

"Indigo..." He sigh before speaking again. "I love you baby." His voice was cracking. "Don't do this to us...please," he continued.

"Bye Tony," I replied, gently placing the phone on the receiver.

My fingers began dialing Rashondra's number before I could think. Just before punching the tenth digit, reality kicked in and I hung up.

Two days later Tony phoned again. I was so happy to hear from him, yet heavily saddened by the thought of him fathering another child out of wedlock.

"Yes Tony I do love you," I responded after he'd asked that ridiculous question. "I'm just hurting right now and need some time alone."

"You know Indigo, I can understand you being shocked at the news. It took me by surprise as well. I can even understand you feeling somewhat sad or disappointed. But I can not understand why your feelings are so deeply distraught that you want to shut me out of your life. Is there something else going on?"

"Nothing else is going on. If you love me, you would give me this time to figure out what I want to do."

"Figure out what you want to do? This is so unlike you Indigo. What is happening to you? So what do you expect for me to do, sit around and wait?"

"No, I want you to go on with your life. If it was meant for us to be together, we will," I said at the end of our final conversation.

Two weeks following that last conversation, Tony called and left a message on my answering machine. "Hi Indigo. DNA proved JaQuez is my son. Please call me. I want to see you. I want to talk to you. I miss you... I love you."

The agony of me wanting to pick up that phone and call right away drilled at me so badly. The hurt and pain I was experiencing at the realization of him having two kids would not allow me to do so.

The past should stay where it is. Which is exactly where I wanted to place Tony. I needed to move forward. But I just couldn't stop thinking about him. That particular situation with him was one of those 'mind over heart' ordeals. Most people will tell you to listen to your heart. I always believed in listening to your mind.

After confirming internally that our relationship was over, I began to crave for Todd whom I hadn't seen in over two years. He called eight months ago just to say a friendly hello. I told him all about my relationship with Tony. He expressed his gratitude and at the same time reminded me that he was still there if needed. Well that was one old bone I really wanted to dig up.

Let me rebuke that devil and keep on going. I'm not about to start lusting for Todd. I don't need a man to make my life complete anyway. As a matter of fact, sex was all I really wanted from Todd. I need to grow up and stop thinking like that. Sex isn't everything. Well, it's still very important to me, I can't help it. I have Todd to blame for that.

As time went on, I never stopped thinking about Tony. I thought about him every single day, one way or another. *Two kids, I just can't deal with that pressure*, I thought.

Is it wrong for Tony to be denied love because he has fathered two kids? Yes that's a lot to ask someone like myself, who doesn't have the same type of baggage. But I loved him then and I still love him now.

Four months later, I received no calls from Tony. Should I have expected to hear from him again after the way I treated him? Yes I did. He's a man. He's supposed to be aggressive. He's supposed to go after what he wanted. Did that mean he truly didn't want me anymore?

I couldn't take it. I had to know something, therefore I phoned Walter, bringing up Tony's name in a round about way.

After somewhat bragging on Aaron, the new man in my life that I'd met three weeks prior, I asked about Tony. *Of course Aaron's not 'all that'. As a matter of fact, he's 'none of that'. I only wanted Walter to think I'd moved on.*

"So how's Tony and Brandi doing? The last time I heard from him, let's see, um, I think it was about four months ago, he mentioned that JaQuez is his son."

"From what he's told me, there is no Tony and Brandi. He's just trying to get to know JaQuez as a son. He has no intimate feelings for Brandi. I think he still loves you," responded Walter.

"Yeah, right. Been there, done that." I said, wanting so badly for Walter to elaborate on that statement. I couldn't. Too much pride. Little did he know I would've dropped Aaron in a heartbeat if Tony came back.

Over the pass two years, Walter and I conversed at least three or four times a month. Although after my break-up with Tony, he never really brought his name up, he was forever asking about Priscilla and Rashondra. On several occasions, I attempted to bury the hatchet and pick up my phone and called them. Plain and simple. Just call. But I knew it wouldn't be simple. I didn't know what to say.

* * * * *

An hour and a half had passed before I realized it. I'd been deeply mesmerized in thoughts about Tony. I wanted him back so desperately.

"What is the doctor doing, performing surgery?" I angrily said to the receptionist after strolling back up to the counter.

"She's just backed up, we'll call you next."

"No, I'm not waiting any longer. I can understand being ten or fifteen minutes behind, but an hour and a half is outrageous. You all should be responsible enough to spread your appointments out accordingly."

"Would you like to reschedule your appointment Ms. Duncan?" snapped the receptionist.

"I guess so, if I haven't died by then," I retorted. After rescheduling I grabbed my purse, tramped out the door.

Chapter 29

Priscilla

"Honey, I'm headed to the office. I have a lot of work to catch up on." Marlon yelled through the midst of the steam from the shower.

"I didn't know you were going in today. You promised you'd attend church with us this morning." He closed the door in the middle of my sentence pretending not to hear me.

After watching him back his car out of the garage from our bedroom window, I hazily sauntered back into the shower. I enclosed my arms around my body and sat in the center of the tub. I rested my head upon my knees and soaked in sorrow.

This was the fifth Sunday he'd promised to attend church with the kids and me, but again, my request was denied by some so-called work at the office.

Why would Marlon rather spend so much time away from home was a question I'd asked myself over and over again. I knew the answer; I knew it all too well. The love I possessed had stripped my thoughts from rationalizing with who my husband *really* is.

* * * * *

Three weeks ago I found a letter in Marlon's briefcase. He'd written it to his psychologist the day after he sent me five dozen of pink roses. I honestly thought things were beginning to turn for the better, until I began reading.

Dr. Johnson,
I almost bit my own tongue last night when I told Priscilla it was hard to say no. I lied about the statement, claiming that being a hard-working, African-American male was the hard part. As much as I love my wife and kids, in actuality, it is very hard for me to say

no to attractive women, especially one in particular, Sarita. She is one woman I purposely forgot to mention to you during our counseling sessions two years ago. A year prior to our first session, Sarita and I were going strong, I mean I spent more time with her than I did with Priscilla. I don't know for sure whether I loved Sarita or not, but I can most definitely say I loved what she did to me. She made me reach my sexual peak like no other woman could, not even Priscilla. Had she not broken things off with me when she found out I had given her chlamydia from Sherry, I honestly can't tell you how things would have turned out. Sherry on the other hand, was one big mistake. Too many drinks at a strip club led me to a nearby hotel for a one-night stand. When Sarita broke things off, she went right to Tyronne. That stung like a bee. I felt it would be for the best anyway because I wanted to do right by my family. That's why I came to see you from the beginning. I truly wanted to do the right thing and be a faithful husband. Well, I thought I was over Sarita until I saw her at Tyronne's funeral. I was drawn to her for comfort. I spent the night with her that night; she would not let me make love to her. I wanted and needed to so badly. She only wanted to be held, so that's what I did. Priscilla didn't argue with me when I returned home the following morning. I claimed to have stayed at a hotel to have time for myself. Sarita came back to me six months ago. I tried my best to fight it, but I couldn't. Although I will never leave Priscilla, I like being with Sarita. I really need to see you doc. How do I let Sarita go and be with my wife the right way? Deep in my heart, I don't like the person I am. I want to love my wife the way she deserves to be loved. Priscilla is the best thing that has ever happened to me. I never meant to purposely hurt her but I've become an expert at that. I just don't know what's wrong with me. Maybe if I start attending church with my family, God will deliver me through this. She tells me all the time that it's the devil that has me doing these evil things. Boy I tell you; the devil has got to be a mighty strong spirit because he sure has me locked down with lust. I love women. I love women. I love women. I need your help. You told me if I ever needed to come back for visits to let you know. Here I am, crying out for help. I want to love my wife the right way. I want to do the right thing. Please call me as soon as this letter reaches your office.
Marlon Turner, Jr.

The copy I made of the letter and sent it via certified mail to Dr. Johnson must have gone unnoticed. If only he would do his job and get my husband back into counseling, maybe things will get better. *God please help me*, I prayed.

Chapter 30

Rashondra

Grandma, Mama, and Nayla stepped off the plane all complaining about the horror of their life, dreading their return flight.

"Gul, ohh Lawdy, everythang hurt on my head but my nose. Give me some medicine rite now. I know you got some in yo pocketbook, big time nurse," Mama said as soon as she spotted me.

"Respiratory Therapist, not nurse," I'd corrected, extending my arms to embrace them all.

Mama begged to stay another week after Grandma and Nayla packed for their return flight home. Initially, Derrick and I didn't come to a consensus on this idea, but eventually he gave in.

Grandma and Nayla left two days after New Year's Day. Nayla had to return to school. She was a sophomore in high school and just as beautiful as can be. She was a splitting image of me physically, hips and all. It's hard to believe my baby sister will graduate from high school in two years.

Mama's week turned into a month. Soon that one month revolved into three. Whenever the subject of her returning home came to surface, she would become very offensive. She claimed I thought I was too good, or 'high and mighty' as she described it, to reach out to a recovering drug addict when needed.

Last month when Grandma called to notify us Mama had been evicted from her apartment, Mama didn't seem perturbed at all.

"Ain have nothin worthwhile in thar. That run down stuff needed to be throwed to the trash any ways. Just watch me Shondra gul, just watch yo Mama. I'm gonna have me some nice furnisher like you gots one day. Just one of these good ole days," she responded.

* * * * *

"Mr. Carter, how are you feeling?" I yelled, in hopes of old Mr. Carter hearing me. Today was his third time being intubated since his three months here. He was admitted two days after Christmas with pneumonia and has been vent-dependent since. He would probably wean from the vent more successfully if he had a tracheotomy. We've been unable to get consent to perform such a procedure. He always refused and he has no family, to our knowledge, to rebut his decision. He looked so pitiful and helpless. I couldn't help but to think about Grandma and Mama when they become his age. There is no way I would just neglect them like Mr. Carter's family has done.

Due to the census at the hospital being extremely high, I've been working sixteen-hour shifts lately. Tonight was slightly different. We're down to twelve patients with six respiratory therapists on the clock. I was delighted at the news of being the 'chosen-one' to leave at eleven tonight.

"The census is down tonight. You look like you need a break. Do you want to leave a shift early?" asked the supervisor.

"You couldn't have asked at a better time," I said, after my last visit to Mr. Carter.

Derrick has been to Japan on business for two weeks. He's arriving home tonight. He's going to be very surprised and happy to see me home early.

I can't wait to see my baby.

Chapter 31

Indigo

When I arrived home, I dug through my medicine drawer for any kind of acetaminophen I could find. I just wanted the pain to go away. I tied a scarf tightly around my forehead to place pressure on the pounding. I stripped down to my panties and jumped under my sheets. It was only five-thirty five. *Maybe a quick nap will help eliminate the pain.*

Taking three five hundred milligram acetaminophen pills kept me out until nine forty-two Saturday morning. I probably wouldn't have awakened then had it not been for the ringing telephone.

It was Aaron wanting to go out to dinner. I really wasn't in the mood for company and asked if he would take a rain check.

"If I can cash it in tomorrow," he responded, not seeming a bit agitated by my so-called rejection.

"Yes, you can cash it in tomorrow."

"That's cool. I'll pick you up around five."

"Okay, see you then," I said to Aaron and then placed the phone on the receiver.

* * * * *

Aaron and I met at a birthday party of a co-worker. I was appalled by his gorgeous looks. Best of all, my mind was in full gear, imagining his dark chocolate bar slowly melting as it slid inside of my milk chocolate cavern. *Lord I just love good sex. It's your fault Todd.*

I was in for a rude awakening two months later. His dark chocolate melted all right. It melted so fast I didn't even feel it. In other words, the sex was horrendous.

Now what kind of intelligent female would I be if I decided to rid myself of him because of sex? There is nothing else wrong with him in my eyes. I keep saying that sex isn't everything so I had to prove that to myself by continuing to date him.

Aaron tapped on my door at five o'clock sharp. *I really wish I could love him. I want to so bad. I really need to get over Tony, the love of my life six months ago.*

Dinner was great. I ate until I was stuffed at 'The Boston Sea Party'. That was one of Tony's and my favorite dining spots. I wish I had the 'Bewitched' hookup. I would've snapped my fingers and replaced Aaron with Tony instantly.

After dinner and a few glasses of wine, Aaron and I showered and headed for the bed. *Hopefully the wine will help entice my mind and body to accept Aaron's lovemaking for what it is.*

The Unthinkable Reunion

Chapter 32

Walter

"What would you like to drink Mr. Lucas?" asked the flight attendant as I settled into my first class seat en route to Atlanta.

"A glass of red wine please, your best."

This trip to Atlanta brings about a feeling of jubilation because I'm going for a good purpose. I haven't been there since Marlon and Priscilla's anniversary party. So much has transpired within those two years.

With me, for starters, I've finally found a babe to settle down with. I've been living the single life for thirty-one years. Yes it's time for old Suave to settle down. Angela is a definite soul mate. I plan to propose as soon as I return from this trip.

My career has boosted drastically from where I was nine years ago. I've gone from late night DJ to one of the top news broadcasters in the metro DC area. Just a week ago, I was offered a position as a talk show host. What more could I ask for? God has truly blessed me. Look out Oprah, here I come.

My relationship with God has blossomed. Although I was reared in the church, during college and right afterwards, I just wasn't ready to give up the lifestyle I had become accustomed to. I loved partying, bedding numerous women, hanging out at the clubs, and smoking a little weed on the side.

By the time I turned twenty-eight, I realized I was taking the wrong path in life. God blessed me tremendously with my career and I felt I owed him something...my soul. At that point, I joined a church and have been an active member since. Besides, I've heard too many corrupt things about hell, and I want no parts of it.

"Excuse me Mr. Lucas, here's your drink. Is there anything else I can get for you?"

"No, not at the moment. Thanks for your kindness."

* * * * *

Rashondra, Indigo, and Priscilla, such beautiful, intelligent young ladies. They shared a phenomenal, sisterly love that a lot of women longed for. I can no longer allow this detachment to continue.

Initially, I was startled by the news that they no longer associated with one another, but for some reason, I fixated in my mind that it was only a temporary disagreement. But as certain events took place and they didn't share that bonding time, I realized there was some seriousness to it. For example, Marlon being released from jail; the trial of Zach; the birth of Priscilla's twins; Rashondra's marriage to Derrick; Indigo's break-up with Tony. Those were the kinds of things they were sure to step in and fill the voids. They weren't happening anymore.

What saddens me even more is the fact that they are yearning for one another as I speak. It's been expressed to me by each of them numerous times.

The primary reason for my visit to Atlanta is to tighten the loose knot they've created. I'm the source of their initial encounter. I was there in the very beginning and watched this friendship mature. I can't allow it to stay apart. I haven't come up with the perfect plan yet, but before I exit this plane, I'll be ready to put my scheme into action.

Whew, I thought, looking toward heaven. *For some reason, I'm feeling this weird motion in my heart, as if the chambers are unraveling. It can't be my drink for I've only had two sips.*

"*Walter.*"

Man, who was that? I thought as I viewed the first class section for any familiar faces.

"*Walter.*"

Who's calling my name? Immediately my eyes were forced shut. There within I saw a bright light that was the image of a man. I felt my flesh trembling.

"*Walter, you asked, and it shall be given unto you.*"

"*What did I ask for Lord?*"

"*You called thy name to help reunite friends.*"

"*Yes I did. I think it's my destiny to bring them back together. But how do I accomplish this Lord? How do I make it perfect again...*"

The bright light diminished. I jolted my head to bring myself back to reality. Instantly, I gulped down the rest of my drink, scared to death of what I thought had happened. A very inexplicable kind of feeling seemed to have pervaded my inner spirits. *Was that really Him?*

"Excuse me Miss, can I have a refill please?" I said to the flight attendant, feeling very confused.

* * * * *

As I was saying about RIP earlier, neither one of them were available to answer the calls I placed last night and this morning. I guess they were caught up in their own little personal affairs.

"Attention passengers and crew members. We are experiencing difficulty with the right engine of the plane. We will have to make and emergency landing. Please place yourselves in crash position just incase we are thrown slightly off course," announced the pilot.

I interlocked my fingers and placed them behind my head. With my face amid my knees, I was able hear the wails of several passengers traveling in coach, drifting through the air.

Man, I'm getting a little shaky myself. They need to stop crying. The pilot said we are making an emergency landing, not crashing. God, please guide this plane to a safe landing spot. I'm not ready to die. You have blessed me with too many good things.

The plane accelerated. *Oh God, please spare us. Don't let this plane crash. I don't want to die yet.* The speed increased.

Instantaneously, that feeling of my heart unraveling was upon me again. *Ooh, I feel sick, God I'm scared.*

"*For God hath not given us the spirit of fear; but of power, and of love, and of a sound mind. It's time Walter, it's time.*"

"*Oh no, time for what?*"

"*For he that passes through in his natural body has a purpose. For God hath chosen you for a purpose; to help rid the world of prejudices against social economic classes. RIP, my son, is just a step in proving the power of God's love can exist in all hearts.*"

"*But I'm only thirty-one years old. I'm a successful black, career man. I just fell in love. What about Momma? What about RIP...*"

"*Greater love has no one than this, that he lay down his life for his friends.*"

As the boisterous wails of the passengers became uncontrollable, tears rolled down my face. The increasing speed of the plane continued.

God please forgive me for my selfishness. I do believe we all have a purpose here on earth. If this is the way you planned for me to reunite RIP... let your will be done. I'm ready...I'm ready to come home.

"Passengers! Crew members! We are about to crash! May God be with you!"

CRASH!! Pain. Blood. Intense Pain. Little Pain. Resting. Waiting. No Pain. White Light.

Fading... Fading... Gone!

RIP... 'til we meet again.

Chapter 33

RIP

This better not be Mrs. Smith calling me about Sean again, thought Indigo as she peered over at her Caller ID to screen the call before answering it.

Tony? I can't believe this. It's been months. Why is he calling me? I'm sure the call Walter placed last night while I wasted my time with Aaron has something to do with this. I should've answered. Had I spoken with him, I'd probably know why Tony is calling me.

"Hello?" Indigo answered after clearing her throat.

"Hi, may I please speak with Indigo?"

The nerves of him trying to pretend he's forgotten my voice. "This is she."

"Hi, this is Tony. How are you doing?"

"I'm doing great," she responded, sounding very chipper.

Taking a sigh, he continued, "Did you hear about the plane crash earlier this afternoon en route to Atlanta from Washington, D.C?"

"Yes, I heard about it. Why do you ask?" Indigo's upbeat persona slowly began to decline as she anticipated what Tony was about to tell her.

"Walter was on that plane."

"No! No! No!" Indigo squealed. "He didn't die did he? Please tell me he's not dead! Please! Please! Please! Oh my God. Nooooo!"

* * * * *

Rashondra hadn't heard from Derrick since he walked out on her the night before due to the confrontation with her mother, Betty. As soon as the phone rang, she grabbed it without even noticing the name on the Caller ID box.

"Derrick, is that you?"

After a brief sigh, Indigo responded, "No, Rashondra. It's Indigo."

The instant silence on the phone line was quickly replaced with short sniffles rippling from Indigo's voice.

Upon completion of that call, grief struck Rashondra immediately. She sat her stiffened body on the edge of the sofa and sobbed deeply.

"Dammit Walter! Why did you have to be on that goddamn plane?" Rashondra said. Her voice rang with anger. "Oh God, why didn't I answer the phone last night? He called me! Why didn't I answer?" she continued.

"AWWWW!!" Her screech was so loud it could've broken glass. She sat on the edge of the bed. With her elbows on her knees, she placed her forehead into the palms of her hands. As she shook her head back and forth in disbelief, she continued to think about the tragic news Indigo had just delivered, over and over again.

Her trembling hands managed to dial Derrick's work number.

"Derrick, come home now please!" she wailed without even concerning herself with why he hadn't called her yet.

"What did Betty do this time?"

"Just come home! Please just come home!"

* * * * *

"Where are you Marlon? I need you sweetheart? Where are you?" Priscilla cried after allowing the phone to fall from her hand. Indigo's news hit hard.

She laid on the bed and continued to weep loudly. "Walter! Oh dear God, Walter! Walter! Why Lord? Why? Why? Why?"

Priscilla's head throbbed as she retrieved the phone from the floor and dialed Marlon's office. Massaging her temples with her fingers was no relief to the migraine she felt coming on.

"Jamaica!!?? He told me Key West! What the hell is he doing in Jamaica?" Priscilla was hysterical, screaming as if she was being mauled. Her vision was slowly becoming cloudy. She sat on the bed in an attempt to regain her consciousness.

"Mrs. Turner, why are you yelling at me? Please calm down. He told me he was going on vacation for a week. I thought you and the kids went with him."

"Where is he staying? Tell me now dammitt! Where is he staying?"

"I'm sorry, I don't know. All I have is his flight information."

Out of frustration, Priscilla slammed the phone on the receiver without allowing another word to be spoken.

She fell to her knees and prayed, "Oh dear God, I feel great pain. I need my husband right now. Touch his heart. Allow him to think about me right now. He needs to call me. Please answer my prayer God. I need him. Please."

* * * * *

Ironically, as RIP mourned the lost of their big brother in private, they couldn't help but to reminisce as they each listen to the sad sounds of 'They Way We Were' emanating their homes through the radio.

'Mem'ries, light the corners of my mind. Misty water-colored memories. Of the way we were. Scattered pictures. Of the smiles we left behind. Smiles we gave to one another. For the way we were...'

Indigo sat in her recliner, arms wrapped around her shoulders, rocking back and forth. Rashondra standing on the balcony, arms folded and head leaning against the wall, awaiting the return of Derrick. Priscilla, still on her knees after her prayer to God, face smothered in the comforter.

'Can it be that it was all so simple then. Or has time rewritten every line. If we had the chance to do it all again, tell me would we, could we. Mem'ries...'

Chapter 34

RIP

Indigo denied Tony's request to accompany her on the flight to Baltimore. Although she'd longed for six months to share his closeness again, she had too much pride to grant him the opportunity to console her. She wanted desperately to believe that she was a 'big girl' and could handle Walter's death without temporary solace from Tony.

After flagging a taxi at the BWI Airport, it didn't take long for Indigo to settle into her hotel room. The steam she inhaled from the shower was a great soother for the rigidity within her body. A little relaxation was just what she needed as she anticipated yet another funeral of a loved one.

Lying on the bed, Indigo thought back on the good times they shared during their college years. Walter and RIP, an awesome foursome. She also thought about the brief conversation she forced upon herself as she delivered the fatal news to Rashondra and Priscilla. She wondered what their reunion would be like under such bereaving circumstances. Although she was apprehensive about the feelings of her friends, she had most definitely matured over the past two years and was ready to make amends. Tears dropped, one by one, as she sighed in an attempt to calm herself down. *Oh my precious Walter, I miss you already...*

Friends and family were to converge at Walter's mother's house for the funeral motorcade. Walter was her only child. Her husband preceded Walter in death when Walter was only fifteen years old.

* * * * *

Four hours later, Indigo gave the front door of Mrs. Lucas's house three soft taps. Moisture diluted her eyelids at the sight of her soul mate. Dressed in a black suit, Tony opened it before she could complete her second rounds of knocks. *I can't break down. I've got to be strong for Mrs. Lucas, just like I was for Grandmama. Big girls don't cry,* thought Indigo.

His warm embrace took her to a place she remembered all too well. A place she longed to venture again, now, and forever. Holding on to the love of her life, Indigo made a quick decision to acknowledge the fact that God made woman a weaker vessel and loosened the hold she had on her tears.

* * * * *

"Priscilla, I just want you to know that I will always love my grandchildren, even if you do decide to leave Marlon for good this time," said Mrs. Hunter.

Marlon's mother picked up the kids and dropped Priscilla off at Hartsfield. She expressed her deepest regrets to Priscilla after learning the news of Marlon's disappearance to Jamaica.

"Are you going to be okay sweetie," Mrs. Hunter asked, holding on to Priscilla's left hand, rubbing it on top. "You look so pale."

"Thanks for your concern. Let the truth be told, I really don't know if I'm going to be all right or not. The doctor gave me a prescription yesterday. I just pray that God delivers me through this."

Priscilla hugged and kissed Marlon III, and the twins, Marlissa and Marlonda, grabbed her luggage from the trunk and somberly strolled through the sliding doors at the airport.

Priscilla had purposely purchased the first two seats on the airplane, using Marlon III as the alias. She was in no mood to converse with any other so called 'well-to-do' first class passenger about who she is and where she works. She wanted to travel in silence and isolation.

After briefly explaining to the flight attendant about the sudden illness Marlon III took on, she advised the attendant not to disturb her for any reason. She grabbed a pillow, secured herself with the seat belt, and turned her back to the aisle. She placed the pillow on the windowsill, finding a comfortable position for her head. During the entire hour and a half flight, Priscilla wept.

Walter is dead. Marlon is no where to be found. There's this uneasy feeling I have about seeing Rashondra and Indigo for the first time in almost two years. Mother's death didn't bring this much suffrage to my heart. I feel like I've been walking through a living hell over the last few days. I feel so weak. God please lift this burden off of me.

* * * * *

As soon as Priscilla entered Mrs. Lucas's home, she bypassed the crowd that was gathered in the living room and went straight to the kitchen. She took the first chair available at the table and requested a glass of water.

Her mind seemed to be stretching in four different directions. Her relationship with Marlon, Walter's death, and seeing Indigo and Rashondra were due reasons for her to experience the intensity that weighed heavily on her. She prayed not to encounter a nervous breakdown.

Walter's Aunt handed Priscilla a glass of water. She nervously fumbled around the inside of her purse to located her prescribed medication. Trusting that she went unnoticed, Priscilla quickly popped two Prozacs into her mouth, drowning them with one gulp of water. She decided to stay seated for a few minutes to relax. She wanted and needed her medication to work instantly.

* * * * *

"Are you okay baby?" asked Derrick as he straightened his tie while they dressed in the hotel room.

"Yes, come here, give me hug me," responded Rashondra.

Rashondra felt a high level of comfort as she allowed her husband to embrace her. He'd been very supportive throughout this whole ordeal. He decided to place their problems with Betty on the 'back burner' so that Rashondra could grieve properly.

Rashondra's preference to rent a car versus flying created a feeling of disbelief. "Baby, do you know how far that is if we drive?" he'd questioned.

"I know it's far, but if we leave a day or two early, we'll have plenty of time to rest. I just feel very jittery about flying knowing Walter was killed on an airplane. Please try to understand."

"Damn baby. ..well okay. We can rent a car," Derrick responded.

* * * * *

Rashondra's walk through the entrance of the door was halted after she saw a visage of Indigo at a slight distance down the hall. Her body stiffened as she stared at her long ago friend, wanting to run to the hands she'd always stretched out. She felt knots rolling in her stomach instantaneously with the nudge from Derrick's elbow in her side. He reminded her that they were still standing in the doorway.

Indigo trailed Tony into the kitchen after a sudden urge of thirst. She had not noticed Rashondra staring at her. "I'll take it straight from the faucet," she said as they walked through the doorway on the opposite side of where Priscilla sat.

There, before Indigo's very own eyes, sat Priscilla, rubbing her forehead with her fingers. She had a look of overwhelming distress. She had lost a lot of weight. She didn't seem to be handling Walter's death very well.

An unexplainable feeling of magnetism began stirring within Indigo as she took miniature steps in the direction of Priscilla. She had no knowledge of what to say or what to do. She was reacting on the unforeseen force that allured her towards her friend.

While Indigo made her way through the small crowd gathered in the kitchen without saying 'excuse me', Rashondra walked through the entrance on the opposite side. She stopped right next to the chair occupied by Priscilla; not realizing whom the occupant was at first.

Priscilla looked up at Rashondra. Their bulging eyes locked on one another as Indigo continued to gradually move towards them.

The moment they had all anticipated had finally come. The astounded looks worn on their faces were evidence that this meeting was more intense than either one of them had anticipated. They stared. Tears swelled. Hearts ached.

Without rationalizing her next move, Indigo's left hand extended toward Priscilla and her right toward Rashondra. The hesitancy in Priscilla and Rashondra's reactions gave Indigo a peevish feeling.

As the first tear trickled beneath Indigo's eyelid, she saw a blurred image of Walter that suddenly disappeared as that tear continued its journey down her cheek. Priscilla and Rashondra must have observed the exact semblance because their hands simultaneously touched, connecting without uttering a sound.

Standing. Holding. Weeping. No words spoken.

Sniffing. No words. Closer. Hugging. Panting. Still...no words. A long, overdue reunion, deemed as lost forever.

Silent thoughts... *I'm sorry. Forgive me. You look nice. Missed you so much. How have you been? How's Zach? Where's Marlon? Pictures of the twins? Congratulations on your marriage. Walter is gone. Heart hurts. I love you. I need you...*

Their moans escalated, unnoticed by the three of them as their silent thoughts were brought out in wails. Derrick and Tony stood behind, understanding completely what was transpiring. Onlookers began to watch with saddened hearts.

"These three ladies were like sisters to Walter," said Mrs. Lucas to the small assemblage of mourners as they wiped away tears. That was her attempt to explain the semi-hysteric wails they had piercing through the air. She was unaware of the two years of separation they'd been through.

"I'm so glad to see you all again. Thanks for the cards and flowers," she added, joining in on their embrace.

RIP welcomed Mrs. Lucas with open arms and continued to shed tears of sorrow, still not uttering a word. There were so many things they cried about. Walter's death was the tragedy that played a major role in their sorrow. It brought them back together. They missed their friendship so much. The personal problems they're enduring; Priscilla and Marlon's marital problems, Rashondra and Derrick's situation with Betty, Indigo's dilemma with Sean, the student from hell, as well as Tony, wanting him back so desperately. They missed having the comfort of one another.

As they stood, hand in hand, the heavy burden that had been the center of their emotions for the past two years seemed to gradually ascend. It felt so spiritual as that overwhelming feeling released itself.

* * * * *

Per Mrs. Lucas's request, RIP rode in the same limousine as she did. Being together lessened their grief and made it a little easier to deal with Walter's death. Derrick didn't dispute when Rashondra told him she needed this time with her friends. He understood completely and was allowed to ride in the second limousine with Tony, Walter's girlfriend Angela, and other relatives.

Priscilla placed herself between Indigo and Rashondra. Their elbows connected as they proceeded down the aisle behind Mrs. Lucas and her sister. There were several familiar faces from college seated on the pews as well as a lot of popular DC locals.

As they approached the coffin where Walter's body lay, the heaviness that burdened Priscilla was more than she could bare. She imperceptibly heard Indigo and Rashondra speak their last words to him before her legs weakened causing her body to topple backwards.

While Indigo and Rashondra knelt beside her, a male usher rushed over and carried Priscilla back down the aisle. Their first instinct told them to follow the usher, but another look at Walter reminded them of the reason why they had to move on to the Amen Corner next to Mrs. Lucas.

I've never been to a funeral before, thought Rashondra. *This is so nice the way they have all these flowers set up. This funeral is so sad. I'm not known to get all mushy, but this is taking its toll on me. When are these people going to stop crying? The church is so crowed, I don't even see Derrick. Damn you Walter! Why did you have to be on that plane?*

Tears ran down Rashondra's face as she thought about the matter at hand. Indigo handed her one of the extra handkerchiefs she retrieved from her purse and placed her arm around Rashondra's shoulder.

"I wonder how Priscilla is doing," said Rashondra in between sniffles.

"I think she'll be okay," responded Indigo, teary-eyed, but not crying. She had cried enough during the moment she met Tony at Mrs. Lucas's front door as well as during the embrace she shared with Priscilla and Rashondra.

"You know, when she fell, all I saw was death," cried Rashondra. "My heart went down with her because I instantly thought I had lost another friend," she continued.

"Come here," Indigo said, squeezing her shoulders even tighter. "Everything is going to be all right. God is going to take care of us."

Prior to their arrival in Baltimore, Mrs. Lucas had asked RIP to speak at Walter's funeral. Indigo was the only one to accept her request. Now the time had come.

As Indigo made her way to the altar, she stood in front of a stand that was positioned on the side of it. She began to unravel the notes she'd scribbled but then decided to speak from her heart.

"History 102. The third day of class. That's when we met. Shortly after our initial meeting, Priscilla, Rashondra, Walter, and I became an awesome foursome for years to come. That class was the beginning. Yes it was the beginning of an extraordinary friendship."

"Take your time sister!" someone yelled from the pews after Indigo paused. She inhaled deeply with all notions of holding back the tears.

"Whenever there was a dilemma, Walter was there to help resolve it. Whenever there was reason to celebrate, he was there with his party hat. If at any moment he felt one of us had stepped out of line, he chastised us back into submission. He was that big brother, he was that dear friend, he was the one you could always depend on, and he never said no. Walter, you were a God sent angel…" *The tears are coming fast. I've got to get a hold of myself. Mrs. Lucas is bawling and so is Rashondra. Now it's rippling my way.*

Taking another sigh, she continued, "An angel that spread its wings wide enough to pull three unique individuals in to form the perfect bond. We couldn't have done it without you Walter. My esteem is lifted as I rejoice in sharing this last moment here on Earth with you. Yes your flesh is gone, but your spirit will live on."

"Praise the Lord sister, praise the Lord!" exclaimed a sister from the back of the church.

"Go 'head, go 'head, tell it sister!" shouted a brother from the left side.

"This world is only a temporary passing for each of us. Walter, your time of departure is now at hand. You have finished your course, and most importantly, you have kept the faith. Go Walter, receive your crown of righteousness!"

The whole congregation was standing. They clapped their hands, jumped for joy, and praised his holy name.

Indigo's message even moved Rashondra. With her hands stretched toward heaven, she camouflaged well with the rest of the congregation.

As soon as the clamor began to decline, she continued, "I've told Granddaddy all about you. He's anxiously awaiting your arrival. I love you Walter. Til we will meet again," she concluded, blowing a kiss at the coffin to the right of her.

As if on cue, a soprano voice from the choir began to ring through the wails of the congregation simultaneously with the sounds of the organ, singing Yolanda Adam's 'The Battle is the Lord'.

"There is no pain. Jesus. Can't feel. There is no hurt. That he can not heal…" she sang.

Thank you Jesus for watching over me as I spoke, Indigo thought, walking back to the pew as the lead singer continued.

"…For the battle, is not yours, it's the Lord."

That was extremely difficult. Thank you for the strength you always prevail within me.

By the time Indigo had taken her seat next to Rashondra, the soprano voice emanated the church with the second stanza of the song.

"There is no sadness, Jesus can not feel and there is no sorrow, the Master is not able and willing to heal," she sang.

My sweet precious Walter, Indigo said to herself as tears gently fell down her cheeks. She embraced Rashondra who was weeping hysterically.

"Remember that all things work," continued the soprano. "They're not going to be all good but they shall work according to God's purpose and his holy will. No matter what. No matter what you're going through. Remember that God sees all and knows all and all he wants to do is use you. For this battle, is not yours..."

As soon as the choir began singing its stanza of the song, everybody in the church were on their feet praising God, even the members of the pulpit. "It's, the Lord. It's, the Lord-ord-ord-ord. Hold your head up high, don't you cry it's the Lord..."

* * * * *

After a very emotional home-going service for Walter, RIP stayed with Mrs. Lucas. They assisted with chores around the house after the last family members had left. When the house was spotless, they all took seats in the den and conversed.

Surprisingly, Mrs. Lucas was able to remember every visit RIP made to Baltimore and Washington, DC. She even asked about Marlon III whom she'd met during a visit to Atlanta with Walter.

Ironically, reminiscing about Walter filled their hearts with joy, not sorrow. It felt good to be amongst the people you love during a time of mourning. Like the old saying goes, 'Cry at birth, laugh at death'.

They talked until they were all exhausted. Mrs. Lucas was curled up on the sofa wrapped in a thin blanket. Rashondra was positioned on the floor in Derrick's arms. Tony laid slanted in the corner of the other sofa with Indigo's head on his chest. Priscilla's head was positioned on Indigo's lap.

* * * * *

Have no sorrow, for I will see you again. Rejoice in your hearts. Your joy, let no man taketh it away from you.

Chapter 35

Priscilla

Mrs. Lucas must have read my mind and realized I didn't need to be alone last night. When she suggested that we all sleep over, the comfort I received was a cushion to my soul.

It's amazing how we squandered two years of friendship due to our own selfishness. Yesterday, it seemed so natural for us to just pick up where we left off. That was enough evidence for me to realize that we do have an extraordinary kind of relationship.

Indigo and I managed to shuffle around a little which placed us on the same flight home. She revealed to me her sighting of Marlon and his female friend at the airport a week ago. Although I was unhappy about the confirmation of what I'd expected all along, it lifted my spirits to know she cared enough to follow up with a PI Check.

"There are no more tears left to cry Indigo. I'm ready for a change." That was all the reassuring Indigo needed to put her brain to work and come up with a great plan.

* * * * *

"Hello," answered Mrs. Moore.

"Hi, may I speak to Sarita," Rashondra said as Indigo and I listened on the three-way calling connection. She'd convinced Derrick to give her the name of Sarita's best friend from high school without revealing our plan.

"Sarita ain't here. Who is this?"

"This is Tangela," continued Rashondra, coughing in the middle of her altered voice with a twang of hoarseness.

"Tangela Taylor?"

"Yes ma'am."

"Hey sugar. What's wrong with your voice? You got a cold?"

"Yes ma'am."

"I ain't seen you in years. How you been doing?"

"I've been fine. How have you and Mr. Moore been?"

"We doing good sugar to be as old as we are."

"Well, I'm in town for two weeks. I've been calling Sarita for the past three days and all I'm getting is her answering machine."

"Sarita, she done gone to Jamaica."

"Oh really, who did she go with?"

"Remember that boyfriend of hers she keep on breaking up with every year?"

"Are you talking about Marlon?"

"Yeah, she gone with Marlon. I don't know what to say about those two. They break up, get back together, and break up again. I told both of them they need to go on and get married. I'm ready for them to have me some grandchildren," she chuckled.

"I know what you mean. I've told her the same thing."

Oh my God. It is her. Damn you Marlon! I thought.

"Here sugar, let me give you the number to her hotel room. Give her a call and surprise her. Bet she'll be happy to hear from you."

"Oh, well, okay, I'll call her."

After getting the telephone and room number, Rashondra promised Mrs. Moore she would stop by to visit before leaving and hung up.

"Yes! Yes! I got the nummmber! I got the nummmber!" bragged Rashondra.

"Thanks for all of your help, but I need to talk to Marlon alone. I'll call you all back later," I said feeling very dispirited.

"No!" retorted Indigo. "You can't call and talk to him. That'll mess up everything."

"Things are already messed up, can't you see that! My husband has been in Jamaica for a week with another woman. I begged him to take the kids and me."

"Priscilla girl, now you know what's up. You know it's time now. It's time to let him go," said Rashondra.

"I know. I just need to talk to him alone. I'm feeling very dejected right now."

"I understand how you feel, but you can't call him Priscilla. Listen to me, okay. We'll call to find out if he's actually there, but you can't talk to him yet. First let's call and ask the hotel if they have a room registered in his name. If they say yes, we will have them ring the room. If he answers the phone, ask for Sarita. If she answers the phone, still ask for Sarita."

"What will Rashondra say to her?" inquired Priscilla.

"Rashondra? Why me? I've done my dirty work for today. Lying to Sarita's mother was enough. Somebody else needs to talk to her. There is no telling what I might say anyway."

"No one is going to talk to her. We'll just ask for her to find out if she's there and then hang up," explained Indigo.

"She's not dumb. She will know something is up if we just hang up," I said, with a 'duh' in mind.

"I don't care. She won't know it's us. Maybe she needs something to shake her up a little. She has no business being down there with a married man anyway, got people thinking he's her boyfriend," replied Indigo.

After confirmation that they were indeed at the hotel, Indigo had plan number two already in mind.

* * * * *

"Priscilla you're gonna have to get a hold of yourself girl," Rashondra said as we sat in the terminal the next day awaiting the arrival of Marlon's slightly delayed flight.

How am I suppose to be acting knowing my husband is about to step off a plane from what was probably a very romantic vacation, with another woman?

The longer I sat the more drenched I became as sweat trickled down my face. Indigo took a tissue from her purse and dabbed at my forehead.

"Do you want me to get you something to drink?" Indigo asked.

"I'll get it myself. I need to get up anyway."

After struggling only about ten feet away, I paid three dollars for a bottle of water. I fingered the bottom of my purse for medication. I quickly swallowed two Prozacs.

When Marlon exited the plane, his arm was wrapped around Sarita's slim waistline. Tears swelled in my eyes.

I thought all of the tears were gone, but the reality of this whole scenario is bringing them back.

"Be strong girl. Just walk up to him and speak. That's all you have to do. Just speak and walk off," said Indigo as she and Rashondra withdrew themselves from the scene, leaving me to face him alone.

How could he do this to me? Oh God, just look at them. They seem to be so happy? My stomach began to knot up. *Why God? Why?* I was drenched in sweat. My head was pounding. Any description that explicated a person in a very nervous state could've been thrown at me.

As the happy couple came closer to where I was standing, my legs weakened. I took tiny steps that placed me within arm distance of Marlon. I looked into his face. He stopped and stared.

I am sobbing heavily internally. There is no way possible he could have even an ounce of love for me. He can't. How could he? I just refuse to accept the fact that he loves me. Look at him. He can't possibly love his family. Damn you Marlon, you are a disgrace to all humans.

"Hi Marlon, " I managed to say.

My voice, hands, legs, everything, began trembling. The same feeling I had when I saw Walter lying in his casket began simmering inside of me. *Keep me on my feet Jesus.*

"Pri Pri Priscilla," he struggled out of his mouth, coughing as if he had a severe case of bronchitis.

What more could I say? I walked away, leaving him there in bewilderment. I walked away, leaving him there forever.

Of course Marlon did the please baby, baby, let me explain plea, but I didn't give in. I was tired. I was tired of the hurt and pain. He had totally disrespected my kids and me in every possible way. I'd given him all of me. There is hardly any *me* left. I've experienced fainting spells as well as a loss of appetite. I can't sleep at night. I have even had thoughts of suicide. Someone will be digging a hole for me next if I don't put an end to this sickness. Like Rashondra said, it's time to let go. I'm tired.

* * * * *

It didn't take long for my lawyer to draw up divorce papers. Surprisingly, Marlon didn't contest. He was out of my life!

Chapter 36

Indigo

Just thinking back on what transpired last week with Sean, the student from hell, I thought I was experiencing some serious drama. But in the end, God prevailed.

Last Monday evening, Mrs. Smith informed me of her brief conversation with Sean's mother. She threatened to sue me for physical and emotional abuse, stating that I purposely threw Sean into the pencil sharpener out of anger because I had run out of work for him to do. You think that's crazy, listen to this one. She also threatened to sue Mrs. Smith for hiring what she calls, 'an irrational' teacher, claiming every time she spoke with me I screamed in her ear.

The anguish I felt after our phone conversation had me considering several corrupt things I could've done to handle the situation on my own.

The bible says 'be ye angry but sin not'. I try, I really try hard, but the devil works his way in sometimes, therefore I did what I could to shake the devil off.

By the end of that week, there was no word from Ms. Rogers. After the last student walked out of my door that Friday, I began to gather my belongings, praying at the same time that I have a safe flight to Baltimore for Walter's funeral. My prayer was interrupted by a call from the office. Mrs. Smith informed me that Ms. Rogers had dropped the lawsuit and moved back to Alabama.

"On your way out, stop by and complete withdrawal papers for Sean," she added.

"Hallelujah!" I walked into the office with a pen already in hand. I was overjoyed at signing Sean out of my life.

* * * * *

When you hear people say 'There is always someone worse off than you', take it for every word it's worth. When I think about everything Priscilla has gone through with Marlon, I should have no complaints.

My heart goes out to Priscilla for all of the pain and suffering she's endured over the last seven years. She has really had her bout with the 'seven-year itch'. We prayed together after returning to her house from our visit to the airport. She had already begun to pack Marlon's belongings. We volunteered to help her complete the task, but it was a desire she wished to fulfill on her own.

Although I feel truly blessed to have my best friends back in my life, a part of me is still missing. That part is Tony.

I think about him day in and day out. Being with him those two days in Baltimore made me realize how childish I was to allow something that happened before I met him, something that he knew nothing about, to come between the wonderful relationship we had developed. I called him Monday evening after returning from the airport with Priscilla and Rashondra. Here it is Thursday and I haven't heard anything from him. Now I'm beginning to feel the pain. I need someone to talk to.

"What are you doing?" I asked Rashondra after she said a tiresome hello.

"Girl, Mama just called saying she'll be over here within the next two hours."

"Is this your first time hearing from her since she left about two weeks ago?"

"Yeah. I've been so worried about her. I can't wait to see her."

"What does Derrick have to say about all of this?"

"Well you know how he feels about her. Before she could hang up the phone good, he was telling me to call the airlines to put her on the next flight back to Ft. Lauderdale. Any way, what's up with you?"

"I'm just feeling kind of sad. Tony has not called me back yet."

"He hadn't? I wonder what's up with that. Maybe he's working."

"I don't know. Do you think he has someone?"

"Well, you never can tell. Men try to be so slick. He acted like he was all into you when we were in Baltimore."

"I know, but he has not called since we've been back."

"Well Indigo, it's not like you gave him a very warm welcome. It seems to me that despite all he said and did, you kept a very unnecessary guard up."

"I know, but I didn't want him to think he could just walk back into my life under those circumstances. We were both sad and needy during Walter's funeral."

"So what I'm hearing is that you don't want him to walk back into your life," responded Rashondra.

"Well, no that's not what I mean. I miss him; I want him so bad. I just didn't want him to think I was vulnerable."

"Okay Miss I-got-myself-together. Don't-need-no-man-to-make-me-feel-complete. You are always preaching to Priscilla about being true to herself and facing reality. I think it's time you practice what you've preached. You miss Tony. You love Tony. You want him back in your life. Stop playing games with yourself and call that man again. Tell him you want him back. Plain and simple. Now that's a done deal."

"Girl that's easier said than done. I don't want him to think I'm running up behind him by calling him two times in a row."

"There you go again with that I-don't-want-him-to-think mess. Honey child you are snoozing and is about to lose that man."

* * * * *

How do I begin, I thought as his phone rang.

"Hi Tony."

"Hi Indigo, how are you?"

"Fine. Did I catch you at a bad time?"

"No, actually, I was just sitting here thinking about you. I didn't ignore your phone call. I've just been very busy."

Yeah, right. Tell me anything. "No problem, I've been rather busy myself. Priscilla has been going through a lot with Marlon. That is why he wasn't at the funeral. So Rashondra and I have sorta been there for her."

"Oh really. Does Marlon know Walter is dead?"

"Yeah, she told him."

"Well I hope everything works out okay for them."

"Things are going to be just fine. The reason I called is because I would like to talk to you about something. Can you come over tomorrow after I get off work?"

"I'm sorry I won't be able to make it tomorrow. I already have plans. What about Saturday?"

"Well that's okay. It's not that important. Besides, I already have plans for Saturday. Maybe we can talk one day whenever we both have the available time."

Why did I lie to him? I have absolutely nothing to do Saturday but sit around in sorrow, wondering who she is. I knew I shouldn't have listened to Rashondra. Now I've got to make up something to tell him because there is no way possible I can let him know my true feelings now.

* * * **

Sitting at the desk in my bedroom, I began scribbling a letter on a piece of paper.

'Tony, I want to apologize for the way I treated you when I found out about JaQuez. I know I put a solid wall between us, but I was hurt. My selfishness played a role in me behaving in a manner that indicated I wanted nothing more to do with you. I admit I was wrong. I really don't know how to explain it, but I never wanted to be apart from you. I guess I was too worried about what other people would think and say versus listening to my own mind, heart, and soul. I attempted to move on with my life. I met and became involved with someone else, but I always thought about you, everyday, one way or another. In the back of my mind I really felt that you would eventually come back to me. It is always easier when the man makes the initial move. I have always hoped to walk into my bedroom and see your name on my Caller ID, but it never happened. Over the last few months, I've felt so alone, but I blame no one but myself. When Walter told me you were not dating anyone seriously, I felt there was hope for us, but I still couldn't make myself call you. At this moment, I don't know what's really going on in your life, but I have to tell you what's going on in mine. I miss you so much. I have never stopped loving you. I want you back in my life.'

Will the letter make a difference? Probably not. I tore it into tiny pieces before tossing the rubble into the trashcan. I walked out onto the balcony to feel the spring breeze that was approaching.

Okay now, I'm a strong, independent, woman who doesn't have to have a man in my life to be a success. Stop crying. Stop crying.

Chapter 37

Rashondra

It was quite difficult to ignore what had transpired between Priscilla and Marlon at the airport. I called her on Tuesday with Indigo on three-way to see how she was holding up. She elaborated on the conversation she and Marlon had when he finally came home, which was three hours after we saw him. When she told us about his reactions toward the news of Walter's death, I thought she was on the verge of thinking reconciliation.

"He broke down and cried. I've never seen Marlon cry before. He was nearly hysterical. Part of me wanted to reach out and comfort him. But I allowed my true feelings to resurface and I walked away, telling him to close the door on his way out," was what Priscilla inevitably said, which gave me a feeling of relief.

Indigo and I advised her to continue to be strong. "Call us anytime of the day or night. We will walk through this with you together."

* * * * *

Indigo and I were the last ones to concern ourselves with feelings of heartache over a man. It was always Priscilla we had to console. Now I finally see my girl Indigo going down. She actually cried when she called back to say Tony turned down her request to meet on Friday.

Feeling bad that I couldn't talk long due to Mama banging on the door, I recommended we all get together Saturday and do some girl things.

* * * * *

"Mama," I said in amazement at how shabby she looked.

"Hey gul," she said, croaking out her words. Her facial expression was as piteous as she looked.

She stumbled through the door, barely able to keep her poise. She held on tightly to the plastic bag that contained a few fragments of her clothing.

I assisted her to the first available seat before asking, "Where have you been? I've been worried sick about you." Derrick just stood there, not saying a word. That sort of made me angry.

"Oh gul, I been just here and thar, some evey whar. Need me some food gul. Whatcha got for yo mama to get her grub on?" she said as she rubbed her stomach, coughing in between.

The black and blue welts bared on her face and arms were exposed easily by her ivory-yellow complexion. Her hair was scattered on top of her head as if there was no such thing as a comb. The clothes she wore gave her the resemblance of a beggar woman. The rancid scent that emanated from her forced me to inhale deeply, as my exhale seeped out slowly. Two weeks were too short of a time span for her to have deleted the ten pounds she seemed to be without. She looked like death itself. She needed to be in the hospital.

"Derrick, will you please go warm up some soup for Mama?"

"Oh hey thar Tar-Baby. I'ain know you was back. Last time I saw ya you had done walked right on out the door and left my gul." She giggled between each word she uttered as she continued to cough.

That cough doesn't sound good at all. I hope she doesn't have bronchitis.

"Ooh gul you shoulda been out thar wit me," she continued. "I done seen me some good lookin mans out thar in them streets. Light skinned, pretty, wit curly hair, just like yo daddy gul."

"Mama, look at me," I said as I grabbed both of her shoulders in an attempt to get her to focus her attention on my concerns. "Where have you been?"

"Damn, here and thar gul! I told cha already! U'on know I'ma grown lady yet? You betta quit queshening yo mama."

Realizing I was getting no where, I sat back on the sofa and decided to continue the conversation after she'd eaten.

"Okay gul, you sittin back on that sofa foldin them arms like you did when you was lil, gettin all mad and stuff. Don't let yo mama git that belt and treatcha like you still is lil." She placed her hand on her stomach and tilted forward as her body bobbed up and down with laughter. She didn't even think about placing her hand over her mouth as she continued to cough.

"Gul ain scarin you is I? You ain said nothin else. Whoa doggy, gul you is stubbon just like yo daddy. Let me gon tell you whar I been. I stayed cross the hall wit Billy two days when I left ya. Then he took me to find Leroy. Took me a week out thar, but I finded him."

"You were out in the streets alone, for a week, looking for Leroy?"

"Naw silly gul, Billy was out thar wit me. He gots him a lot of friends. They gave us all the food, reefer, crack, cocaine we needed. Went to Leroy's and stayed three days foe I got to fightin wit some ole gal of his wantin to move back in his house. Gul you shoulda saw yo mama. I kicked me some ass big time. Had blood running all down her face. She won pretty no mo."

The life of a drug addict. She's talking, smiling, and laughing as if she's telling me about a good movie she'd seen. She probably doesn't even realize she's telling me she's been out there on drugs. I knew it. When is enough going to be enough?

"Then I jumped on Leroy for disrespectin me wit that gal. He thought he was gon put it on me talkin bout I got too many people out there hookin me up. Claimin I'm sleepin wit Billy and all. Gul I told him Billly ain't nothin but a lil fag. Watch how he switch his ass. Just like you and me. He gon git jealous cause I done met me some folks through Billy that just gives me my stuff free. He ain't likin that at all and I'ain likin that other woman over thar."

"Here Mama, eat your soup" Derrick couldn't have come at a better time with the bowl. I really didn't want to hear anymore about her life on the streets.

We left her alone and sat at the kitchen table. Derrick hadn't spoken a word since Mama had come back.

"After she eats, I'm going to see to it that she has a nice warm bath and put her to bed. I'm taking her to the doctor in the morning for a physical. What are you thinking about?" I stretched my arms across the table to grab his hands.

"You know how I feel baby. She can't stay here."

"Look at her," I said with tears swelling in my eyes. "Do I just kick her back out on the street? She's not going to make it. I can't do that to her. She's my mother."

"Rashondra, when are you going to realize that you can't fix your family. I don't mean anything bad by this but you grew up in the ghetto, surrounded by drugs and gang life. You were fortunate. You had a break and you ran with it. Most of the people don't get out like you did. Your mother has been on drugs since you were a child and you are now twenty-nine years old. Do you really think she wants to stop? She's been in and out of rehab for years, but eventually falls back into the same hole. She just can't stay here. I don't even want her up here in Atlanta because it's going to cause too many problems within our relationship. Don't you think we went through enough with Zach?"

"You don't get it do you? I don't care how bad Mama and Zach turned out to be, they are my family. I love them. I am living proof that there's a better way of life. I was there and like you said, I got out. I did everything I could to help Zach up until the day he was escorted away in handcuffs and shackles. Am I wrong for wanting to help my Mama like that? I don't have another Mama," I cried.

Before Derrick was able to retort, Mama was screaming from the living room. "Gul! Gul! Come hem!" she screamed, coughing between each word.

I rushed into the living room only to find bloody, dark yellow sputum all over her dingy clothes. Barely able to speak, she muttered, "I thank I'm dying gul. Thank I'm goin home to glory," she added as her voice faded away. Her head fell between her knees as she slumped over in the chair.

"Oh my God! Derrick, call 911!"

One Year Later

Chapter 38

RIP

"RIP is in the house! Oo'ah! Oo'ah! RIP is in the house!" they sang in unison as they danced to Rashondra's favorite song. She refused to allow eight months of pregnancy hinder her from 'shaking what her mama gave her'.

Everyone gathered to observe RIP as they laughed and danced in the basement of Rashondra's home. The way the spectators shouted and applauded, you would've thought they were auditioning for some type of talent search.

Derrick's prior plan to surprise her with a thirtieth birthday party was curtailed when she announced her pregnancy. Since her due date is only a month after her birthday, he decided to combine the two celebrations into one.

They continued to dance right through the next song. "Y'all gon' make me loose my mind, up in here, up in here. Y'all gon' make me go all out, up in here, up in here." they sang.

"Girl you need to slow yourself down. You're going to shake something loose in there. You are not in college anymore," Indigo said to Rashondra while she and Priscilla slapped each other high fives.

That only motivated Rashondra even more as she maneuvered her arms and shoulders to add new movements to the 'Prep'. Now she was really out of season with that dance. How about a decade or so later.

"Whew, I'm going to take a break," said an exhausted Indigo.

Rashondra grabbed her by the arm before she had the chance to walk away. She attempted to coerce Indigo into a dance she'd seen at one of the football games.

"Come on Indigo girlfriend, let's do the 'Dirty Bird'. This is how you do it," said Rashondra. She bounced from side to side, as her elbows inevitably flapped like a bird. Her loaded belly flopped in the middle.

Surprisingly Priscilla caught on to the flapping quickly. She looked just as ridiculous as Rashondra did. While they enjoyed their 'new found' dance, Indigo squirmed away from the little spot they had created as a dance floor.

Tony reached for Indigo's hand as she approached him.They walked to an area of the basement that was away from the small, assembled crowd.

"So that's what y'all wanted to show everybody, how you all partied in college," inquired Tony.

"Yeah. We had to do it for old time sakes. We used to have the student center rocking every Friday night. The way you all were standing around watching us party was a carbon copy of the way it was 'back in the day' also."

"Well it seems like you and Priscilla need to lubricate your bones a little because with heavy load and all, Rashondra was out there shaking it," added Tony.

"She's always been like that. Nobody could out-dance her in college. She was and probably still is one of the wildest female dancers around. Rashondra will put a shake dancer to shame." Indigo smiled at Tony and kissed him gently on the lips.

* * * * *

Things couldn't be better for Indigo right now. She's back in college working on her Master's degree, engaged to her soul mate for life, and blessed with two of the best friends you could ever ask for. Life is good and she thanks God for it.

When Indigo invited Tony to visit her the Friday after Walter's funeral, he was unable to comply with her request because he had prior plans. Two days later, Indigo continued to feel the torment of his rejection. During her moments of heartache, she resolved that suppressing her true feelings would only make matters worse. She had to remedy her situation whether it ended happily or not. She called Tony that Saturday morning and advised him of her cancelled plans, which were none to begin with. He came over and the cards fell into place perfectly. He'd yearned for her just as much as she'd yearned for him. They admitted the love they treasured in their hearts. They both hoped for the day to come that their souls would open up and allow the other's love to come in.

That summer, Tony and Indigo flew to Hawaii, just as they had planned in the Bahamas two summers prior. She returned from her second vacation with a sense of security about their relationship because Tony had proposed, and she'd accepted.

Indigo had been afraid of what people would think and say about her settling for what was less than *her* ideal dream guy. She pondered over and over again about the reactions she would receive from her family and peers if she accepted a relationship with a man who had not one, but two kids. 'You love whom you love', she had concluded. She loved Tony and decided not to allow the fact that he was a father come between the distinctive love connection they had.

Indigo had exerted too much energy into maintaining that 'nineties' woman persona. Having Tony back in her life gave her a new perception for the millenium.

* * * * *

"Come here baby, you know you need to sit down." Derrick grabbed Rashondra's hand and led her to a rocking chair he'd brought down from upstairs. "I'm sure Lil Junior has knots upside his head the way you were out there agitating him," he added as he rubbed his hand across her stomach.

"I know what I'm doing. Did you forget I'm I a medical personnel? There's nothing wrong with a little exercise. Now, go get me some orange juice...pretty please."

Rashondra settled back into the chair and began to rock back and forth. *Damn Jr. Please stop kicking me. I'm sorry okay,* she thought as she grabbed her stomach. She let out a soft grunt each time he kicked. *I'll tone it down when I go back out there. Ooohh! Awwww! Okay, I won't go back out there.*

She continued to hold her stomach and rock as she observed some of the dancers 'raise the roof'. A smile slowly crept across her face. She felt so happy.

* * * * *

A year ago, Betty passed out right before Rashondra's very own eyes. She was admitted into the hospital for a few days and treated for walking pneumonia. Normally that type of pneumonia is mild, but because it went unnoticed for several days, it had become a serious situation for her.

Before the ambulance arrived, Derrick called Rashondra's grandmother to make her aware of what he thought was a death experience for Betty. In a panicky state, Rashondra's grandmother called her son, the one her husband had taken with him the second time he'd left her, to advise him that Betty had been rushed to the hospital, nearly dead.

Although Derrick mistakenly over exaggerated, Uncle Richard flew down from Nevada to be by Betty's side. He hadn't seen his sister in thirty-eight years.

Ironically, he's a Counselor at a drug rehabilitation center in Nevada. He convinced Betty to go back with him for treatment. That was also a good way for them to make up for lost time. Betty's life is totally different now and it's all for the better.

Two months following the drama with Betty, Rashondra and Derrick moved into their house. It wasn't long afterwards that they discussed starting a family. With the medical background Rashondra had, she timed her fertile period just right. After the ultrasound confirmed she was carrying a boy, Derrick was already prepared to name the baby after himself.

"We're going to call him Lil Junior," he said after the news.

"I don't think so. Nicknames these days sound too ghetto. Well, maybe we can go with Lil Derrick. We'll see."

* * * * *

Life had been a struggle for Rashondra since the day she was born. She thanked God she was able to keep a self-reliant and courageous mind. She thanked God for blessing her with Indigo, Priscilla, and Derrick.

* * * * *

"You are sweating sweetheart. I didn't know you were out there dancing that hard. You still got it in you."

"Well, there's not a lot of *it* left. I haven't danced in such a long time. I feel like I've just completed a round of Tae Bo. Advanced mind you. Hopefully I'm not sore tomorrow morning. I need a drink of water," responded Priscilla after she and Rashondra finished their dance.

"Don't worry, I'll give you a good massage tonight. You'll be in good shape for service in the morning. You know the devil will do anything to keep us from hearing the word of God. I'll be back in a minute with your water."

Priscilla looked toward the ceiling and recited a little prayer to God. *Thank you so much for touching Marlon's heart. Thank you for saving him, delivering him out of the hands of the devil.*

* * * * *

A year ago, Priscilla pleaded with her lawyer for a hasty divorce. Without any refutes from Marlon, their marriage ended two weeks after she'd filed.

Three weeks after the termination of their marriage, Marlon joined Priscilla's church. He continued to attend every Sunday thereafter.

One Sunday afternoon after a very emotional service had ended, Elder Rogers called Priscilla into his pastor's study. He advised her of

Marlon's request for him to speak with her. Marlon wanted Priscilla to be aware of what had been transpiring in his life since their divorce.

Two days after the divorce, Marlon attempted suicide. He couldn't deal with the stress of losing his wife, son, and twin girls. He called on Elder Rogers at his bedside in the hospital. Elder Rogers placed his hand upon Marlon's forehead and prayed to God. He asked God to cast out that lusting spirit that had been riding Marlon's back for years. He asked God to deliver Marlon out of the world of sin. In return, Marlon promised he would become a member of the church.

The same Sunday Priscilla sat in Elder Roger's study, she'd witnessed something during service beyond her imagination.

When Elder Rogers called members of the congregation to the altar whom wanted prayer, Marlon was present. Before Elder Rogers could lay his hand on Marlon, he asked for the microphone and began to speak.

"Dear Father. I'm standing here before you and the congregation of this church to plead forgiveness. Because of my sins, I have hurt a lot of people, especially my family. According to your holy word, if we confess our sins, you will forgive us and cleanse us of all unrighteousness. Cleanse me Father, make me whole. Satan is a mighty powerful spirit and he gets his satisfaction out of watching us sin. I want to beat the devil at his game. Touch me Father. Save me Father. Get out of my way Satan because now my body and soul belongs to God."

Marlon concluded by accepting Jesus Christ as his Savior in front of the congregation and asked to be baptized. Priscilla knew he had changed.

"He wants his family back. Do you have any desire to be with him?" asked Elder Rogers.

Being true to herself, Priscilla couldn't lie. She'd never stopped loving him. "Yes, I miss Marlon. The kids miss him. I trust in you Elder Rogers, through your counseling and prayers, I believe we can make it," responded a teary-eyed Priscilla.

Three months later, they were remarried. They had a very small ceremony with family and a few friends. Uniquely done, Marlon, Priscilla, and the kids were baptized together at the end of the ceremony.

* * * * *

After Rashondra opened the gifts she'd received for both her birthday and the baby shower, RIP walked outside, away from the crowd, onto the balcony.

Indigo reached out and grabbed Priscilla and Rashondra's hand. They stood for a short while stealing a moment of silence. Tears slowly fell down the sides of their cheeks. At that particular moment, their minds were focused on the same thing.

"Walter, I know you are looking down from heaven, smiling at what you are witnessing this very moment. Had it not been for you, we probably would've never met. I will forever reserve a special place in my heart for you. I miss you so much. Til we meet again," said Priscilla.

"You knew our hearts when we were apart and we know that's why you called the three of us before you boarded that airplane. Even during our separation, not one conversation went by that you didn't ask one of us about the other. You were a true blessing to us. I will miss you always. Til we meet again," continued Rashondra.

"My dear Walter, I truly believe we all have a purpose here during our passing time on Earth. It was your destiny to show the world that people can bring their own uniqueness into a relationship and create a perfect bond. Maybe you didn't know it was us, but I thank God he brought you into our lives. From beginning to end Walter... from beginning to end. You brought us together from the very beginning and made a way for us to reunite at your end. Til we meet again," added Indigo.

A white cloud gathered across the sky as RIP looked toward heaven and said one last personal prayer in silence. They knew it was a sign from Walter acknowledging their presence.

Releasing their hands and breaking the serenity, Rashondra shrieked "Oohh! Ouch!" She rubbed her stomach and continued, "I think it's time we went back inside. Lil Derrick wants some cake."

With Rashondra in the middle, their elbows interlocked. Giggles were heard ringing through the stillness of the night as they headed back toward the basement.

... There is a friend that sticketh closer than a brother.

R.I.P.
...'Til We Meet Again

To order additional copies of *RIP*:

- Contact your local bookstore with the ISBN number 0-9703122-0-2
- Postal orders:
  Send a check or money order for $10.95 plus $2.50 for shipping and handling to:

ARA Publishing
P.O. Box 511
Morrow, GA 30260-0511

- Coming soon: Online ordering. Check with a major online bookstore for available purchase date. Please provide them with the title of the book or the above ISBN number, or email me at snywash@aol.com.

Please complete the form below and send it along with your payment.

Name:_____

Address:_____

City:_____ State:_____Zip:_____

Telephone:_____

Email:_____

Quantity _____ X $10.95 plus **$2.50 per book** for shipping

Total amount enclosed:_____

R.I.P.
...'Til We Meet Again

To order additional copies of *RIP*:

- Contact your local bookstore with the ISBN number
  0-9703122-0-2
- Postal orders:
  Send a check or money order for $10.95 plus $2.50 for
  shipping and handling to:

ARA Publishing
P.O. Box 511
Morrow, GA 30260-0511

- Coming soon: Online ordering. Check with a major
  online bookstore for available purchase date. Please
  provide them with the title of the book or the above ISBN
  number, or email me at snywash@aol.com.

Please complete the form below and send it along with your
payment.

Name:_____

Address:_____

City:_____ State:_____Zip:_____

Telephone:_____

Email:_____

Quantity _____ X $10.95 plus **$2.50 per book** for shipping

Total amount enclosed:_____

R.I.P.
...*'Til We Meet Again*

To order additional copies of *RIP*:

- Contact your local bookstore with the ISBN number 0-9703122-0-2
- Postal orders:
  Send a check or money order for $10.95 plus $2.50 for shipping and handling to:

ARA Publishing
P.O. Box 511
Morrow, GA 30260-0511

- Coming soon: Online ordering. Check with a major online bookstore for available purchase date. Please provide them with the title of the book or the above ISBN number, or email me at snywash@aol.com.

Please complete the form below and send it along with your payment.

Name:_____

Address:_____

City:_____ State:_____Zip:_____

Telephone:_____

Email:_____

Quantity _____ X $10.95 plus **$2.50 per book** for shipping

Total amount enclosed:_____